RIVALS
AND
RETRIBUTION

OTHER 13 TO LIFE NOVELS BY SHANNON DELANY

13 to Life
Secrets and Shadows
Bargains and Betrayals
Destiny and Deception

RIVALS AND RETRIBUTION

A 13 TO LIFE NOVEL

Shannon Delany

St. Martin's Griffin

New York

RIVALS AND RETRIBUTION. Copyright © 2012 by Shannon Delany. All rights reserved. Printed in the United States of America. For information, address St. Martin's Press, 175 Fifth Avenue, New York, N.Y. 10010.

www.stmartins.com

ISBN 978-0-312-62518-4 (trade paperback)
ISBN 978-1-250-01590-7 (e-book)

First Edition: August 2012

10 9 8 7 6 5 4 3 2 1

Dedicated to my brother,
who knows me completely
and still manages to love me,
even on my worst days.

Everyone needs someone in their life
like him, and I am tremendously fortunate
to have him as my own.

RIVALS
AND
RETRIBUTION

PROLOGUE

FIVE HOURS AGO IN JUNCTION

The girl enters the barn, slipping between hay bales and a stack of buckets. It is that rare time in winter when hay smells like springtime to her, bringing both the scent and sensation of hope. The temperature difference between the inside of the barn is striking against the brisk pull and drop of the air outside, and Jessie tugs off her knit hat, brown hair tumbling out to brush against her shoulders. She tucks her gloves in her pockets, unzips her jacket, and prepares to clear her mind by doing some good old-fashioned manual labor.

She's never shied away from work. She's not the type who thinks herself too pretty to earn calluses on her hands or muscles in her shoulders and back to match her strong arms and legs. Few people have called her pretty, but few people's opinions matter to her.

And the people whose opinions truly matter? They're her dad, her mother (now dead more than half a year), her best friend, Amy, and her Russian-American ex-werewolf boy-friend, Pietr Rusakova.

Pietr thinks she's beautiful.

And to a teenage girl in a tremendously complicated situation, sometimes that's all she needs to keep going.

Jessie reaches for the pitchfork. But she stops, her hand outstretched, frozen, in midair. Her mind jumbles through images, flashing back to the time Pietr and another boy from her high school got into an epic rumble here, crashing into hay bales and rolling across the paddock outside, each using their paranormal abilities to fight for control of Jessie: Derek to possess her body and the power he could leech from her, and Pietr to protect and own her heart.

Her head buzzes with warning, her scalp prickling as if Derek is still somehow nearby.

Part of him *is* nearby, she knows—there is a part of him that lingers, unchecked and roaming inside her head, even after his final gruesome moments connected Jessie, Sophia, and the girl Amy calls Jessie's frenemy, Sarah.

It was here Derek tried to kill Jessie's pride and joy, her four-legged best friend, the chestnut mare, Rio. He used the pitchfork.

Shivering at the memory, Jessie decides against the tool in her hand and grabs the nearby shovel instead.

Rio is the first horse to spot her and lets out a happy snort of recognition. The other horses each respond in their own particular way, with a toss of a mane, a nod of a head, or a single stomp of a hoof—trying to get Jessie's attention first.

But there is no competition. Rio always wins. When it seemed no one else was there for Jessie, Rio was her stalwart companion, her faithful friend. She listened to all the complaining, crying, screaming, and stomping with barely the flick of an ear, and after each of Jessie's rages or depressions ended, Rio pushed her snout into Jessie's back or shoulder and made the girl move forward again.

More than a horse and more than a pet, Rio is a member of Jessie's family—a family whose number has dwindled with the sudden death of Jessie's mom. Jessie props the shovel by the wall and picks up the brush hanging by Rio's door.

"Hey, girl," she says, opening her stall door and sliding inside to stand beside her, her hand on Rio's cheek and drifting down the well-muscled neck to trace gently along her graceful shoulder and back.

Jessie rests one palm on the mare's rib cage, the soft-bristled brush following the sleek and gentle patterns her short coat grows in.

"I just don't know what to do," Jessie confesses. "He's different. Changed."

Rio paws the floor, straw crackling beneath her hoof.

"I know, he was *supposed* to change—to not be this half-man, half-wolf that was dying as fast as he could live. I expected *that* change. . . ." Jessie moves back to the horse's head and begins brushing out her dark mane. "I expected victory," she says, her voice slow. Tired. "But I never thought a single victory could feel so much like defeat."

Rio pulls away, stomping a hoof. Jessie makes shushing noises, realizing she's pulled a little too firmly on Rio's mane. She's too focused on herself—again.

"Sorry, girl," she whispers, adjusting her grip and pressure. "I had different expectations. I thought I'd get all the heat and the fire that was Pietr but without the danger of him being hunted because he was a wolf. I thought I'd have the passion but not the limitations. But it was a devil's bargain. Maybe it was destiny that he could only be Pietr—this studious boy—or Pietr: the quickly dying werewolf. Maybe I can't have it both ways."

She focuses on separating one stubborn tangle, determined that today something will go right.

"The thing is, I told him I'd never let go. I promised I'd stick by him. . . . And when I said that, I meant it. But it's harder than I thought. He's so very different. He's not the Pietr I knew at all. It's like he's not the Pietr I *want*."

She jumps, her cell phone vibrating in her pocket, and she pulls it out. Seeing Pietr's face, she pauses.

It's the first time she's ever ditched anyone. And as much as she thinks she still loves him, it's freeing to know she can step away to clear her head. She still has enough independence to take a few hours away and think of things other than were-wolves and Mafia and the madness that so recently swirled around her.

It's reassuring to know he cares enough to notice she's gone.

Unless he's calling for some other reason . . .

She sighs, not ready to face an answer she fears, and turns off the phone, returning her attention to Rio.

The mare's coat glistens, and Jessie steps toward the stall door. She freezes, noticing a strange and sudden stillness fall over the barn. All the horses turn their attention in one direction, all eyes fixed on one location.

A slender young man stands near the entrance, his short red hair bold against sharp and pale features, his nostrils flaring. Catching her scent, his narrow lips turn up in a smile that borders on the terrifying.

Gabriel has found her.

Although most girls might balk, scream, or run in a blind panic knowing a werewolf from a new and dangerous pack has tracked them all the way home and that they are alone, Jessie isn't like most girls.

She can't afford to be anything but an individual. So she sucks in a breath, straightens her back, and shoves back her shoulders.

"Hey," she says, her bravery a bluff. "You need help with something?"

"Yes," Gabriel says, striding closer. "Yes, I think you can help me with something, Jessica."

Her eyes slide, examining her options. Out the back and she'll wind up in the main paddock and pasture. Out the front and she'll be nearly nose to nose with Gabriel.

Decisions, decisions . . .

"What can I help you with? If you wanna learn to ride a horse, I can teach you. But I don't do impromptu lessons."

"Come out here and we can talk about scheduling something," Gabriel suggests, his smile unfurling into a grin.

"I'm fine where I am," Jessie says, her stomach churning as her feet remain still in the stall's straw.

Her lips press together in a frustrated line, and she mentally berates herself. She'd known when he sniffed her in the hallway at Junction High that he'd be able to find her anywhere. She'd expected trouble, and yet, there she was, unprepared. Again.

"So when's a good time for you to come back and start lessons?" she asks, her eyes scanning the area for potential weapons. Her gaze falls to the brush in her hand, and she smirks at her own pitiful luck.

Considering all she's lost, the one thing Jessie Gillmansen has managed to keep throughout everything is a sense of humor. Certainly it's grown darker and more fiercely cutting, but at least it's remained.

She sizes her opponent up, glad she's continued training in hand-to-hand combat with the only non-werewolf member of the Rusakova family: Alexi. He's taught her to be swift and sly. To deceive with her body language.

And if there's one thing Alexi's good at, it's the art of deception. History's greatest traitors? Judas Iscariot? Benedict Arnold? They've got nothing on Alexi. His entire life's a lie.

But the fact remains, no matter how well trained Jessie is, or how sturdy her farm girl build, she's going to be facing down a werewolf. And that shifts all the odds against her.

He stands at the stall's door, his hand resting on the handle, his face close to the wide-set bars. "Looks like there's a schedule out here, a calendar of some sort," he says. "We should look at it together. I'd hate to come up with a time that we find out later just won't work."

"How very considerate."

He shrugs, the grin spreading to gleam maliciously in his eyes. "I do my best."

Jessie's hand slides along her hip, reaching subtly into her jeans pocket to withdraw her phone, but Gabriel notices and yanks the door open, leaping into the stall.

"I wouldn't," he snarls, grabbing her wrist and pulling her tight to him.

"Ow!"

"I'd say I'm sorry, Jessica, but I'm not. You're the means to an end for me—the greatest gift I could give someone. The weird thing is I don't even know why you're so valuable to her. I mean, I get that you're connected with curing werewolves. But we don't want the cure. We're happy being who we are. And that's something most people can *never* say." He pauses, stepping back to drag her forward. "And the fact you're dating Pietr? I couldn't care less. But you'll help me achieve my goals. And I'm very much into achieving my goals. So come with me, like a good girl, and do exactly what I tell you to."

"The hell I will!" Her booted foot slams down on his instep as her elbow catches him in the gut.

He's barely winded.

She shoves away from him, past Rio, and falls against the door leading to the pasture. The rush of cold stings her face as she shoves the door open, but he's grabbed her waist and hurls her to the ground. Rio snorts and dances away, struggling not to step on Jessie as she thrashes beneath her attacker on the straw-covered floor.

With a spin Rio jumps them, rocketing past, and out into the cold. The door swings back and forth, squealing, and Jessie pounds on Gabriel's face and chest with all the strength in her arms and hands and all the anger roiling up inside of her—anger at him and anger at herself because she's again playing the role of the victim.

Next time, she promises herself, *I'll be ready next time.*

The only problem is, she needs to live through *this* time in order for there to be a next. She begins to wail on him with her knees and feet, kicking and yelling.

He's unfazed.

She bites him.

He shouts in pain, blood pouring from the teeth marks in his ragged cheek, and rolls away from her.

With his pinched and sharp features, he probably wasn't considered good looking before, but now the likelihood is even less.

But he'll heal. Quickly.

It's a blessing if you're in love with a danger-prone werewolf like Pietr was before he took the cure, but it's a curse if you're trying to fight one off and you're simply human. If you're only a normal girl.

But Jessie hasn't been normal for a while now, and the things she's learned about what lurks in the small town of Junction has made her reexamine her lifestyle and choices several times.

She used to think Junction was just another dull small town with no excitement. Now part of her is wishing she'd been right.

She plows into the other stall door, forcing it open, and grabs the shovel leaning against the wall.

Gabriel is back on his feet and outside the stall right after her—just in time for her to swing the shovel and barely miss his head.

"Dammit!"

"Come on," he coaxes, reaching his hands out, arms spread wide. He wiggles the fingers closest to the wall, a distraction Jessie's seen Pietr and his elder brother, Max, use when they spar.

So when he comes at her with his other hand, she's thinking about an important difference between werewolves and starfish. Other than being covered in fur. Or having to live in salt water.

And she strikes, the shovel's blade pinning his hand to the wall for the space of a single, throbbing heartbeat. Caught, he struggles a moment before pulling free in a hasty blur of panic and rage.

With a soft thump, two of his fingers drop to the hay bale below.

Unlike starfish, werewolves can't regenerate parts that are cut off. Like a middle and ring finger. Of course, unlike werewolves, starfish don't have fingers to begin with. . . .

"No more scrrrewing around—" he growls, his face

contorting as his teeth grow into wicked and curving ivory points.

Yes, if he'd ever been considered handsome before, he's far from it now.

With a grunt of effort, Jessie tugs the shovel's blade free of the wall and swings it again, connecting with Gabriel's shoulder as his fist connects with the side of Jessie's head.

Limp, she falls into the straw alongside the shovel.

Grinning and bleeding, Gabriel leans over his prize.

She wakes in the dark, her hands stuck behind her back, a gag in her mouth.

She tests her bonds and winces when the fine hairs on her wrists tear out as she twists.

She focuses on her surroundings, trying to get a clue about her location.

In the movies a bright heroine can save herself from her captors if she learns enough to use her location against them. But this isn't a movie. This is Jessie's real life.

Plus werewolves.

It's not long until Gabriel is back and wrenches her onto her feet. With no explanation he forces her out into the breeze and makes her stagger a distance, blinded by snow flurries before he shoves her just hard enough that she falls.

He leaves Jessie then, seeking his true quarry—the alpha female and leader of the pack he considers his family: Marlaena. She's on the second floor of the dive motel they're staying in—a dive motel, yes, but still much better than their normal living quarters.

Her long red hair, a few shades deeper than his own, falls along her shoulders and frames her face, setting off her high cheekbones and fierce mouth and making a fiery curtain that threatens at any moment to obscure her teasing eyes. He pauses to catch his breath, to get his mind and mouth under control. He's risked a lot doing this and he's about to find out if it's all worth it.

If he'll finally win the role of alpha.

And the girl—Marlaena.

She's leaning against his usual rival for her attention, the broad-shouldered, dark-skinned Southern boy, Gareth. The gentle gentleman of the crew who acts more the lover than the fighter, but Gabe's seen him draw his claws and bare his teeth.

Marlaena's wanted Gareth since the moment she first saw him back in the sticky heat of Mississippi. He'd just been released from jail on good behavior. Good behavior was the last thing Marlaena expected of her kind.

They'd attracted like polar opposites always did.

And Gabriel had hated Gareth since the moment he'd realized . . .

He clears his throat and waits.

Nothing.

He clears it again.

Gareth turns to face him first, his eyelids low over purple irises, giving him a sleepy look. His dreadlocks shift, and Gabriel catches sight of the beads the other girls have recently added to their hair ends.

He hates Gareth a little more for that.

"Can we help you?" Gareth asks gently. He spots Gabe's hastily bandaged hand and the chunk of flesh missing from his face. "You okay, man?"

Marlaena glances his way now, too, finally noticing Gabe's existence.

"Yeah. I'm fine. And, no, *you* can't help me," Gabe says to Gareth. "Just Marlaena," he clarifies. "I need to speak to you. Alone."

She squints at him, finally noting the blood that marks him. For a moment his heart speeds and he thinks that she'll be worried about him. But his hope is short-lived. She sighs. "Right now?"

"Yes."

She had hesitated to even get in the backseat with him and help staunch the bleeding when he'd been shot. . . . So why does he still want her? Why does he hold out hope?

He repeats himself, "Yes," and adds, "now," for good measure wondering why, after everything, he still crawls and begs for any scrap of attention from her.

"Wait here for me?" she asks Gareth.

"I'm still on duty, 'Laena," he says with a smile.

Gabriel chokes down a growl, dabbing his cheek with his bandaged hand. 'Laena was his nickname for her first. He was her number one before Gareth was even discovered. He'd established precedents Gareth was benefitting from.

"Guard, guard, guard," she chuckles, rubbing her hand along his chin.

Gabriel turns and heads toward where he's stashed Jessie, motioning just once over his shoulder for Marlaena to follow.

When they finally descend the steps, he leads her to an area not far from the motel.

She glares at him, already tired of this wild goose chase. "What's going on, Gabe? Why the secrecy?"

One last time he clears his throat and works up his courage. "You're way more complicated than most of the girls I've dated," he admits, scrubbing a fist across his forehead. He's already bluffing. He hasn't dated many girls at all, so most of what pours out of his mouth next is a mix of theories and hypotheses. "Some girls like candy; some are into flowers or jewelry—but you don't care about any of that."

Her hands settle on her hips, her fingers curling into tight fists. Cocking her head to watch him, he can tell she's not sure where this is going, and she's certain she doesn't like it.

"But we're not dating, are we?"

"We sure as hell aren't," she replies.

"And it seems there's nothing I can do to change that . . ." He looks at her from out of the corner of his eye, weighing things, and shifts his weight from one foot to another.

Her mouth is working awkwardly before she even manages to get the two small words out. "I'm sorry?"

"Yeah. Well. I don't even know when your birthday is—you realize that? No one does. That's how distant you are. But I've run with you for more than a year, so I must've missed it. And I think that sucks: missing birthdays. We don't get many. We should celebrate each one."

"Gabriel."

His head snaps up, hearing his name on her lips, but the spark lighting his eyes gutters when she says, "I don't want anything from you."

"I know. You're amazingly self-sufficient. But, as you've pointed out, *needing* and *wanting* are different things. And I noticed something you *need*."

She blinks.

"I'll admit, I couldn't get *exactly* what you need, but I've found the means to an end. This gift I'm about to give you—"

Her nostrils flare, pulling in the surrounding scents, and her eyes pop wide open in recognition.

The scents of horseflesh, hay, and a simple floral deodorant flood her nose.

"—will provide you with a way to get the thing you *really* need." He jogs a few yards away and drags back Jessie. He grins at the look on Marlaena's face.

Jessie growls, a bruise discoloring the side of her face where Gabe's been rough, retaliating as he drags her before the girl he's trying so desperately to impress.

He shoves her forward, but Marlaena steps back and lets her land on her knees, Jessie's eyes rolling at the impact.

"So," Gabriel asks, "do you like your present?"

Marlaena's eyes shift from him to the writhing girl at her feet, wheels turning inside her head. She reaches down to ruffle Jessie's hair, grinning at the way her captive fights against her touch. "It's perrrfect. I don't just like it—I *love* it. And I know *exactly* what to do with it."

CHAPTER ONE

Alexi

I folded the morning's newspaper and set it down on the kitchen table, the headline of the Big City section reading, "Stocks Soar for Wondermann Corp." As intrigued as I was about what caused Mr. Wondermann's decidedly dangerous business to quadruple stock values overnight, the antics of my siblings Max, Cat, and Pietr, and Max's girlfriend, Amy, demanded my more immediate attention.

"So I said to him," Max began, pointing at Pietr, " 'I thought she was with *you*.' We had split up for a little and—"

Cat stepped in, still carrying a shopping bag from their recent outing to the mall. "And *I* said: 'You mean to tell me you've lost Jessie?' " She gave Max a hard look before returning her gaze to me. "He manages to lose his sneakers and at least one sock out of most of his pairs—and do not get me started about how very remote the TV remote becomes once he's used it—but to lose an entire person?"

"*I* didn't lose her!" Max bellowed, glaring at Pietr instead.

I cleared my throat, and all eyes were on me, my position as eldest brother and previous alpha a help. "Are we quite certain Jessie has not just gone home?"

They all looked at one another.

"Seriously? You think I didn't try calling her?" Amy asked me. "She's not answering her cell."

"Does she always answer her cell?"

"I had Pietr call with *his*," Amy said, as if that was all the answer I needed. It was. Jessie would always pick up a call from Pietr.

"Who was responsible for Jessie last?" I asked.

"Don't ever let her hear you talk like that," Amy said. "She'll kick your ass."

"Language," Cat warned with a sniff.

I shrugged. "She has a gift for getting into trouble."

Amy leveled her gaze at me. "Pietr's in charge of stating the obvious. And just because a thing is true, it doesn't mean we say it out loud," she scolded.

Max chuckled. "We were at the mall. Pietr and I hit the Game Shop. The girls were trying on clothes. Is it any surprise they lost track of her when Cat was distracted by what color makes her boobs look better?"

"It's green, you oaf. And they don't need to look *better,* but it does somehow make them appear bigger." She paused, blinking at him in frustration. "And that was most certainly *not* the issue," she added with a *hrumph*. "Jessie said she was going to catch up to you two and talk with Pietr."

"Well, it seems obvious she did not succeed." Unease unfolded in the pit of my stomach. "It is very unlike Jessie to simply . . ."

"Pick up and leave?" Amy asked.

"*Da*. Unless . . ." Turning to Pietr, I asked, "Were you somehow a jerk to her?"

"*Nyet*," he said, defensive. "I barely paid her any attention at all—"

Cat and Max groaned in unison.

"Jerk," I confirmed, nodding my head.

"You've been kind of aloof since you got cured," Amy stated more gently, reaching for Pietr's arm.

He looked down, shoulders slumping. "I never intended for that to happen. We searched the mall. . . ."

"This may all be quite simple," I assured him. "Call the Gillmansen household."

They blinked at me.

"Use the landline," I clarified. "Her father may be home. Or Annabelle Lee. Either might have answers."

Pietr nodded and pulled out his cell, punching the proper button. "Mr. Gillmansen? *Da*. Is Jess around? *Nyet*. She is not with us." He looked at us, worry etching a crease between his brows. "He is yelling for her now."

We heard.

Pietr's focus returned to the phone. "She is? *Nyet*. *Da*. I understand. We will be there immediately." He headed straight for the door.

"Hold up," Amy said, grabbing his arm. "You said 'she is.' She's there?"

"*Nyet*," Pietr returned, paler than his normal pallor since taking the cure. "Rio is loose in the paddock. Spooked. Her stall door is hanging open."

Amy pressed the heels of her hands into her eyes and groaned. "This is bad." So fast he jumped in surprise, she grabbed Max's arm, saying, "We need a tracker."

Max did not need encouragement. He nearly beat us to the front door.

We piled into the convertible, Pietr, Amy, and Cat buckling into the back while Max took the driver's seat and I, as the girls said, rode shotgun. It was a very American phrase, sounding far more dominant than it was in reality.

The Gillmansen farm was not a long drive in good weather, but peering up through the windshield I realized we were not entering optimal driving conditions. Snow fluttered down from fattening clouds.

Travel might take significantly longer, and if Jessie's horse, Rio, was spooked, Jessie was most certainly in trouble. Time was, again, not on our side.

Marlaena

Leaning forward, I peeked out through the thin sliver of space between the door and doorjamb and looked down the motel's second-story breezeway toward Gareth's room. He'd be napping now, his shift guarding us recently over.

I didn't get it. What did Pietr see in Jessica Gillmansen? Why'd I even care? She was like anyone else in the world: brown hair, brown eyes, a medium athletic build . . . freckles spotted her nose and cheeks like any country girl who'd stood in the sun for a few minutes. She was a simple human being living in small-town America.

Absolutely unremarkable in every way.

But Pietr, who seemed every inch the alpha, saw something in her. Not that I cared. I didn't want to see any redeeming quality in her. For some weird reason she felt like competition.

Kyanne stalked along the breezeway, watching the parking lot below, keeping an eye out for trouble.

Maintaining a guard at all times was one thing I insisted on even though the motel *seemed* safe. I *seemed* like just an average college-age girl, but that was far from reality.

Gabriel teased me about not trusting anyone. He was very nearly right. I didn't trust anyone but Gareth. And he was the main reason I didn't trust myself.

Not far away, another reason I didn't trust myself—Jessica Gillmansen—was stashed in a forgotten storage shed. Her very existence made me undeniably insane. It had only been an hour since Gabe had delivered her as a belated birthday gift and I needed to decide how everything was going to play out. And decide what—or how—to tell Gareth.

God. I rested my forehead on the door. Where I was raised, kids wore those WWJD bracelets to ask themselves what Jesus would do. My guardians, Phil and Margie, pushed religion on me so hard I rejected it. I was more worried about what Gareth would do.

A door clicked open at my other side and Gabriel came into view, his eyes popping wide when I opened the door before he raised a fist to knock.

"Hello."

His eyes raked over me, taking in my thin cotton pajamas and pausing so long in his examination of my low-cut top that I thought he had to be memorizing the statement scrawled across my front. "It says, 'Sleep Is for Quitters.'"

He blinked up at me, his mouth opening. I stopped him before words—or drool—came. "If you're done staring at my tits, say whatever you came to say."

He pursed his lips and dropped his line of sight again to

piss me off. I smacked him, my fingers tingling in the after-
math of the sudden strike.

He touched his face, my palm hitting the same spot just
starting to heal from Jessica's defensive strike. He worked his
jaw, testing it. "You can't think you're sleeping tonight . . .
not with *her* here. . . ."

I shrugged. "This doesn't have to go down tonight." I
needed time to think.

He cocked his head, his naturally narrow eyes becoming
sparkling slits. "I'm not sure."

"Not tonight, honey." The only thing I wanted to think
about was getting rid of Jessica without Gareth knowing.

I began to close the door on him, but he wedged his shoe
between my door and its frame. "Are you going to screw this
up?"

"*I* don't screw things up. I make things happen."

A smile twitched at the corner of his lips. "I hope so. This
could make big things happen for us. You just have to be
ready."

"I'm ready. I just need . . ."

"What? What do you still need?"

"Time."

He snorted. "How much do you think you'll have before
they get here? It won't take them long to realize she's missing
and then connect us to her disappearance."

"I need time," I insisted, shoving him back so I could slam
the door shut. Silent and seething, I waited there until I heard
him walk away, muttering.

Dread lodged in my gut, I knew I needed to talk to Gareth.
Always on my mind and nudging his way into my heart, Gareth was the one I trusted. He'd help me see things clearly,

although it seemed whenever I was near him all I could see was *him*.

Until recently. Now being around him made me think of Pietr Rusakova. And that made me as queasy as knowing that I had Jessica in the shed made me happy.

Alexi

Rio was still racing around the paddock when we arrived at the Gillmansens' farm. Leon and his youngest daughter, Annabelle Lee, edged toward the horse with soft words and slow gestures.

I caught Leon's eye, and he nodded toward the barn. He had noticed something inside and wanted us to see it, too.

Max's nostrils flared when we stepped into the richly scented interior of the barn. I coughed at the hay and the dust motes swirling in the air.

"You might not want to be here," Max said to Amy, resting a heavy hand on her shoulder.

"Why?" Her eyes widened, and her mouth drew into a little "o" of fear. "Why, Max?" She started to move around him, but he looped his arm around her waist and pulled her close.

"There's blood ahead," he said, his eyes searching hers.

"Whose blood?"

"I don't know yet."

"It's a lot, isn't it?" she whispered. "For you to smell it over here."

"It is a significant quantity," he confirmed.

"I want to know whose it is," she said, determination setting her jaw. "Now."

"Then stay here and let me work." He gently pushed her back so she stood at arm's length from him.

She eyed him a moment and, as he turned toward what must have been the site of the fight, she burst past him with her best runner's sprint.

He roared, but as fast as she had run past him, that fast again she came to a stop.

"Oh. God."

It was a substantial amount of blood. It marked the wall, spraying and dripping down its length and leaving sloppy drops at close and regular intervals from there to the barn door. I was on the scene in a moment, searching for clues as Max pressed toward the wall.

"Oh. Look." Amy pointed to the floor and I squinted to see what she had discovered. My stomach turned on itself. Fingers.

Amy and Max reached a conclusion at the same time. "Not hers."

We breathed a collective sigh.

"Those are some guy's fingers," Amy said. "So who . . . ?" She looked at Max and me for an answer.

"Gabe," he muttered. "His oily scent is thick here."

Pietr stiffened. "Gabe's Marlaena's second in command. Why would he take Jess?"

Max shrugged. "You piss him off?"

Pietr shook his head.

"Not everything is about Pietr, as much as he might believe the world revolves around him," I reminded. "Now think. What motivation does Gabriel have? What does Gabriel want?"

"Marlaena?" Max asked with a shrug. "She's a hot little number."

"Standing right here, Tiger," Amy snapped, hands clenching into fists on her hips.

"Not that I noticed," Max backpedaled. "But what male in a pack wouldn't want to be the alpha's partner?"

"Is that what it's always about?" Amy muttered. "Control?"

"*Nyet*," I said. "Not for all of us. But"—I hesitated before grinding out the most difficult combination of words to make sense of in any language—"I think Max is right."

"If Gabe wants to be alpha, why take Jess?" Pietr wondered aloud.

"As an offering to Marlaena?"

I countered Max's question with my own. "But why *Jess?*"

"Because Marlaena wants . . ." Amy paused. "Wait. Because Gabe wants you—"

Pietr's eyebrows shot up.

"Not like *that*," Amy said with a snort. "Let me finish. He wants you—*all* of you—to go after Jessie. Maybe he wants a fight," she concluded.

I nodded. "He wants to be alpha, but he does not have a chance of winning Marlaena. So he is uniting the pack beneath him through a foreign war strategy."

"A what?"

"Come," I said, leading them back toward the modest house. "It is a traditional strategy among governments that when things are going poorly at home—domestically—the way to get people's minds off the failure of their own leadership is to make someone else appear to be a bigger enemy than they are. Start a foreign war and people unite beneath whoever declares it."

"That's insane," Amy muttered.

"Study your history and you will see it may seem insane, but it works time and time again."

"So we go with the 'start a foreign war' theory," Pietr muttered. "Fine. He wants a fight, he'll get a fight. Let them unite under Gabriel. We can worry about the fallout later. Our priority needs to be getting Jess back safely."

"Agreed," I said. "Let us do so. Now."

Mr. Gillmansen followed us to the house, and unfortunately *now* was minutes from my designated *now* as we explained the situation and told him why he should not come along and why *we* were the best solution.

I found myself being creative about the last bit.

We, of course, *were* also the problem.

Without us in Jessie's life, she never would have become entangled in such strange and dangerous situations. In the end, Mr. Gillmansen offered his truck, saying, "Four-wheel drive."

Annabelle Lee dashed inside and back out of the house again, and held out three flashlights to me. "You may need these."

"Maglites," I said.

Annabelle Lee nodded. "Jessie's favorite type," she said with a shrug.

I reached out and gave her a quick hug.

We took the flashlights and squeezed into the cab. Pulling the truck out of their gravel drive and onto the country road I allowed myself a moment to speculate while Max, Cat, and Pietr argued what we should do next and Amy punched holes in their plans.

If we had never come to Junction, Jessie would have never known us—although she was doing significant research on the Phantom Wolves of Farthington. Perhaps she still would have crossed our path.

I shook my head. What were the odds that a chance meeting regarding her research would have sparked such a mutual interest as had developed between Pietr and her? Love at first sight? That was not how things truly worked.

If we had never come to Junction, Jessie's life would have remained relatively simple. Nice. She would have dated some-one who attended school with her for years, not a recent arrival who happened to be a Russian-American werewolf, an *oborot*, as my people said: one transformed.

The boy would have been from a family with a more le-gitimate income than that obtained through the black market and hustling pool tables. He probably would have been a bright, handsome, clean-cut sort of guy.

Not unlike Derek.

I blinked. She *had* dated Derek.

With or without us, Jessie would have found the same danger. But without us there would have been no Max to make a rescue from Derek's bedroom when rescue was most definitely needed.

Derek had proven himself to be one of the most insidious of our opponents: a charming football player with a bright future and tremendously destructive psychic abilities allow-ing him to manipulate anyone with a touch. Even though he was dead, it seemed he had left a handprint on the psyches of Jessie, her friend Sophia, and Sarah Luxom.

I slapped the steering wheel, noting the silence that had filled the truck. Our appearance in Jessie's life had been a blessing of sorts, considering.

What a screwed-up place small-town America was. "What is the battle plan? Home first?"

Pietr opened his mouth to respond, but Amy glared at him. I had missed something.

Pietr shut his mouth again, and Amy began: "You're going to take me to the house. I'll get a gun—"

I turned in my seat to better look at her. "Exactly how much weapons training do you have?"

She tried to stare me down.

I clenched my jaw and stared back. "How much?"

She looked away, her lower lip sticking out and her chin trembling before she puffed out a breath and regained control. "None," she admitted. "But you need as much help as you can get, and I don't want to be sitting at home just hoping for the best. . . ."

Max reached out for her, but she pushed his hand away.

"Amy," I said in a voice both soft and firm, "we cannot have someone untrained going into a fight. It is more dangerous for all of us. A gun"—I paused, having her full attention—"is as dangerous in the hands of the untrained as it is in the hands of the enemy. You may have the best of intentions, but without the training to back them up, you, my dear, are more a liability than an asset."

"Then teach me so I'm no longer a liability," she said, crossing her arms.

"We will," I promised. "If that is what you want, we will. But it takes time, and we have none to spare today," I said. "Our first stop should still be the Queen Anne. I presume we should then head to the motel where they are staying."

Pietr leaned back as far as he could, his brow lowering. "*Da.* That is a logical place to start."

"Has anyone wondered how they're affording a motel?" Amy asked.

Pietr and Max turned to look at her.

"Seriously?" Amy sighed. "Okay. Maybe I'm more valuable to this crew than I realized." She wiggled in her seat belt. "There's a lot of them. A lot of werewolves. And werewolves— at least *these* werewolves—are territorial. They like having room to move. So it's not as if you can stack them like cord-wood. You can only get a few in a room. Maybe four—that's the legal maximum, anyhow."

Max peered at her.

"Long story. Let's just say there was a really long week-end in a motel with a bunch of us when things were really bad at home." She shrugged to dismiss it, the topic marked as off-limits.

Max slipped his hand over hers.

"So there's what—thirteen of them? That's like three or four rooms. Let's say three rooms every night. Even at a dive motel's rates, that adds up. Fast."

"We know they are not averse to theft," I pointed out.

"Right. The vending machines, the candy bars at the Grabbit Mart that Jessie saw Gabe take . . . petty stuff."

"The owner of Skipper's wound up dead," I said solemnly. "That was a theft."

Amy's lips pursed. "I didn't know that."

I nodded.

"Okay, Skipper's is by the Blockbuster, right? What do you think he took in a day? Several hundred—maybe a thou-sand dollars? I mean, it *is* after Christmas, so people have Christmas cash to burn—"

"Or Christmas bills to catch up on," I reminded her. "Let us be generous. Say he took in two grand a day."

"Fine. Two thousand dollars. Three hotel rooms a night . . ." Her eyes rolled up in thought, her lips turning down. "I don't think you can even make it a month in a dive motel for that. . . . And they've been wearing much nicer clothing. . . ."

"You are really paying quite a lot of attention to them, are you not?" I asked.

"You sound impressed."

"I never expected you to be so involved."

"I have my reasons to be invested," she assured me, her gaze falling on Max.

He smiled.

"So I think they're being sponsored by someone with resources. Someone with deep pockets."

Pietr's eyes narrowed. "Who?"

Amy twitched. "There's only one person who comes to mind. Are you sure Dmitri left Junction?"

The temperature dropped at the mention of his name. The idea that "Uncle" Dmitri was lurking around and had made connections with the new pack after Pietr did his best—sacrificed the wolf within himself—to be rid of him . . .

We did not answer her. The chance she was right was too frustrating to put even in monosyllabic words.

Max rolled down his window, sticking his face into the biting cold. The breeze tore at his eyes and turned his cheeks pink. "Maybe I'll pick up her scent when we get closer," he finally said, closing the window and slumping down, his eyes on the landscape rushing by.

"What will we do when we find her?" Pietr asked me.

I gave him a sidelong glance. "Whatever is necessary," I said with a coolness my racing heart betrayed.

"Hurt Marlaena? Kill her?" Pietr asked, peering out the window.

"Whatever is necessary."

He nodded and mimicked Max, slouching down in misery. "And if there is no scent to find—if they've covered their tracks so well there is no trail to discover? If Jess is gone—forever?"

I pulled the truck over so fast we skidded, everyone jerking against their seat belts. "There is something you are not telling me." I studied his impassive face. "Why would anyone kill Jessie? What else is going on here, Pietr? Kidnapping Jessie I understand to an extent. It seems nearly standard operating procedure in Junction. Things run smoothly, everyone feels comfortable and plans for a better future, and then it is time for someone to endanger a nearly average girl who lives on a wonderfully unremarkable horse farm. I think it is time to consider getting Jessie her own personal bubble," I concluded.

Pietr looked at me in the completely dramatic-hero fashion he had cultivated and—I peered closer at him to confirm my suspicion—*da*, he had *perfected* since meeting Jessie.

"It is completely logical they would take Jessie. It makes us come against Marlaena and engage a foreign war strategy. But *killing* her . . . Why would Marlaena want Jessie dead? How does she benefit?"

He shook his head, the mop of his hair falling into his eyes. "I have a feeling," he muttered. "There is something more here—something deeper . . . like someone wants to get at me by hurting Jess. . . ."

"Dmitri is far from your biggest fan," Amy said.

Both Pietr and Max looked at her and then away again. None of us wanted to believe Dmitri had returned, regardless of how likely it seemed.

CHAPTER TWO

Marlaena

"Gabriel, you are truly something," Dmitri said with a smile. "Taking the Gillmansen girl to lure Pietr to us . . ."

I didn't like how the smile twisted on his face. Yes, having Jessica Gillmansen as my prisoner gave me a bit of a high, but knowing Dmitri agreed with it made me question every bit of that amazing sensation.

Gareth slipped out of his room and onto the breezeway to stand beside me.

Our conversation ended.

Gabriel looked down into the parking lot; my gaze followed his, focusing on an old muscle car in the third row. In my peripheral vision someone hurried into the space beneath the extensive balcony and out of sight.

Huh.

Gareth's hand was on my arm, and I spun to face him.

"Good to know my presence is so influential. Gareth, destroyer of conversation."

I smiled, even though he wouldn't approve of what we had been discussing. I needed to keep him in the dark a little longer.

He was so kind and compassionate, so willing to be the cowboy in the white hat, or the knight, coming to everyone's rescue. He was the best of us. And I was going to keep dragging him down into the gutter with us. Just like Kyanne said. I pulled them out of one gutter to get them shot in another.

Some alpha I was.

I'd use the gift Gabe had given me, persuade Pietr to—what was I trying to persuade him to do? Let us stay in Junction? He didn't care if we didn't make any trouble . . . or have any fun. . . . What did I really *want* from Pietr? My palms pressed against the banister so hard the metal bit into me.

Did I want his pack to join ours? Yes. Why? It'd be an upheaval if he or Max tried for the alpha spot and . . . I cast a sideways glance at Gabriel. . . . I had plenty of trouble already.

Jordyn and Londyn opened the door to their room. "Uncle Dmitri!" they cried, hopping up and down like two schoolgirls.

I sighed. Because that's exactly what they were—two schoolgirls.

As young as they were chronologically, I usually translated their lives into wolf years and so forgot their actual ages. We'd been through so much it aged us, made us old souls. Old, worn out, embittered souls.

Dmitri turned on the charm, grinning and slapping his hands together. "How are my beauties?" he asked as they bounced forward, their nostrils flaring briefly to scent him for gifts. He brought them little treats now. Candies and odds and ends, jewelry and trinkets, things that he called *baubles*— and things Darby called *shinies*.

Useless things.

Things everyone desperately wanted—brand-name sneakers or purses—things no one really *needed*.

"He's buying them," Gareth muttered, watching more pups scramble for his attention.

"He's *providing* for them," I clarified. "Better than we can."

"When was the last time we *honestly* tried?"

I got hung up on his emphasis on *honestly*.

"We haven't tried doing anything *honestly* for months now," he added, moving closer to me. So close I smelled the mint on his breath. "We could, you know? I have ID, and my record was expunged after Mississippi. I could get a job." His gaze swept the parking lot and beyond. "There has to be work here—even in this podunk town."

I snorted. It seemed so simple. So moral. Get a job, feed the family. "Where, Gareth?" I asked. "Where would you work? What would you do?"

"There are burger joints in Junction. I can work a fryer or a grill."

My backbone slipped, and I bent across the banister, letting my arms slide over its edge so they hung limp. "You can't." My hands dangled loose from my wrists, useless.

He straightened, puffing out his chest as he sucked in a deep breath. "Of course I can," he said, like working as a fry cook would be some challenge to gallantly surmount.

"But, you're so smart . . . ," I whispered. "It's a crime to make you do menial labor."

He chuckled, the noise making my stomach tremble. Or

maybe it was how he stood so close that made my body act that way. . . . "There are far better men and women than me working what you call *menial labor*. People with degrees in education and psychology and the arts. Amazing people who had big dreams but small means. People like that, they sacrifice their dreams—or delay them—so their families make it. This pack *is* my family. I'd give anything for them."

"Jesus Christ."

I gawked at Gabriel, having forgotten he was there.

"Seriously, Gareth. You're just dying for your own cross and crown of thorns. Sacrifice this, sacrifice that. Give until it hurts. Who ever gave anything for *us*—even a damn? No one. Families failed us. Friends failed us. The system—*you* of all people know better than anyone—the system failed us. So why feed it with our sweat and blood?" Gabe held the banister between whitened fingers and then dropped to do presses against it, his arms rippling with long, lean muscle as he hissed out his frustration. "If you want to feed the system and get nothing in return, be my guest. But don't expect us to be so self-sacrificing."

"I don't expect *you* to do it, Gabriel," he said.

With a grunt Gabe pushed back from the banister and whipped around, heading after Dmitri. He paused a few yards away, looking over his shoulder at me. "You and I have something planned, don't we?" He didn't wait for my answer, but stalked away, self-confidence marking his stride.

Gareth looked at me, suspicion marring his features. "You two have plans?"

I swallowed. "Not like you think . . ."

He raised his hands between us. "It's okay," he stated, backing up. "It's not like you and I made any plans." He shrugged and, giving me a sad smile, turned and left me on my own outside our rooms.

Jessie

Inside the shed where they'd stashed me the frost on the ground melted under my cheek, shoulder, hips, and side, just long enough for moisture to wick into my clothing and chill me. Sound was muffled by the snow I guessed was still falling outside. I couldn't be near any houses or well-traveled buildings because, lying there, awake the entire time, I knew no one had been by since they'd dumped me.

I ground my teeth into the gag and focused. I liked to think I'd come a long way since I first met Pietr, but lying bound and gagged, I wondered exactly how much I'd truly grown.

A smarter girl wouldn't have gotten kidnapped—again—in the first place. A smarter girl would have thought to leave some trail—it sounded a little Hansel and Gretel, sure, but didn't survivors of abduction usually do something clever to help their heroes find them? Didn't survivors drop a bracelet, a necklace, a cell phone, or tear out the brake lights from the car trunk they were transported in? Sure, I was unconscious for part of that, but survivors . . .

I swallowed, realizing.

Survivors.

Maybe I wasn't slated for survival.

I squeezed my eyes shut, trying to close out the thought.

Jessica Alice Gillmansen, body discovered in an old shed because she was TSTL.

Survival of the fittest—maybe this was finally the proof; I wasn't fit to survive.

Behind my eyelids like a movie recorded with a shaky camera, images came into focus and my stomach roiled in rebellion.

Derek. I was going to be sick.

Even better. *Jessica Gillmansen, body discovered in an old shed, where she'd choked on her own vomit. Not even her kidnappers had the satisfaction of offing her, because she was, simply, TSTL: too stupid to live.*

I fought the bile back down and sank into the vision, knowing the remnants of Derek, dead but not truly gone, were rising to the surface of my brain again.

I floated behind the eyes of someone just a few feet tall, walking down a long hallway, fancy rugs underfoot, paintings thick with pigment hanging in long blurs of color on either wall. I passed a low-set window and strained to catch my reflection in its sparkling glass.

Derek at age six, maybe?

I—he—paused outside a door that was open a crack, pressing his face against the space between the door and its frame. Inside were two people: a quiet-looking woman with a soft body, narrow nose, and sharp eyes; and a tall man with golden hair and strong features. . . . There were aspects of Derek in both of them. They had to be his parents.

Someone spoke in the room, but neither Derek's mother's nor his father's mouth moved. Someone was with them.

"It is survival of the fittest, and we are breeding the fittest humans ever. It makes sense there would be some casualties."

"Casualties," the woman gasped, and I—he—*we* looked closer. Her makeup had run, tears streaking down her face.

"You make it sound like we're in some war. We just lost a baby. . . ."

"It was a miscarriage. Unfortunate, that's true. But you're young and healthy and you still have Derek."

"Some consolation that is," she whispered, lowering her head.

"You will try to have another child. Your genetics are absolutely amazing. . . ."

"You arrange all this—everything—" she retorted, "as if we were show dogs to be bred and sold."

"No. Nooo," the mystery person said, a woman by the pitch of her voice, and suddenly she was in view. A slender brunette with her hair tucked up in a conservative style. My breath caught, recognizing her. Dr. Jones. "We are simply encouraging good matches."

"'Encouraging good matches'? Is that what you call taking DNA samples and arranging marriages?"

"No. I call that prudent science and evolution."

"Mary. Stop harping on the woman. She's just doing her job."

"And is that what we should do? Treat all this, our marriage, our children"—she caught herself with a gasp and corrected herself, saying—"our *child*, as a job?"

He looked at her, stoic and aloof. For a long minute he watched her, letting her cry quietly. "You do know survival of the fittest doesn't mean survival of the strongest or the fastest—the ones who survive and thrive are the ones who *adapt*. You need to adapt to our special circumstances." He turned to Dr. Jones. "I apologize for my wife, Doctor. She's emotionally distraught over the loss of our baby. We both are aware that Derek is a prize asset, very trainable and potentially the first in our line."

"So you will both get back on the job shortly," Dr. Jones confirmed. "And adapt to your circumstances."

"Of course."

Derek's mother just hung her head and we stepped back, the images fading away and leaving me in the dark of the old shed, colder than ever, one thought in my head: *adapt to survive.*

Alexi

"Are you sure I can't help?" Amy dogged my steps, following me from room to room in the Queen Anne as I opened closets and pulled out gun and knife cases and other things that had become tools of my rather unsavory trade. My time with the black market had served me well. By being one of the bad guys so frequently, I knew how to handle the same sort of people when I had to switch my black hat for a white one.

"Amy," I finally said, setting one case on the foot of my bed and popping the latches so it sprung open. "If you want to help, assemble that." I pointed to the gleaming Glock.

She stared at me.

"Then stay out of my way," I added, grabbing the gun and slamming it together before I opened the Baggie containing the scrap of an old T-shirt still damp with gun oil and wiped down the gun's muzzle.

She crossed her arms, and the stare became a glare. "I just want to help get Jessie back."

"I know. But right now there is nothing you can do but stay out from underfoot and wait for our return." I handed the Glock to Cat. "Unless."

"Unless what?" Amy asked, stepping closer.

"Do you pray?"

She swallowed. "Occasionally" was all she committed to, finding something fascinating about the floor nearby rather than keeping her eyes on mine.

"Excellent. Now would be a wonderful time to reconnect with your god. Pray for us." I brushed past her, Cat close behind, Max still in the dining room with Pietr, laying plans.

"You must not hesitate if the moment comes," Max was saying.

"I have not recently been known for my mercy," Pietr snapped at his brother. "Dmitri believes—"

"*Da*," I interjected. "Dmitri *believes* you killed those people at his orders. But we know you got them out. You were not a murderer—you were their salvation. The premeditation of murder is more than you might be up to."

"And," Cat added, "if Amy is correct and Dmitri is back in the picture . . ."

"There will be additional trouble and perhaps a necessity to premeditate such a severe act. Hesitation may cost us in lives. *He* will surely have the proper bullets."

"And with only one wolf . . . ," Amy whispered, looking at Max pointedly.

"I will be careful," he assured her. "I have much to return to. But, Pietr, if Marlaena . . ."

"I am prepared to kill her," he muttered.

Something heavy as a stone sank into the pit of my stomach. He said the words, but his tone was wrong—his body language soft and lacking determination. He was not being honest with us about something. Or perhaps not being honest with himself.

Perhaps he did not even know what it was. . . .

I squinted at him, examining his posture. Something was wrong beyond the fact he was still a werewolf—minus the wolf.

"We need to go," Cat said from the door, her coat, hat, and gloves on once more. She looked more the part of a fashion plate than someone on a rescue mission.

"*Da*. We must."

We gathered the last odds and ends that defined us as being officially at war and left Amy and the comfort of the house for one more dangerous adventure.

Marlaena

They were bouncing on the beds, doing jumping jacks and moves that'd make a simple human cheerleader jealous of their agility and grace. "Down!"

Londyn bounced one more time, grinning.

My growl knocked the bounce out of her and she slipped off the bed to land nimbly on the floor, pouting.

"Why, *why* must you ruin everyone's fun, Marlaena?" Dmitri asked, giving the pups his best *She sucks the life right out of the party* look.

"If they create a disturbance, we get complaints. Then the motel's manager will kick us out or raise the rent."

Dmitri shrugged. "Do I not handle all the bills?"

"Just because you can handle the bills, and possibly the manager," I said, my gaze drifting to the bulge in his waistband where he kept one gun (there were others), "doesn't mean we need additional attention." I glared evenly at each pup. "So keep it under control. You got me?"

They nodded slowly, lips drawn into thin straight lines.

"Under control," Kyanne repeated, each syllable separated. "Thank goodness you lead by example."

I was on her in an instant, my hands wrapped around her neck, my face so close to hers I brushed the hair hanging across her forehead.

"There you go again," she croaked. "Leading by example . . ."

Strong hands gripped my shoulders and a mouth was by my ear, whispering, ". . . now. Leave her be. Shhhh. 'laena . . ." Gareth's hands slipped around me and traveled the slow lengths of my arms to get to where my fingers pressed tightly to Kyanne's throat. One by one he loosened them. "Shhh. She's a *child*. She's disappointed. She's not challenging you. . . ."

I rolled back, limp against his chest, my eyes burning with anger. I was trapped in a world where I couldn't do anything right. The pack was turning against me.

My family was falling apart. . . .

"Thanks, Gareth," Kyanne said, bitterness in her voice. "*She's a child,*" she repeated. "Awesome. Like *I'm* the immature one."

"Shhh," he urged her. "Then don't admit to being immature," he agreed in a calm whisper so close his breath heated the edge of my ear. "But if it's not that—"

"Brave," she snapped. "I'm being *brave* enough to speak up."

"There's a thin line between bravery and stupidity," he concluded, his tone so calming it made my skin crawl. His even pitch reminded me of the lapping of the ocean on the shore. Steady. Dependable.

I closed my eyes and focused on breathing. I heard Kyanne scramble away from me. I concentrated on the rise and fall of Gareth's chest, the strong beat of his heart, the soft sound of his breathing, his existence anchoring me . . . and I took sanctuary in that moment.

"Get up, Princess," he whispered. "Let's take a minute. Just you and me, okay? We'll have us another stroll."

I grunted and let him help me to my feet. He slipped an arm around my waist and, guiding me out of the motel room, paused on the long balcony.

The door closed and the volume inside the room rose once again. But Gareth held me—stopped me from going back inside to shout some more.

"I don't know what I'm doing," I confessed. "I'm . . ."

The room grew silent, and shadows hinted at figures leaning behind the curtains on the far side of the picture window.

Gareth nodded. "A stroll," he said, turning us as one and starting us on our way.

"They're going to get us in trouble," I protested. "They'll get us noticed."

"Since when did you worry about trouble?" He tugged at the ends of my hair, teasing me. My bright red hair had been an issue for the guys for a while, Gareth being quick to point out how memorable redheads are. If we really didn't want to attract attention, I should dye my hair. Go brunette. Be just like the less memorable majority.

So I hadn't.

"I get it. I'm a hypocrite."

"Don't," he whispered.

"What?"

"Don't be like that. Not with me."

"What do you mean?"

"You're so all-or-nothing. Hot or cold. Love or hate. It's like there are no settings in between. You take things too far sometimes."

"I commit. I'm not wishy-washy," I defended myself.

He smiled at me. "There you go again. It's not being wishy-washy to just take it easy sometimes."

"They can't be breaking beds."

"They weren't. They were bouncing on them."

"Ugh."

"Something's eating you up inside," he said, pulling me tight to him. "Tell me what it is."

"I can't." I thought about Jessica Gillmansen. Duct-taped and hidden away. About Pietr and the way his image ghosted around in my head.

Gareth's hand slipped from around my waist to hang beside him, his fingertips brushing mine. They stroked the inside of my palm, and the world blurred and tilted as I struggled to keep breathing. "Come with me," he said, fingers encircling my wrist.

I nodded, feeling fire brush my face as my ears fought to decode his tone. "Yes," I replied, not caring what he was trying to do because at least he was trying to do it with *me*.

He slid his magnetic key out of his pocket and tugged me toward a door. Room 206.

Gareth's room.

My vision swam.

"I need you—"

I didn't hear the rest of what he was saying because the sound of the ocean—of my pulse fuzzing out—filled my ears. Gareth *needed* me. . . .

The door opened, and we slipped inside, his body snug to mine. Even in the dim room I could see the strong angles of his face: the sharp jawline and crisp cheekbones, the broad and supple lips that rested a thumb's width from the base of his aquiline nose. And the powerful eyebrows, so much like the bend and sweep of a blackbird's wing. . . . Beneath which his lavender eyes lit with just a hint of the wolf's red.

Moving backward, my calves bumped up against the edge of the bed and my breath caught. He bent down, flowing like deep, dark water, and untied my shoelaces, slipping off my sneakers. Then his eyes met mine again and he grinned, his lips twisting at one end. A sliver of white showed from between them as they parted to reveal his perfect teeth.

"Ready?" he whispered, stepping on the heel of one of his sneakers with the toe of the other to shirk them both off.

I nodded, mute. With Gareth, I felt ready for anything.

His hands closed around my waist and he lifted me onto the bed. The grin, all devil now, widened, the beads at the ends of his dreadlocks bouncing.

He jumped onto the bed and looked down, stooping over me, the entire mattress rocking. He took my hands. "Up, Princess," he said, rolling his weight back and forth so the bed moved like the waves on an unsettled ocean.

"You're kidding," I whispered, glad the bad lighting hid the blush rising in my cheeks. "You brought me here to . . ."

"Bounce," he finished with a laugh. And, holding my hands, he started bouncing in small but growing increments and forced me to join in as his jumps got bigger and crazier. . . .

I laughed, my head rolling back as the sound poured out. I was bouncing, my feet quick to leave the fluff of the comforter and reach for the ceiling instead.

Gareth laughed, watching me, his eyes crinkling as his mouth opened to let out bigger and bigger laughs—laughs that bordered on shouts of joy.

And then, suddenly, his face became serious—intense—and he stopped his jumping, his legs spread wide to keep his balance as my own jumping died down, my face getting as serious as his.

"What?" I asked, reaching for him. "Is something wrong?"

"No," he replied, his tone flat, eyes shining. "You were laughing."

I nodded.

"Everything's right." He grabbed me by my shoulders and kissed me. *Hard.*

CHAPTER THREE

Jessie

Noise outside the shed made me peel my eyes open again. I was still nauseated from my last vision of Derek. Being inside his head—or, more properly, having him inside *my* head—was unsettling at best.

Had Derek been bred like his memory showed? Had some dark agenda been going on in and around Junction for years? What sort of group would arrange marriages in today's society just in hopes of getting kids with freaky super powers? Sure, it wasn't like the bite of a radioactive spider was enough to do it (and how many people would volunteer to try, spiders being creepy and all—especially the ones with hairy legs), but getting married to someone just because of the kids you might produce seemed even worse.

What sort of group would have that much power over people to encourage that sort of behavior?

Of course . . . Derek's parents did both come from money. Perhaps *that* was how the other half lived—bizarrely.

There was a scratching noise at the shed's door. Too light to be a wolf or dog. . . . A shadow moved in the little space between the doors, and a small nose with whiskers poked its way into the opening. A mouse wiggled inside and pulled itself up on its haunches to sniff the air and peer at me with tiny black eyes.

Snow peppered down from a small hole in the shed's roof, flakes tumbling not far from the mouse's twitching whiskers.

Great. Add insult to injury by dumping me in a mouse's nest. I growled and thrashed toward it, and it let out a little squeak and dodged back out the way it had come. The brief sense of victory I had was quickly replaced by the knowledge I was still trapped. Still bound and gagged and helpless.

Alexi may have trained me to fight hand to hand, and Wanda may have increased my combat shooting capability, but no one had trained me for this scenario. Once again I was on my own—left to my own limited devices.

I didn't want to do this anymore. I didn't want to constantly worry about the rivals of werewolves and their relationships or retribution for me just being me and loving who I wanted to love and living the way I wanted to live. . . .

I was babbling.

Something chewed at the edges of my vision, and a shiver ran through me, making me tremble from the inside out. I felt him like static when laundry was fresh from the dryer on a winter day, making the hairs on my arms prickle and rise even covered as they were in my long sleeves and jacket. I itched with the sensation of Derek again taking hold of me, and I cried out as the view of the shed's interior was violently ripped away and replaced with the quivering view of another posh room in what I could only presume was Derek's expansive home up on the Hill.

This room had a carefully appointed ceiling, trimmed with crown molding—like the stuff you saw in restored historic houses that had been relegated to becoming museums. Wallpaper with delicate and organic scrollwork coated the walls and gave the place an air of being untouched and unchanged over many decades.

I gasped, my focus coming back to someone standing right before me. I heard her before I saw her. She was gagging. . . . I squinted through Derek's eyes, and she snapped into crisp detail—as did the stinging sensation ebbing through my cheek. It was his mother. Choking. On her tears?

"Mommy's sorry," she said, wiping clumsily with the back of her shaking hand at the water that raced out of her eyes. "But you have to focus. You have to master this lesson before she arrives, otherwise . . . " Her eyes closed and more tears seeped out. "Auntie will be here in less than an hour, Derek," she insisted. "And you have to show her . . ."

My lips—his lips—were moving, and I heard us say, "I don't want to do this anymore. I don't like this."

"I'm sorry, baby," she murmured, wiping at my cheek, her fingers coming away wet with Derek's tears. "This is why you were born. When you've learned all these lessons, no one will ever rival your power. Don't you want that? To be powerful? To never be afraid?"

"I want to go play. . . ."

"I'm sorry," she whispered, her eyes flashing. "Most of us don't get what we really want." Her head hung a moment, and when she looked at us next, her jaw was set and firm even in that soft-looking face of hers. "You can take some time away after Auntie comes and sees that you've learned your lessons. That you're fit."

We nodded.

"Now focus on *her.*"

I gasped, seeing a woman in a jogging suit slumped in a nearby chair. A woman with blond hair hanging loose around her shoulders, and strong features that I'd come to recognize too well now. I knew her even without her signature ponytail.

Wanda.

About ten years ago.

"Be gentle, but be firm. We don't want to reduce every visitor to a drooling idiot like we accidentally did that Bible thumper. All you need to do is slip into her brain and find what she most wants to do in life. . . ."

Our gaze focused on Wanda, and the skin of her forehead seemed to peel back and her skull unfolded and we were absorbed into her gray matter. In a moment we stood in the foyer of a dimly lit house.

"Hurry, baby," a voice oozed out of the woodwork of the hallway and spurred us forward.

"Hurry, hurry—find the door. . . ."

"It's not here," we hissed, spinning to again view all the doors lining an impossibly long hallway. A hallway that, the more we tried to look to see its end, to see where we had entered, the longer it stretched and the more doors popped into existence to fill the walls.

"It is there. It has to be," Mommy urged us. "You don't have much time. She must have some defenses."

"Does she know it's me?" we asked. "That I'm the one setting the trap?"

"No—not at all. She just knows someone is. But it doesn't matter what she knows or how she can adapt. You are better.

Stronger. More able. Find the door. Open every one of them, if you must."

And we did. We raced down the hall, throwing doors open wide—doors to Wanda's memories: her first kiss, her prom, her entrance exam for the academy . . .

"Stop, stop!" Mommy shouted. "Too much too fast . . . She's struggling. Look at the doors. Focus on your goal. You'll see a sign. There's always a sign."

We stood stock-still, spread our feet shoulder-width apart, and balled our hands into fists. Down the hall about halfway to forever the wall had distorted into a door that wobbled and glowed.

"Got it!" we shouted as we rushed toward it and flung it open.

We paused inside a tidy office space. Only as wide as we were with our arms stretched straight out at our sides, it was still a happy place with potted plants on the desk and a huge assortment of colorful books and pictures filling a few tall bookshelves.

"Do you see her life's desire?"

We examined the area, running our fingers across the spines of books and watching their titles rearrange themselves, letters rippling and falling into unreadable jumbles at our touch and then straightening again, shaking themselves and climbing back into their proper order and place.

"Is it temporary? What I'm doing?" Derek asked.

"Only if you let it be," Mommy answered. "But you can change a life forever if you just try."

"Forever," we whispered, making our way beyond the bookshelf.

On a wall hung a whiteboard.

Words were carefully written in a dozen different colors of

marker, each in friendly, bubbly handwriting. Kindness, Sharing, Love, Gentleness, Reading, Writing, Arithmetic, Friendship, Self-Esteem, Good Manners, Self-Worth, Science, Art, Social Studies, and Phys Ed were each in a circle with a line extending from it back to the largest bubble of them all, with two words written in neat, large script in the board's center.

TEACH KINDERGARTEN

Our heart raced. "We've found it. There's a whiteboard with her goal," Derek said. "She wants to be a teacher."

Mommy laughed, and deep inside Derek, who was deep inside me, I shivered at the sound. "Well, that will never do," she said. "Pick up the eraser and let's make up her mind for her."

I fought him. I begged him. *Don't do it,* my mind screamed. *Don't erase her dream and replace it. . . .*

But he grabbed the eraser and went to work, his arm sweeping the height and width of the board to wipe it clean. To wipe out any trace of her dreams and desires.

"It's not coming off. . . ."

"Put your back into it," Mommy commanded. "Push your will onto hers."

I was going to be sick, but there was no way I could. I was without form. *He* was without form. . . .

I was watching the memories of a ghost.

The queasiness passed as he worked with a fierce passion and the words began to disappear.

Mommy wasn't just erasing Wanda's future, she was changing Derek's by letting him tamper with another person's soul.

Inside his head, I cried. For both of them.

"Now what?"

The floor beneath our feet shifted, the boards buckling.

"Mommy?"

"What is it?"

"The room is . . . tilting. . . ."

"Oh. Very good. She knows something's wrong. She's strong enough to rebel. Be quick, baby. You need to write the new goal and get out."

Back the way we'd come the door swung open and closed like a chewing mouth as the entire office slanted.

"What do I write?"

"In the center, write: 'Work for the CIA.' Then surround it with these words: 'Shoot, Train, Fight, Work, Battle, Justice, Blood, Compete, Rise.'"

We scrawled the words on the whiteboard, connecting them back to her goal with a trembling hand.

The walls shuddered, pictures dancing off hooks and nails to crash on the floor and throw splinters of glass at us. "Finished!" we screamed.

"Not yet," Mommy said as we grabbed hold of the whiteboard's tray to keep our footing. "Grab all the markers so she can't rewrite her destiny."

I heard the smile in her voice and I shivered again.

We grabbed the sliding markers and shoved them into every pocket as things fell off the bookshelves and rolled under the desk. "Done!"

"Good boy! Now get out of there!"

We let go of the whiteboard and slid toward the door, kicking it open and bursting out into the hallway.

The ceiling undulated, tiles popping loose and flying in our direction, and Derek screamed, "Ouuut!"

We were back in the room with Mommy, her face so close to ours we pulled back in surprise. She patted our hand.

"How did I do?" we asked, panting from our efforts.

"Beautifully. You didn't give up, and you adapted to new circumstances. You're a survivor," she said proudly. "Now let's get things ready for Auntie's arrival."

I plummeted back into my own head—or he seemed to be vomited out of mine—but his mother's words stuck.

"You didn't give up, and you adapted to new circumstances. You're a survivor."

It was like Derek was sharing a lesson with me. With a groan, I kicked my feet out in front of me and rolled up onto my butt. The blanket fell off my shoulders, but it didn't matter. Energy from Derek's memory still washed through me beside the roaring headache. If I was going to survive this, I had to adapt.

And I was determined to survive.

Marlaena

My brain spilled out of my ears as my lips parted for Gareth's kiss. His mouth was all cloves and cinnamon drenched in honey, his lips somehow both soft and firm, his tongue delicately probing along the edge of my mouth, precise as a cautious finger.

I sucked him down, filled my head with his smell, his taste, and wrapped my arms around him, letting my hands glide over the powerful muscles of his back and come to rest on his hips, just above that magnificent ass of his. He pressed me so close against his chest that my boobs ached, squashed against him the way I was, but I didn't care. Because this was me and Gareth. Together. The way I'd wanted things to be for so long.

And then he pulled back from me so slowly I followed him, bending toward that delicious mouth like a moth drawn to the buzzing bulbs outside each room at the motel. "What?" I whispered—no, I *gasped*. Parts of me were on fire, parts of me buzzed with an energy—a hunger—I never felt except when I was chasing my prey, fur and flesh and hot, sweet blood just a hairsbreadth away. "What is it?"

So close I couldn't see his mouth, I still knew he smiled because of the way the corners of his eyes crinkled. His dreads rubbed against my forehead, a bead bouncing across the tip of my nose as he shook his head. "You are so beautiful. So strong." Then he stepped back on the bed, and my world tilted as my feet tried to compensate for the shift of the mattress beneath my feet. "But we should . . ." His arms dropped away from me, and he took my hands off his hips and held them, watching them intently as they curled limply in his own.

My hands looked as pale and weak as skim milk against the richer and warmer tone of even the palms of his hands.

"We should take things slow," he said softly.

I yanked my hands away, the sting of rejection sharp. "Fine."

He grabbed my hands again and took advantage of his better balance, pulling me close once more. "I'm sorry?" he asked, searching my eyes for some clue.

I pushed back from him and caught myself as I tumbled off the edge of the bed, making my stumble look more like a dismount. Barely. "It's completely logical," I admitted, fighting to keep the acid from my voice. "You don't want the responsibilities that come with being bound to an alpha and . . . well . . ." I brushed the hair back from my eyes and straightened, throwing my shoulders back and my boobs out. Yeah. I had great boobs. And I made damned certain he knew it. And that he knew he wouldn't be touching them for a very long time. "And I'm an alpha. I can't just go screwing around with someone who can't shoulder responsibility."

He opened his mouth to object, but before he could say what I'd guessed all along—that he wasn't shirking responsibility—I added, "I have to think of the pack."

His mouth closed and he nodded. "You're right," he said as a conciliatory measure. "I'm not good enough for you."

I blinked. I thought of Jessica Gillamansen, duct-taped and gagged nearby. My stomach quivered. *Gareth* wasn't good enough for *me*. It was the furthest thing from the truth.

"I like you, Gareth," I admitted, my heart quivering at my willingness to put words to my feelings. "But you're right. Slow is best. Maybe pause or stop is even better."

Before he could say anything else, I left, letting the door slam behind me.

Alexi

I fought to keep the interior of the truck's windshield from fogging up between the heat of Max's breath and the cold of the blustering wind.

"And exactly what will we do when we get to the motel?" Pietr asked.

"Max will scent for their rooms—" I leaned forward and rubbed my sleeve against the windshield to give myself a swatch of vision.

"Or Jessie," Max stated, his nose to the open window.

"And we will confront Marlaena and demand she return her."

It seemed simple enough.

"And if they put up a fight?"

"We will give them the fight of their lives."

"And if Dmitri is there?"

"We'll argue over who gets to kill him," Max muttered.

I shook my head.

"There will be no killing unless we're left with no other choice. They are *oboroten*. They are like us—like you," he corrected, looking at Max.

"They may be *oboroten*, but they are nothing like us. They are thieves—"

"And very likely murderers," I reminded. "There is one shopkeeper less in this small American town, and I am willing to bet it is their fault."

Max stretched in his seat. "And we know what that means," he stated, folding his arms behind his head. "You don't make bets you aren't sure of winning."

"I would bet you are correct," I confirmed, easing more weight onto the truck's gas pedal. "But the fact remains they are *oboroten* and should be given a chance at being something other than our rivals."

Marlaena

I crept down the motel's stairs and around the back of the building to watch them, sipping substandard coffee. It was still coffee, at least. A totally legal upper with a dark and grim flavor perfect to reflect my mood.

It wasn't like I was going to sleep tonight, anyway.

Dmitri and Noah scuffled a minute in the clearing between the motel's back wall and the single line of trees marking the property's boundary.

Dmitri barked out a laugh and threw Noah back to land

on his ass. I nearly threw my cup and shouted, but the pup's blond hair just ruffled with the impact, his cheeks pink from the cold, his mouth open with something between laughter and a gasp of surprise. Laughter won, and he nodded at Dmitri and popped back onto his feet, brushing the snow off his jeans.

I stayed still and quiet, sucking up the scent of my coffee and watching them.

Crouched nearby, Terra huddled under a hoodie, grinning and clearly impressed by Noah. They had joined the pack at nearly the same time. I'd nearly rejected her—she didn't fit in anywhere, except with Noah. He had convinced me that she needed to be part of the family.

But she was still "a square peg trying to fit into a round hole," as Margie would have said.

Of course, our entire pack was made up of square pegs, if you thought about the rest of society.

Dmitri reached out a hand and signaled at Noah to advance on him again.

Noah grinned and rushed him. Dmitri simply stepped aside, letting him barrel by. "You fight like Maximilian Rusakova," he called as Noah skidded to a stop, bits of snow flying up from his sneakers. "You are expecting to use your body's bulk as a weapon. But look at yourself."

Noah did as he was told, his gaze scraping down his own body. How did he see himself? As the skinny, pimply faced kid with poor posture that his parents always told him he was? As the geeky boy whose quiet intelligence made him a target for his peers at school? Or as a young man with a wolf raging inside?

Dmitri shoved his shoulder. Playfully. "You are strong, there is no doubting that. And clever. But you are not built like a tank. You cannot afford to act like you are, either."

Noah grunted. "Okay, so what do I do if I can't out-muscle someone?"

"Outsmart them instead."

He nodded solemnly, a smile slowly stretching his slender lips. "That I can do."

Dmitri chortled, and I slipped back the way I'd come, letting Dmitri again get Noah into a fighting stance.

Jessie

I looked around the shed, my eyes as adjusted to the low light as they could be. There were a few tools left abandoned in its rusty hulk, which only strengthened my hypothesis that wherever this shed was, no one other than my kidnappers would be opening its doors soon.

An old hoe with a broken and splintery handle, a shovel—I was liking shovels more and more after lopping off a couple of Gabriel's fingers with one in a pinch. *Pinch.* I snorted despite my predicament. Pinching was one thing Gabe wouldn't be doing easily ever again. Not with his right hand.

The gag molded to my smile and I tested my wrists against the duct tape binding them. Still snug. I needed to correct that. I needed my hands free in order to have any chance of getting out of here alive.

Unless they wanted me alive . . . But why . . . ? Why did I feel like bait for some trap?

I scooted around to get a better view of my surroundings. An old lawn mower, a gas can—probably empty since I couldn't really smell fumes seeping out—and . . .

That'd do nicely.

Propped against one hard rubber wheel was an old lawnmower blade. If I could just make sure it stayed still . . . I looked at it and where it rested and tried to keep the picture carefully in my mind as I edged my way back around so my stiff but grasping fingers were closest to the blade. I carefully reached out toward it and tried sliding the duct tape along one edge of its blade, but it rocked and I caught my breath and froze, afraid it would roll back and totally out of reach.

Tentatively I caught hold of the blade with one hand and tugged at it until I heard it scrape and roll forward over the wheel. I grunted. Yeah. Niiice. Right into my back. That'd bruise.

I grabbed it again and gave a little shake, but it stayed still. Adjusting my position, I stroked my wrists along the old blade's length, rubbing and rubbing until I heard the duct tape begin to give way, threads popping as I continued, layer by layer, chafing metal against my wrists in order to free them.

My shoulders began to ache, but my hands—my hands began to move farther apart by increments of millimeters as I sawed through the tape.

Adapt to survive. I could do this.

With one last pop, the tape tore loose and my hands fell limp at my sides.

I shook my shoulders, urging life back into my limbs. I stood up and stretched.

I tried the door and heard chains rattle outside. No good going out that way.

I picked up the shovel and swung at the hole in the roof. It puckered with a horrible creak and groan—as loud as the noise the *Titanic* probably made when it split. More snow fell in, but I'd barely made a dent. And the last thing I wanted to do was alert my captors to my attempts at escape.

I was trapped.

Dammit.

Looking at my red and worn wrists, I nearly started to peel the tape free of them, but I thought better of it. Better to maintain appearances.

Better yet to find a weapon so that reality was far from what it appeared.

I rooted around the tilting shelves of the shed, nudging baby food jars filled with rusting nails and screws of all sizes out of my way as I looked for an easily concealable weapon.

I was faced with only two viable, but grim, options: a flat-head screwdriver (like a distant cousin of an ice pick) and a trowel with a long and narrow point, its edges sharp for masonry.

Decisions, decisions . . .

Shrugging, the pain in my shoulders and arms made me want to yelp. I bit my lip, scrunched up my face, and rolled my shoulders until the pain was just another part of me. A very angry, motivated part of me. And the whole time I held the screwdriver in one hand and the trowel in the other, weighing my decision. Which was the best weapon?

I finally decided on *both*.

I sat back down, grabbed the discarded blanket, and prepared to wait for my rival for Pietr's attention.

Or Gabriel.

I didn't really have a preference.

Alexi

"Shit." Max's single exclamation summed up the sentiment in the truck as I slowed at the sight of a line of brake lights up ahead.

"Language," Cat said.

"Can you see what is going on down there?" I asked him, slowing the truck down and bringing it to a stop so we had plenty of space between us and the car immediately ahead.

"From the lights . . ." He leaned forward and stared out the windshield. "It looks like a tree fell. Wires are down."

"Ah. Country living," I surmised. "Do we know another path to the motel?"

"I would use my phone's GPS, but . . ." Pietr held his cell up, moved it around, and even touched it to part of the truck's metal frame in hopes of getting it to act as an antenna. He growled—a weak sound in a boy who used to be a wolf. "No signal."

We all tested our phones.

"Nothing," I concluded.

"Bad traffic is not something that should hamper a rescue," Max muttered.

"*Pravda*. That is true," I reported, swinging the truck's nose into the opposite lane and performing a less than elegant K-turn on the narrow road. "We shall not allow it to hamper our efforts for long," I assured him. "Jessie will just need to hold on a bit longer."

Marlaena

Outside his door I bent over and tried to catch my breath. Oh, sweet Jesus in Gethsemane, I'd really done it this time. I'd let him reject me outright. I'd given him the upper hand. And even after that—after he'd all but drawn first blood, I'd naïvely admitted that I felt something for him. That I had some emotional connection with him—even as lame as "like" was.

Damn it. I straightened and focused on the dimming light in the sky. It would be dusk soon. I'd let time slip away from me. How long until Pietr and his gang realized that Jessica was missing? How long until they figured I had something to do with it and came hunting us?

God. The sickness swelled in my gut at his words. He wasn't good enough for *me*. . . . We both knew it was a lie. But how could an alpha who was higher in rank than Gareth still have to climb to be his moral equal?

Maybe if I just released her . . . Maybe there was still a chance all might be forgiven. Maybe I wouldn't be falling into what suddenly felt like some snare Gabriel had set. For *me*.

I headed down the nearest stairs and skirted the motel until I came to the old storage shed back in the lumpy snow. Dry stems of uncut weeds and tall brown grass bent under clumps of snow. It was an area of the property no one cared about anymore. The only sign it had been visited recently were the tracks our footsteps had made in the snow that kept refilling as more snow fell.

I pulled the key out of my jeans pocket and rubbed the lock with my thumb to clear the frost from the keyhole. The lock rattled off the chain, sliding with a *clunk, clunk, clunk* as I dragged it through the holes in the door.

Tugging the door open, a thin beam of light fell across the bound and curled form of Jessica Gillmansen and the ramshackle mess of odds and ends rusting away near her.

Jessie

The noise of chains startled me before the door opened, light falling across me, just bright enough bouncing off the snow outside that it made me squint. My cheek was as cold as the dead ground beneath it; my ear ached. My nose had begun to run and sting not minutes after the two of them first locked me away, and now the inside of it felt thick and sharp with ice crystals. I tried to relax, to make myself appear asleep in hopes that Marlaena or Gabriel would mistake me for being less of a threat than I was.

Or at least less of a threat than I *hoped* I was . . .

I kept my wrists together behind my back, pressing them so tight the bones ached and my skin—raw from the tape I'd sliced through against the dull blade of the old lawn mower—stuck together. I opened my eyes just enough to peer out the scant space between my negligible eyelashes. The silhouette cleared in my vision.

Marlaena.

The bitch was back.

My fingers itched in the cold, itched to wrap around her neck so that I could warm my hands throttling her. But I stayed still, my fingers tightening on the screwdriver and trowel as I waited for her to come closer. I had no idea what I'd do when she finally was next to me. I only knew I had to do *something*.

Something desperate.

CHAPTER FOUR

Marlaena

I shuffled toward her, my eyes focused on her face to see if she was awake. Her eyes crinkled briefly—the movement of someone trying to fake sleep.

I did the same thing when I lived with Phil and Margie so I could hear the prayers they said over me late at night when they thought I was fast asleep. They had to be more embarrassed by me than I'd ever expected, knowing what they said and the frequency with which they said it.

They must've thought I was the Devil incarnate.

Seeing me with Jessica taped and gagged in a rusty shed would only confirm their suspicion.

I blew out a breath, and her eyes twitched again.

Jessica Gillmansen was definitely faking.

Fine. It'd make it easier to explain things to her and set her loose. Wouldn't Phil and Margie be surprised?

And wouldn't Gareth be proud? If I ever told him. I took a

step closer to the prone girl. I could never tell him. Better just hurry up. Get her out of here and apologize . . .

"Jessica," I said, nudging her with the toe of my boot. "Jessica."

She groaned and opened her eyes slowly to glare at me.

"It's over," I stated, leaning across her body and stretching my hand out toward the knot that tangled in her hair and filled her mouth with foul fabric.

Jessie

"It's over," she said, reaching out to grab my throat. Before I could say a thing, someone behind her delivered the line instead.

"It sure as hell is!" Gareth's shout made her jump and I took my chance, lunging at her, my hands free and holding the screwdriver and trowel I'd found among the junk in the shed. I swiped at her face, and she leaped back with a shout as the trowel bit into her cheek and left a ragged cut from her eye to her jawline.

"You bitch!" she shouted, lunging at me, hands going for my makeshift weapons.

But I stabbed and sliced at her, keeping her back. "Takes one to know one," I snapped, my eyes widening when I saw hers narrow in response to my taunt. *Someday, Jess,* I warned, *someday you'll learn when to keep your mouth shut.*

Her hand went to her face and came away slick with blood.

"Not so pretty now, huh?" I shouted. *Dear God. Maybe I'd learn that lesson eventually, but it sure wasn't sticking today.*

"'laena!" Gareth shouted from behind her. "What—what is the meaning of this? Why the hell do you have Jessie—"

"Stop!" she commanded me. The hand not holding the wound on her face was up, palm out. "Just *stop!*"

For a moment I hesitated, seeing something new, something different in her eyes.

Repentance?

"Gareth—it's not what it looks like . . . ," she whispered, far from the alpha role she normally played.

She was . . . apologetic?

But then Gabriel slipped up beside her, their combined bulk pushing me farther back into the shed, my feet tangling in the discarded junk.

"Gabe—get out of here," Marlaena demanded, her tone terse. "Let me fix this," she said, her attention split between me and the two guys. "It's over. . . ."

In the thin space between their shoulders I saw Gareth move forward, reaching for Gabriel—to move him out of the way. And then—a shadow crossed behind Gareth and, as I focused on what was going on behind him, Gabe got past Marlaena, his hands clenching my wrists, shaking the trowel and screwdriver out of my hands with a growl.

I looked pointedly at his bandaged hand and sneered despite the pain in my wrists, saying, "Not eligible for the five-finger discount anymore, are you?"

With a snarl he raised his fist and brought it down sharply.

Marlaena

"Dammit, *no!*"

Gabe cuffed Jessica and she fell, limp, to the ground, causing him to smirk.

I turned back to Gareth, my hand still on my cheek, trying to find the words, to explain I was going to free the little wretch—to apologize. . . .

But Dmitri was behind him, as smooth and fast as a shadow, and raising a gun, he brought its butt down sharply on Gareth's head. Gareth blinked once at me, his mouth falling open as his knees gave way and he sank to the ground a heartbeat before I could even shout a warning.

"Damn it!"

Gabe turned to Dmitri and grinned at us both.

But all I could think was that Gareth would wake up remembering two things: that I'd kidnapped Jessica Gillmansen, and I'd let someone get the drop on him.

"*No,*" I whispered, the breath ghosting out of me along with any hope he'd understand. That he'd forgive me this stupid, stupid mistake. "Oh, *no* . . ."

I stopped myself from rushing to him. From grabbing him and cradling his head in my lap. Barely.

I was in too deep.

Swallowing whatever thing swelled in my throat, I narrowed my eyes, pushed back my shoulders, and stretched to my full height. I could not allow them to think I was intimidated.

I was the alpha.

"Dammit," I snapped again.

Dmitri holstered his piece and shook his head at me. "He will be fine. He will not even feel it when he regains consciousness—how do you say it? When he *comes to?* The benefit of being *oboroten, da?* You barely feel anything."

I swallowed again at those last few words.

You barely feel anything.

Then why did my chest clench and ache at the sight of
Gareth on the ground? And why did knowing how bad I'd
screwed things up this time make it suddenly so impossible
to breathe?

Alexi

The road conditions were far less than optimal as we made
our way back to Junction's main street, got a cell signal, and
subsequently new directions. Our slow speed only intensified Pietr's growing panic.

"Something's wrong, I know it," he said.

"*Da*. Of course something is wrong, Captain Obvious.
Jessie's been kidnapped," I pointed out.

Pietr glared at me.

"*Again*," Max drawled. "Do you think our Jessie is a magnet for trouble?" he asked offhandedly.

"At one time I believed you were attracted to her, so *da*.
Yes. She *must* be a magnet for trouble," Cat stated, picking at
her fingernails.

Max growled a laugh, but Pietr failed to find the humor.

"Can't we go faster?" he asked, leaning forward to rub the
dashboard as if that would change things.

"We will do her no good if we die in a fiery crash," I stated,
my teeth gritted against the frustration I felt. "We will make
it to the motel. Soon."

Pietr looked at me, his eyebrows arching with worry.

"*Nyet*, not as soon as you want."

"As long as it is soon enough," he whispered. "That is all
that matters."

Marlaena

"Unfortunately," Dmitri was saying, "this little mess means we must move up our plan. She is more dangerous than you thought, and with Gareth knowing you took her . . ."

"*I* didn't take her," I protested.

"It looks that way from where I'm standing," Dmitri said coolly. "And it will most definitely appear that way to Gareth." He nudged Gareth's limp form with the toe of his boot.

"Don't do that," I demanded, going down on my knees beside Gareth. I rolled him over, sliding my hands under his armpits and tugging him up so that his head lay in my lap. I brushed the hair back from his eyes, my hand trembling.

Dmitri shook his head. "You are an alpha. Act like it."

"I am," I said with a snarl. "I am protecting my pack. I was releasing Jessica so that she would not bring the others against us."

Dmitri bent forward at the waist, bringing him nearly nose-to-nose with me. "As much as you think you should release her, as much as you know it is what Gareth would like, deep down you know you want her to suffer. She has something you want, *da?*"

Images of Pietr filled my head, slipping across every bit of my brain and I fought it all down, holding Gareth more tightly. "No," I croaked out. "I have all I want right here. Right now."

Dmitri glowered at me. "Liar." He shrugged. "Or perhaps . . ." He focused on my face with an intensity I had only seen him use when sparring. "Perhaps you do have all you want here and now. Perhaps this is a *need*. . . ." He chuckled and straightened. "It does not matter anymore. It is all semantics, *da?* The wheels have been put into motion. The juggernaut of destiny is now on the move. You owe me Pietr. Remember. We have a bargain. The safety and comfort of your pups for Pietr Rusakova."

Dmitri focused his gaze beyond my shoulder and I heard Gabe grunt behind me. "She's not as light as she looks. Farm girls must be packed with muscle."

Putting his hands behind his back, Dmitri swayed on his feet, his mouth twisting in a sly smile he turned on me. "Winter in the northeast is a particularly harsh time when one is homeless. And hunted. Did you not lose Harmony in Chicago?" he chided. "It would be awful to lose another . . . And they are so young. So innocent. They look to you to protect and guide them as an alpha should." He tilted his head, his eyes hard. "Will you back out on me and see your pack put on the streets?"

I looked away, clenching my jaw, and focused on Gareth lying as if he slept in my lap. I could go along with Dmitri. I could lose Gareth's love for me. Or I could lose more lives.

Love might—eventually—be recovered. My brain pounded against my skull. Love might be recovered, yes, but lives . . . Despite my natural body heat and insulation against the cold, I shivered, realizing.

I had no money to keep us housed and fed and safe.

I had no allies.

I had no options.

As much as I wanted Gareth's love, I *needed* my pack to be safe.

Need always won.

I gently slid Gareth's head off my lap and watched Dmitri bind his hands. It would barely slow him down, but slowing him down was necessary.

"Put her in the car," Dmitri said to Gabriel.

I rubbed my head. "You," I said to Dmitri, trying to regain some semblance of control, "make an excuse for us to the pups. And tell them to stay inside. To keep the doors locked, ignore the phones, and to not let anyone—not *anyone*—in until we come back."

He grinned. "I will reword it so none of them wets themselves with worry," he muttered before walking away.

"Do you know what we're doing?" I asked Gabriel. "Where are we even going?" I'd thought we'd have more time. I needed more time, time to plan.

Why did time always run like water through my fingers?

"Where are we going?" I repeated.

He grinned at me, cocksure. "Straight to Hell," he said, closing the trunk on Jessica's body. "But at least it will be warmer there."

Alexi

The glowing sign blinked from off to on and back again ahead of us, unsure what dusk was—day or night? Missing a letter and a numeral, the sign read: OTEL. "There it is," I said, thrusting out my chin.

"The motel," Pietr said. "Max?"

"Yeah," he replied, his voice merely a whisper. "This is definitely the place. It smells of wolves."

We pulled into a parking space and quietly exited the truck, each watching for any sign of the pack or Jessie. Max's nostrils flared as he tried to work out where the scents thickened, which way we should go to find them—or avoid them.

"Here," he said, jogging toward the steps. "Wolves upstairs. I'd guess that's where the pack's rooms are." But he froze at the base of the stairs, his eyes narrowing with wariness. "Amy was right," he said slowly. "He's been here."

Cat adjusted the gun in her jacket pocket, keeping her hands hidden, her bright blue eyes roaming. "Is he still here?"

"I cannot be certain. . . ."

Pietr was already bounding up the steps, giving us no choice but to follow him.

Up we went, cresting the stairs and turning down the long, slender cement porch that stretched like one continuous balcony.

Max stopped us at room 204 and signaled Pietr to come back. "This is one of their rooms."

Pietr pounded on the door, and my face and palm slammed together. Cat and I jumped back, flanking the door. Pietr had always been impulsive, but never so socially inept. Cat and I pressed our backs to the wall.

The hint of noise from inside had come to a halt.

Max shook his head. "Stupid," he said, looking at Pietr.

"Ironic," I said, looking at Max.

Max pressed his lips together and spared me a brief glare. "You've scared them," he said to Pietr. He rapped on the door with his knuckles, making a simple sound. A nonthreatening sound completely unlike Pietr's previous attempt. "Look," he said, just loud enough for the pups inside to hear him. "We just want to talk. One of our friends went missing. We're hoping you know where she is."

Nothing but silence.

"She's part of our pack. You'd want us to help if someone in your pack was in trouble, *da?*" he tried. He glanced at me, cupping his mouth and speaking in the barest whisper. "Movement inside."

The curtain that hung heavily across the big picture window stirred, faces pressed to the glass. I relaxed my pose, looking more like a man bored with waiting than one ready to storm a room of werewolves in a hail of bullets.

"It's Max, by the way," Max said. "Max and Pietr and Alexi . . ."

"Is Cat missing?" someone asked from inside.

Max looked at me, and Cat flattened herself more completely against the wall to his right. "Would it matter to them if Jessie's missing?" he whispered. "Do they see her as part of our pack?"

"Be honest with them," Cat returned softly. "Perhaps a change of pace is exactly what they need."

Max nodded. "*Nyet*. Cat is here and safe."

"*Allo*," Cat called out cheerfully.

"Then who . . ." Distrust crept into the pup's tone.

"Do you remember the human girl who came with us to the campfire party you guys had?" Max asked, thankfully not adding, *You know, the event after which we nearly died in a strange car accident?*

"The pretty redhead?"

"*Nyet*," he said. "That was Amy." He tried again. "Do you remember the brunette? Jessie?"

"The one who didn't dance much?" they asked.

"She has a poor sense of rhythm," Max tried.

"And timing. Do not forget her bad sense of timing," I muttered, watching the snow start to thicken just beyond the lip of the roof.

"She didn't howl much, either," another pup grumbled.

They were not Jessie's biggest fans.

"Her throat was sore that night," Pietr said. "She would apologize if she were here to."

"Pietr?" More faces pressed to the glass.

"*Da*. It is me," Pietr answered, trying to smile. "Jessie is gone. She has disappeared and I must find her. Can you help me?"

The bolt clicked open, the chain slid across, and the door opened for us.

Marlaena

When people claimed "the Devil made me do it," I had to believe they meant "Uncle" Dmitri.

I'd left Gareth out cold, *in* the cold, and I was beginning to wonder if there was any way I could ever come back from the dark place Gabriel and Dmitri had towed me into. Jessica still lay unconscious in the trunk; Gabe was driving, with Dmitri riding shotgun. I was stowed in the backseat like a disgruntled kid on the most hellishly dysfunctional family road trip ever.

"She's pouting," Gabe muttered, looking back at me in the rearview mirror.

"She is a female. They are often moody."

"You're just a ray of sunshine yourself," I retorted.

He ignored me, saying instead to Gabe, "She will get happy soon. Very soon. I will have Pietr and I will leave you with the money you need to make it into springtime and without having the hassle of trying to appease me."

"That *is* happy-making news," I said, staring out the window. The car slowed, taking us more cautiously up one of the roads leading into the mountains ringing the town of Junction like a crown. Outside, the snow continued to fall, lightly at some points, and then it suddenly washed across our windshield like a foamy ocean wave crashing and we crawled a few feet forward, nearly blinded by a whiteout, until it cleared again.

The only good part about it was that we didn't have to worry about any other traffic on the road. Almost no one else was crazy enough to be out in weather like this.

"This is insane," I said, curling in on myself, my cheek to the cold glass of the window. "We should let her go."

"I think it is time you stop suggesting that and go along with the established plan," Dmitri advised.

"I wasn't involved in establishing any frikkin' plan. I wasn't even consulted," I protested.

"You haven't been in the right state of mind," Gabe stated.

"What is the right state of mind for a kidnapping? Dangerous? Risky? Crazy? That's all I see when I look at you two."

"No," Gabe snapped. "You've been pining over Pietr Rusakova and you're so blind to it all that you don't even realize that's what you're doing."

I puffed out a breath in exasperation. "I am not *pining*. I do not pine. And I certainly don't pine over Pietr Rusakova of the chess club."

"Debate team," Gabriel corrected through gritted teeth. "He's on the debate team, not the chess club, and you *know* it."

"Wait. Is that why you're going along with all this, Gabe? Because you think this'll get Pietr out of the picture—Dmitri said he'll take him—and then what? You think it'll open the way to *me?*"

I laughed bitterly when he hunched over the steering wheel, glowering at the road ahead.

If you could still call it a road . . .

"God. Why don't you get it, Gabriel? I don't want you. I'm sorry, but I don't. And I don't need you. I . . ." I stopped myself from proclaiming my love of Gareth. Barely. "And I don't want Pietr Rusakova, either. I mean, I'll admit it—as an alpha, it's fascinating to watch a rival alpha with his pack. They're totally different from us. And he, well, the fact he's cured, no more werewolf there—it just makes it even weirder. But I've wanted Gareth for a long time. Everyone knows that. Accept it."

"I should be the alpha."

"Gawwwd," I groaned. "Then leave, start your own pack. Hell, I'll even give you a little of the money Dmitri's going to give us, if it makes it easier." I picked at the back of Dmitri's headrest. "If I go through with this—get Dmitri Pietr and he leaves and leaves us with money," I said, "would you finally go then, Gabe? Go and never come back?"

"Is that what you really want?"

"It's more than what I want," I admitted slowly. "I think it's what we both seriously *need*."

His knuckles whitened on the steering wheel, but he said nothing.

CHAPTER FIVE

Alexi

Pietr paced the length of the room, fingers clenching into fists before relaxing again as he tried to keep calm. "So you have not seen Jess?" he asked, all eyes on him.

The pups shook their heads.

Max had disappeared back down the steps on the trail of some scent he wasn't ready to talk about. Cat sat on one bed, pups nestling around her as she played with their hair and complimented their clothing, and I sat on the other bed, feeling we had gotten nowhere since we'd arrived.

Pietr looked at me, his distress plain. "Where could she be?"

The door opened with a billow of snowflakes, and Max paused on the threshold to stomp the snow from his boots. "No answer to that yet," he confirmed what we all feared. "But I think I've found a valuable clue."

Gareth stepped in behind him, snow coating his jacket and jeans and in his hair, a torn-up length of rope hanging in his hands. His gaze hopped from face to face, taking a quick accounting of his pack, and he sighed, his eyes finally falling on Pietr. "I may be able to help you," he said. "But I'm afraid by helping you find Jessie I'll also help them get what they want."

Pietr's voice was low. Dangerous. "What do they want?"

"You."

"Then let's give them what they want. Every bit and more," Pietr said, his eyes bright with hate.

Gareth shook his head, his mouth twisting down. The pups rushed him, flinging their arms around him. "You're only human now. You can no longer do what you used to," Gareth said, sighing. "Perhaps you'd better leave this to the wolves."

Cat stood up and cleared her throat. "About that . . . ," she began, placing a hand on Pietr's arm. "There is something we have kept from you, little brother. Something you must know."

"Tell him in the truck," I urged, standing to slip my coat back on. "And the pups?"

"Stay here," Gareth said, petting their heads and smacking their shoulders. "Be careful and be smart. I will be back as soon as I can."

"And the others?" one pup asked.

"I will bring back whoever is left and worthy of being your family," he said, tilting the pup's head up with a finger beneath her chin just before he turned to the door. Only I was close enough to see the way his eyes flashed red and to hear him say beneath his heating breath, "And the rest can rot in Hell."

Jessie

I woke in the trunk of a car, jostling along what I could only guess was a lumpy country road. I was freshly bound and gagged and if I'd thought my shoulders had ached before at the tension brought on by having my wrists pulled so tight behind me, it was nothing compared to the pain that burned in them now.

But . . . I wiggled my fingers and tugged at my wrists. It did not feel like they'd had duct tape handy this time. As raw as my wrists were, I could still work with less than perfectly knotted rope. And from what I'd seen of Gabriel, he was as much a Boy Scout as he was an angel.

Which was clearly not at all.

I listened to the muffled sounds of voices on the other side of the car's backseat as closely as I could, trying to determine how many people rode in the seats ahead of me, and who they were. The voices were frustrated and disillusioned.

And sounded distinctly like Gabriel, Marlaena, and Dmitri mid-spat.

I closed my eyes again, allowing my mind to drift away from the jouncing trunk and dissolve into what remained of Derek's thoughts as I worked the rope with numb fingers. I needed to find a way to utilize all my assets and combine every bit of knowledge I had to get out of my current predicament.

Derek's memories had offered up odd but useful suggestions before.

He had answers. Weird, creepy answers, but they were still answers. And that was what I wanted.

Answers.

Help from any source.

The right answers might give me a way out of this.

I thought of Derek. I remembered how he'd seemed at Homecoming—before I'd known any of the truth about him, and he was there, filling out the spaces in my brain, spreading like floodwaters creeping beyond riverbanks to ooze across low-lying hayfields.

My brain shuddered and my heart raced as my world dissolved and his popped into focus.

We were with Wanda again—*within* Wanda again. Although the décor in the hallway had changed, become crisp and clean and nearly sterile with very few images hanging on the walls, I still recognized it as hers.

Derek skipped down the hallway, only a few years older than the last time I'd been here, and shoved open a door. Inside was a beautiful park, filled with trees and flowers surrounding a fountain and an assortment of statues. In the branches, birds chirped merrily.

We'd found Wanda's happy place.

But the birdsong ceased and the sky darkened as we bounded across the threshold.

"She's built better defenses," we said.

"Never mind those—find the icon."

We headed toward the burbling fountain, seeing the statues spread out not far from it. These were of ordinary people, built of granite, all of them posed and frozen in some action that seemed part of their nature.

We paused in front of a tall man with broad shoulders. He wore a button-down shirt, and an exposed gun holster like a detective might wear on the job. He looked like he was in his late forties, strong creases beginning to show around his mouth and across his brow. He had decidedly few laugh lines. On the base of the statue was written a single word: BOSS.

"I have him," we said.

"Excellent." Mommy's voice filled our ears. "Now make him shine in her eyes."

Derek pulled out a can and shook it. He held it up to the statue and sprayed the paint liberally all over the man so that he was covered in a sparkling coat of gold and our arm ached. "Now she'll notice him. . . ."

My mind balked. Wanda was being manipulated into *noticing* her boss? What sort of ramifications would that have? I speculated, beginning some mental math before Derek's mother burst in on our shared thoughts again.

"Good work," Mommy assured. "Now get out of there."

We turned back toward the fountain, but our knees turned to jelly and we staggered the distance to the doorway, gasping. "Can't . . . drained."

"Don't quit on me now."

Air brushed our face like a warm breeze in a world where the temperature was dropping in jumps of tens of degrees. And the air—the sweet breeze that carried just the faintest scent of Mommy's brandy-spiked coffee—whispered, "Rest. Regroup. *Feed.*"

Grasping the door frame we lowered our head and dug our fingers into the wood. We fed, pulling from the door frame and wall until wallpaper and plaster cracked and flaked and the ceiling began to sag.

"Not too much," Mommy warned, her voice edging into a hysterical tone. "Derek, Derek—you need to let go—get out before she buckles or you'll be trapped. . . ."

But we were high on the sensation, our head full of clouds, our feet so light if we let go of the wall we might drift away, lost. . . .

"Derek—*now*," Mommy commanded.

But her voice held no power, no authority. It was a whisper among the dark rain that now fell in the forest of Wanda's mind.

Then everything shuddered and the high was snatched away, replaced by a throbbing headache.

"Out. Now!" A voice boomed like a crack of thunder as lightning raked the sky.

"Father," we said with a gulp, and let go of the door frame and raced out into the hall, the door slamming shut behind us. We ran down the hall, back toward the main doorway and out into her brain, vaulting backward out of the gray matter, skull and flesh, and slamming back into our body—Derek's body.

Our eyes peeled open, the throbbing behind our skull so intense we bent over to catch our breath and try to clear the fireworks that burst across our field of vision.

"I told you that you had to be tough with him. If you're weak, he'll be weak. And the little bastard will ruin everything we've worked so hard for on this project." Father leaned over us, grabbing us by the shoulder and forcing us to sit up so fast, we thought we'd die. "Quit screwing around. You have a job. Do it. We can't afford a screwup like the last time. Get yourself under control." Then he strode out of the room, slamming the door shut behind him.

We rubbed our head, our eyes screwed tight against the light in the room that seemed to want to pierce our eyelids and drive into our eyeballs like railroad spikes. "Where's he going?" we asked, our voice thick with misery.

"Out to see some woman, no doubt," Mommy hissed. She patted our hand in a conciliatory gesture. "But don't you worry. How do you feel?"

"Rested. Ready to tackle anything."

"Excellent."

And I knew that resting and regrouping mentally was what I needed to do, too.

So I closed my eyes and thought back to my training as a competitive shooter, thought back to calming things, and let my pulse and my breathing slow.

Alexi

Rescue attempts are seldom as easy as they appear in the movies. And so it was true of our circumstances. Max's superior nose tracked them easily to a particular mountain road. Thanks to the borrowed truck, we roared toward it.

Roared was an apt description not because of our amazing speed but because of the more amazing lack of any truly discernible muffler on the beast we rode.

Cat had explained the flaw in the cure to Pietr and so he pouted, even less useful than before as he wracked his brain to decide how he might break past the cure and be *oborot* once more.

"If the car crash didn't trigger it . . . ," he grumbled.

Cat patted his hand. "The car crash happened too fast. I think the change must be triggered by a building desperation. Perhaps you must be close to death. Or perhaps someone you love . . ." She looked away.

"That is far from encouraging. But you don't know if that is what it takes to trigger the wolf's return," he said, catching her gaze and holding it with his.

She shook her head, dark curls tumbling around her heart-shaped face. "*Pravda.* I do not know. There seems no certainty in this."

"Then I guess today we will find out exactly what it takes," he said, setting his jaw stubbornly and once more turning to face out the window.

Marlaena

We parked the car, and Gabe hefted Jessica over his shoulder, carrying her to a large lump in the snow. He dumped her on the ground, and she kicked him, growling as savagely as a simple human could.

I laughed in spite of everything. "What's that?" I asked as Dmitri and Gabe brushed snow off the lump.

"Our transportation," Gabe explained, tugging a blue tarp away from the lump to reveal a sharp-looking pair of snow-mobiles.

I had always wanted to ride a snowmobile. . . .

And I had never been allowed.

"It's far from a ladylike pursuit," Margie had scolded me when I'd mentioned the possibility. A group of my friends were heading to a ski lodge way up in the mountains. It was going to be chaperoned. Safe. There was even mandatory church attendance on Sunday. In short, it seemed like the perfect diversion for winter break in an area where you had to head to the mountain peaks to find anything like winter.

But Phil and Margie had agreed: The trip would be laced with temptation, and I was ill-equipped to make good, moral choices.

That was before I let my grades slip.

Before I stopped caring about things, because why bother trying to make good choices when you never got any choices to make in the first place?

Before I started earning a reputation that made the girls hate me and the guys vie for fifteen minutes alone with me behind the school.

Even though what they wanted only took ten.

At most.

And it was before I made my first change—terrified and alone at the first sleepover I'd ever been allowed to attend.

At the church Phil preached at.

My throat tightened. Yeah. The third verse of "Kumbaya" had been waaay more memorable than anyone ever expected it to be.

I'd wanted only a few things and I'd been denied all of them until I disappeared and made my own way.

"You're kidding me, right?" I stepped over to the sleek machines and ran an appreciative hand across one slick chassis. "How much farther is it? I mean, if we expect them to catch up to us sometime during this century . . ."

The faster this was over, the faster I could start to try and make amends—get my pack away from everything that was so wrong and so dangerous. That's what we needed to do, I decided, looking at Dmitri and Gabe.

Gareth would agree. But maybe he'd think I was just as bad an influence. . . .

"We have the perfect staging area," Dmitri confirmed. "Not far from here. But I prefer some small comforts in my old age. Let the others walk, run, or lope their way to us."

He turned one snowmobile on, the engine firing up with a noise much like a contented purr.

"Not like Pietr can lope anymore," I said, loud enough to be heard over the engines.

Dmitri smiled. "He will lope when the moment is right."

"Wait. What?" My brows tugged in tightly.

He thrust a helmet into my chest, his smile becoming a wicked grin. "There is still wolf within him—you need not worry. We will force it forward." He put his helmet on, and Gabriel wedged one on Jessica before sliding one on his own head.

"We tried triggering—"

Dmitri tapped the side of his helmet and motioned for me to put mine on. I did. "They are smart helmets," he explained. "Voice-activated." He mounted a snowmobile and laid Jessica across it before him. "I would not get any ideas if I were you," he warned her. "We will be going quite fast and it would be unfortunate if you decided to volunteer as a mogul for their vehicle to vault."

Gabriel mounted up and turned, patting the spot behind him. Awesome. I was going to have to ride with my arms wrapped tight around him. Someone was totally thinking he'd hit pay dirt with this idea. Making sure my groan of protest was audible thanks to the smart helmet technology, I took a seat behind Gabe and locked my hands in front of his stomach.

"You may continue," Dmitri said as we started off.

"Thanks so much." I watched the scenery ghost past us. "We tried triggering the wolf with the truck crash, remember?"

Jessica's growl filled my helmet until Dmitri gave her a swift smack across the back.

"No wolf—no over-whatever."

"*Oborot*," he corrected.

"Whatever. It didn't happen then—why now?"

"It requires the appropriate stress and proper timing," he said grimly. "Timing is the key to everything."

"Yeah, well, so far our timing's sucked. And Jessica, well, hers isn't any better," I muttered.

"Remember the deal. You get me Pietr Rusakova and I'll be nothing but a memory. And evidently Gabriel will make himself scarce as well. You can only win by doing this."

I thought about it. I could be rid of two devils with one dramatic choice. Maybe I could rebuild things with Gareth. Maybe once he realized what I had to do to save all of us—the sacrifice I had to make . . .

Gareth understood sacrifice better than anyone. Surely he'd understand this if it freed our struggling family from Gabe and Dmitri.

"Just what exactly do I have to do to hold up my end of the deal?" I asked, regretting my willingness to go through with it as soon as the words fell out of my mouth.

"You will trigger the wolf inside Pietr," Dmitri said as if it were as simple as breathing.

I snorted. "And how exactly do you suggest I do that?"

"When the moment is right, you will kill Jessica Gill-mansen."

Alexi

Between Max's nose and the standard American four-wheel drive, we found where they had parked their vehicle.

"Slash the tires?" Max suggested.

"*Nyet*," I said. "We may need their vehicle on the way back down the mountain. I want all our options open," I explained.

Max nodded. Pietr and Cat were already up ahead, examining tracks.

"Two snowmobiles," Cat reported.

Max's eyes seemed to lose focus, and I knew he was

listening. "They haven't gotten very far. We can—" He began to jog forward.

"Wait!" I caught him and looked at each of my siblings. Gareth was of little importance. Family was always the most important thing, and that was no different now. "They mean for us to catch them. They are only getting ahead of us to set the stage—to fix the snare." I weighed the flashlight in my hand.

Evening was sinking into the mountains. This task would be easier for the *oboroten*.

Gareth nodded. "We need to go more carefully now than before. Gabriel's impulsive and passionate—hotheaded—but he's clever. And with Dmitri's training . . . caution is the better part of valor," he assured.

"What about Marlaena?" Max asked, his voice gruff. "What does she bring to the party?"

Gareth shook his head, his eyes sad. "I do not know. I did not think she would ever go this far . . . for anyone," he added, his voice softening.

"So she's our wild card," Max said.

"Ugh." Cat shivered. "I hate when you use that term. Do you remember the last time you used it?"

Max blinked at her.

"It's the same thing you called Derek: our wild card. And you see how well that turned out. We are stuck with bits of him—perhaps forever." She snorted in frustration.

"What?" Max defended. "It's just a name."

"*Da*," Pietr said darkly. "What's in a name?"

"We must go," I urged.

"I'll go on ahead," Gareth volunteered, starting off at a ground-swallowing stride even in the snow.

"Excellent," I said. "Perhaps he will draw enemy fire and we will be rid of more of them when this all is over."

Their path was clear and bold—too clear for my liking. While Gareth scouted ahead I sent Cat into the treeline on one side of the path while I took the other, trudging through sudden piles of snow where the canopy broke and significant stretches of forest that were covered in crunching pine needles and peppered with the last traces of sunlight. We flanked Pietr and Max on their way up the hill.

I expected all eyes to be on Pietr.

I expected a trap.

I did not expect to get so close to the mountain's bald top without even a stir or a whisper from the shadows. With every step we drew closer to the peak—a dramatic setting for a dramatic werewolf alpha and her captive—the more nervous my stomach grew.

What was I missing?

I peered across the open path, where Pietr and Max pushed their way forward in the track left by the snowmobiles' skis and bellies, and into the woods beyond. A slender beam of light announced that Cat still kept pace with me.

Gareth paused suddenly up ahead, his gaze raised to a spot at the mountain's very top.

They were there. At the tip of the mountain's highest rock outcropping Marlaena stood in snow that glittered beneath the rising moon's light, a half step behind a figure who was bound, gagged, and kneeling awkwardly in the white powder, her dark hair waving and snapping in the breeze.

Jessie.

Pietr began to run.

CHAPTER SIX

Jessie

"He's really something, isn't he?" Marlaena's voice boomed out. "He has the makings of an alpha—a hero," she added. "Oh, hell," she muttered. "I really don't care for monologuing, and there's no harm giving you a voice *now*. . . ."

She ripped the gag's knot out of my hair and tore it from my aching mouth. My eyes went wide as I wobbled close to the mountain's edge.

"Go ahead. Speak your mind. Get out all your words—you might not have many left."

I growled and found the words I thought whenever I thought of Pietr. "He doesn't just have the *makings* of a hero," I retorted, "he's been a hero. And he will be again. He's nothing like you or your pack of thieves and troublemakers."

She snorted. "We'll see about that. . . . It's a funny thing, really, how similar we are just below our skins." She looked me up and down, her mouth twisting. "You having only one skin, it makes you far less understandable—far less compatible than we wolves are to one another."

"Is that what all this is about? Compatibility?" I snarled. I was getting so sick of every frikkin' psycho wanting to get her claws into Pietr. Sure, he wasn't wearing his specially crafted necklace to combat his animal magnetism, but since being cured he didn't have much magnetism. "If you're looking for love, can I suggest an online dating service?"

Leaning toward me, her eyes locked on mine, she froze, staring at me as if she was contemplating my words. Deeply. As if she was confused, puzzled by her own actions. "Love?" she whispered. "I'm not looking for love with Pietr. . . ."

Her forehead scrunched up, creasing, and for another long minute she was simply silent. Finally she regained her attitude and hit me with another question. "How many times has he had to rescue you, Jessica?"

"Too many."

"Don't you get tired of playing the hapless victim?"

Hapless victim? I could shut her up and tell her about the men I'd killed defending myself and my friends, but no matter what my reasons—what my justification—had been, I hated talking about it. And boasting about it was wrong on so many levels. . . . I seethed silently and tried to twist the ropes around my wrists to better work the knot with my fingers. Because, yes, although she had me trussed up like a pig for barbecue, Gabe hadn't run rope between my wrists to keep his tangled mess in shape. He had definitely not grown up in the country where knot-tying was still a useful skill.

I was thankful he was a rookie.

"How does it feel to be so utterly useless you need someone to rescue you?" She nudged my knee with the toe of her boot.

I tugged at the ropes biting into my wrists. "Come closer and I'll tell you all about my feelings."

"Ha. Like you're a threat. You're just some lame-ass fairy-tale princess in need of a prince's rescue. God. I hate those stories. Maybe that's why I hate you."

"*Hate* me? You don't even *know* me to hate me." I shook my head and squinted toward Pietr's distant figure. "Maybe you just hate anyone who's better than you." I laughed. "That's gotta be a *looong* list."

"You really aren't very smart, are you? Here I am, able to roll you down the mountainside, and you're getting attitude."

I shrugged. "I was the same way with a *previous* psychotic attacker," I admitted, thinking back to my encounter with Marvin in the school hallway. "And a jerk who wanted me dead because of what I could do for the werewolves," I added, remembering Officer Kent at the gun range. "But hey, there's something to be said for consistency, right? And maybe the third time's the charm—though there's nothing charming about *you.* . . ."

She returned to watching Pietr make his approach.

"Geez. Whatever happened to *them?*" I wondered out loud. "Oh. Yeah. They're *dead*. Both dead. Sucks to be on the wrong side." I didn't bother adding I hadn't killed either of them.

Still downhill a good distance, Pietr paused, assessing the situation, his left hand twitching at his side, signaling to someone behind him? Let it be Max. For such a sexy slacker, Max always came through when he was needed.

Marlaena didn't notice. Her eyes were fixed on Pietr. "Marlena," Pietr called, "what are you doing?"

"I have a working theory," she shouted down the hillside, compensating as the wind tore her words away. "I think Jessica hasn't been one hundred percent honest with you. My sources tell me—and I think you'll agree they are in *the know*—that cures like yours can't truly end what's effed up in your genetics. The cure you took? A temporary fix. A stop-gap measure. It *masks* your true self—doesn't cure a thing."

Pietr froze a moment, considering. He licked his lips as he weighed his words. "Jess wouldn't lie to me."

"Why not? She's lied to everyone else. So what would stop her from lying to you? What makes *you* so special?"

"Love," I answered simply. "Love is what makes him so special. But Pietr, she's right. Cat and I didn't tell you everything about the cure. We only found out by accident the night the company was blown to Hell. And when we told Alexi, he wanted time to come up with an alternate plan. He wanted to have a complete cure before you'd demand it."

"See? She lied to you, Pietr. She omitted pertinent facts and put you at a disadvantage."

His body language barely changed, only stiffened a little. He was coping tremendously well. Like he already knew . . . We had both tried so hard to always be honest with each other. We hadn't always succeeded, but we'd tried.

"And Pietr . . ." The breeze shifted and so did Marlaena on the gravel beside me, her back straightening and her chin lifting. I looked up and saw her nostrils flare. "While you're asking for answers, why not ask Max why he's *still* a werewolf?"

We'd seen Pietr force Max to take the cure, but none of us witnessed his final change. And Max had remained more Max-like than any of the other Rusakovas had remained like their *oborot* selves.

Pietr turned back down the hill and shrugged. "Max?"

Max stepped out from the deepening shadows and also shrugged, like a little boy caught taking an extra cookie from the jar. Then he unfurled his most devilish grin and aimed it at Marlaena. "We've been through this already, Mar, but if it makes you feel better . . ." He cleared his throat and faced his younger brother, giving him the most pained look he had in his arsenal of expressions. God. "What was I supposed to do?" he asked. Dramatically. There were even hand gestures.

Max knew, like I did, his drama bought us time. I refocused on the knot near my wrists, ignoring how my fingernails bent back as I plucked at it.

"I couldn't leave us defenseless," Max said. "I understood your grief and I get what drove you to force the cure on me, but it wasn't how I'd handle things. So I spit it out and locked myself up a while. I got sick," he admitted, "puked a bunch. But you didn't get enough into me to make me go through the final change." Max looked back at Marlaena. "Huh. That felt pretty good, getting that out. It's like therapy in the wilderness," he said through a grin. "Some people pay a helluva lotta money for that, I guess."

Marlaena was unimpressed.

Max's grin snapped shut and his brow lowered, his forehead heavy and shadowing his eyes. The boy was designed for drama. And he was exactly what Amy needed. "Maybe that could be your career path—kidnapping girls and getting their boyfriends' family to fess up." He clapped his hands together in front of him and cocked his head. "Of course it won't be much of a career if you die here today."

Marlaena's boots scraped in the gravel and snow as she widened her stance, adopting a fighter's pose. But she clapped, slowly and loudly, at the spectacle before her. "Now, Jessica, tell Pietr the rest," she urged. "Tell him what breaks the cure."

Silent, I continued working the ropes.

"Tell him," she demanded, nudging my hip with her boot.

A few pebbles fell off the edge of the mountain and tumbled down into the ravine. She froze, seeing the same thing.

My throat tightened, watching the stones fall and bounce their way to the bottom. How would what *I* said or did at this moment really matter?

I could tell him the truth, warn him about the unreliable burst of adrenaline it took for the wolf to jump back out of his skin and take over once more. I could agree there was no cure that was permanent at this point and there was no way to know when a werewolf's life would end.

Chances were good that Pietr wouldn't die immediately after changing back.

Chances were good he would still have years before his werewolf nature drove him to an early grave.

And chances were also good that no matter what I did or said, Marlaena was going to shove me down the mountainside.

But *chances* were still only chances.

"It's a burst of energy," I said. "It's a dumping of so much adrenaline into your system—so much fear or passion or angst or pain—that it pushes you past your limits. Your body breaks through the mask of the cure."

"Thank you, Ms. Science. Now. Shall we have a demonstration?" Marlaena asked, leaning over my shoulder and gently rocking my entire body so that more pebbles and a small puff of crystallized snow fell free and disappeared into the gap in the mountain's teeth.

"*Nyet!*" Pietr shouted, sprinting as he pushed his body. "Marlaena—tell me what you want—I'll do it—*Anything!*" The knot was finally coming loose under the pressure of my prodding fingers, the coarse strands of it biting into my skin. But it was working. In a minute I'd be free. . . .

They were still yelling at each other, and then, out of the corner of my eye, I saw Gareth.

"Don't" was all he said to Marlaena. Just one simple and soft word as he reached out a hand for her—or for me. I had no idea which of us he was trying to save at that moment or if he wanted to somehow save us both. . . .

The way she looked at him . . . something in my heart faltered seeing that expression—even on *her* face.

"You don't understand," she whispered. "You never do. You never will."

Pietr was nearly to me, the look of terror plain across his face as he realized he was too slow. . . .

Wolf again, Max raced in ground-swallowing strides, overtaking Pietr. . . .

The *crack* of a gunshot reverberated across the mountaintop and Max rolled, his head tucked, tail like a flag suddenly loose in the wind.

I screamed for them both.

Max tumbled into the trees, leaving nothing but an awkward and bloodstained path in the snow and an explosion of white when he landed with a thud against a tree trunk.

Leaning suspended from a harness high in a tree across the clearing was Dmitri, the barrel of his gun still smoking.

"Help me understand," Gareth urged Marlaena, approaching slowly and steadily.

"I don't even understand. . . ." And then her hand took a rough grip on me, squeezing my shoulder so tightly I knew it was bruising beneath her fingers. "But I think this is a lesson we all need to learn," she said.

"What?" Gareth asked. "For me, 'Laena, don't . . ."

Marlaena hesitated.

We were both frozen on top of the mountain, and not

because of the crushing cold. Pietr rushed toward us, Gareth's fingertips nearly at my sleeve as Marlaena's grip tightened on me and Dmitri lowered his gun and took aim.

At me.

If Marlaena wasn't going to end me, he would.

Their images blurred and faded into the darkness and I was again in Derek's head, gasping as my world—the present world—was ripped out from under me.

"She needs to move. Get inside quickly, push her, and get out."

We vaulted into Wanda's brain, stood inside the hallway that made up the heart of her head, and stared down at the doors. One vibrated in the wall as if it knew our intention. Without a second thought we yanked the door open and stepped inside.

Before us was a chess board filled with figurines in black and white. The red squares among the army of figures were marked with words; scrawled across each in Wanda's own handwriting was the name of a city or town in the local region. "There." We pointed as one, reading Junction. Derek stepped forward to grab a pawn and shift it to the spot, but I recoiled, seeing that each pawn was a figure of Wanda.

"Move," he insisted, sliding the pawn forward.

"More," Mommy urged. "Shift them all to that position so that the message is understood, so that the need is fierce." And we did.

The chessboard beneath our feet slanted, shifting, the ground rumbling below us. "Move," we shouted as everything tilted and we were thrown from the board. We screamed, racing back toward the open door.

"Hold on," Mommy cried, and everything went black, my vision clearing just enough . . .

"You can't save everyone." Marlaena's voice broke through the fog fuzzing up my brain.

. . . and I took the best advice I'd gotten in the past few hours.

I *moved*.

Marlaena shifted as the gun fired, pulling me back—out of harm's way?—but not before the ropes binding my wrists came free and I'd grabbed her pant leg, unbalancing her and sending us both tumbling. Damn it—whose side was she on?

All I heard were screams: hers, mine, Pietr's, and Gareth's.

Then there was the noise—and the sharp and bitter pain—as my body barreled down the mountainside, crashing awkwardly into snow and stone and chunks of trees and mashing the breath and the thoughts out of me, but not the will.

My arms and legs pinwheeled, flailing, but my hands kept grasping stubbornly for anything that might slow my progress down the steep slope. The snow and ice made grass and vines impossible to find, and when my hand suddenly snagged in something I screamed at the pain burning through my left shoulder as my body suddenly ripped to a stop, my hand caught in the root of a downed tree. "Breathe, just breathe," I whispered, my right hand trying to find a grip and pull me up to alleviate the weight that pulled on my shoulder and wrist and made me scream and curse.

I dug into the snow with my right hand, feeling carefully—and quickly as my fingers became numb—for another root or a branch or an oddly shaped rock . . . anything to help me move up the mountainside instead of continuing down.

I cried, tears streaking out the only heat on my stinging face. The taste of blood made me guess a split lip was among my many injuries. All of me ached, bursts of sharp pain intersected with throbbing dull pain, and my vision swam with more than tears.

About five feet below me and to my left I heard Marlaena whimper, clinging awkwardly to something that was protruding from the stubborn snow still clinging to the cliff side.

I crawled up far enough to take the weight off my left hand and shoulder and, looping my right arm through another sturdy-looking tangle of roots, I pulled my left free with a sob. "Not good," I whispered, every tendon burning and every bone and joint loose and springy as old rubber bands. "But alive," I realized with awe and a sudden burst of joy as I looked up the steep cliff face and saw just how far I'd fallen.

With a swallow, I looked down, past Marlaena's struggling form, and assessed my options.

The bottom was actually closer than the top. Maybe, if I could control my descent, gravity would do most of the work for me instead of having to fight it in a struggle to climb back to the top.

My stomach churned. My head felt murky and thick. I wondered what was happening far above me. Marlaena had hesitated, changed her mind, and Dmitri had taken a shot at me instead? Shit. How were Max and Pietr? And Gareth. I even worried on Gareth's behalf. He was the most reasonable member of Marlaena's pack.

Of course, I probably would've given credit to any member of Marlaena's pack who tried to save me. Maybe my forgiveness was too sweeping.

But Pietr . . . Where was Pietr? I craned my neck, looking back up, and screamed when I saw the answer hurtling toward me, large and dark and powerful with eyes like hellfire. Wolf. He skidded and clawed and fought the ravine's pull the whole way down the slope.

He came straight for me with nothing but my battered face and his seething rage reflected in glowing *oborot* eyes.

We connected, a *poof* of air slamming out of our bodies and shaking the tree's roots so hard the entire thing rattled and Marlaena flew free as I also lost my grip. Pietr's front legs morphed into something more human, sleek and furred but ending in hands, and he grabbed me and pulled me firmly against his chest and stomach.

He tucked and rolled, letting gravity take control but shielding me with his body—a canine roll cage—the whole way down. Above us I dimly heard the sound of something else tearing down the cliff face and for a heartbeat my gaze caught the image of a midnight-colored wolf charging head-long down the slope, paying no mind to his own body's harm—only one goal in sight: Marlaena.

Gareth.

Pietr and I came to a jolting stop—as if every part of our impromptu journey downhill hadn't been jolting—and I breathed deep, my lungs shaken and rattling, my teeth aching in my jaw and my mind full of one word: *OW*. My fingers twined in the dark hair of his wolf's pelt (never had I imagined a hairy back to be so appealing), and snuggling against his thickly furred chest, I did a quick mental accounting.

I was still alive.

Pietr was still alive.

Pietr was a wolf again. But more important than back hair or battered faces, Pietr was still alive.

Max . . . ?

I whimpered, straining to look up the way we'd come.

Pietr shivered against me and his form wavered, trembling like a mirage around its very edges as he fell back into his human form. Reaching up, I stroked my fingers down the side of his cheek, faint stubble rasping against my fingertips just long enough to wake sensation in them. "You're going to freeze out here like that . . ." I winced; even unzipping my coat to open it and pull Pietr into it with me made tears well up in my eyes.

"Stop," he whispered, grabbing my zipper with one hand. "You need it more than I do now. I'll be fine. We just need to hurry back. . . ."

I adjusted my grip on him, my fingers twisting into his hair and pulling his mouth down to cover mine. I pressed myself against him and it only took one heartbeat before he reciprocated, and all the intensity and the heat and the hunger—everything I had hoped for and missed so desperately—came back to him on that slippery slope.

I wanted to scream. Not because of the pain that worked like a cheese grater across every bone in my body, but because Pietr—*my* Pietr—was back.

He pulled away from me, his lower lip still between my teeth, his brilliant blue eyes sparking with red like someone had set off flares in their wild ocean depths.

He blinked. And shuddered.

I released his lip and tried to come back to my senses. "My Pietr," I whispered.

He rumbled out a purr. "We need to get up top."

"Yeah," I agreed, choking back my hesitancy. "I hope Max . . ."

He nodded and readjusted our position with a grunt. "Max'll be fine. And do not worry about *us*. I am here," he assured me. "We'll be fine."

"Better than fine," I insisted, pressing my face into the crook of his neck, my nose tickled by the short hair near his ears.

The groan to our left pulled our attention that direction and we looked as one.

Marlaena lay on her side, her hair a long, stringy mess of red, her eyes shut, her face splotchy and red with scrapes and scratches already healing. Even the slice I'd given her across her cheek had pinched together and started to smooth.

Gareth, still wolf, was looking very, very worried; nudging his alpha with his snout he whined for her attention . . . whined for her to regain consciousness. It was the most affection I'd seen him give her.

He shimmered and became human again, tugging her limp body into his lap and cradling her head in the bend of his arm as he made soft noises at her. Gentle noises. "Come on, Princess," he whispered. He had to be the only guy bold enough to call someone like Marlaena *princess*. "You're too hardheaded to let a little tumble end it all. . . . Come back, 'laena. Come back to me." He kissed her forehead. "I'm not ready to learn that lesson you want so bad to teach me: that you can't save everyone," he confessed. "Not yet—not with you. Let me save you, 'laena. Come back."

"We should help him," Pietr murmured, his lips brushing a curl by my ear.

"Helping him means helping *her*," I reminded him. "And at the moment I'm pretty firmly opposed to that course of action." My fingers grazed his forehead, trying to erase the crease that marred his beautiful brow. I brushed his bangs back and pressed a kiss to his temple. "Let's go—get topside and find Max. And . . ."

"And Cat and Alexi," he muttered. But he was studying the two of them with an intensity that rivaled the one he'd only recently found for his schoolwork.

"Pietr," I whispered, my palm sliding down to flatten against his chest, "we need to go. . . ."

His heart was racing.

Gareth shook her gently, saying, "Don't you dare try to convince me that—"

Marlaena's eyelashes fluttered, and her eyes slowly opened, fixing on Pietr's face. "You can't save everyone," she whispered.

Something in Pietr tightened beneath my touch, and his heartbeat vaulted to an even faster speed.

Marlaena's expression shifted, her eyes going wide with shock, something sparkling in their depths. Fear. Absolute terror turned her florid face pale as milk.

What had her so scared? Being alive? Or what she had nearly done? Or . . . ?

"Pietr. You're trembling. You must be cold," I whispered. "Come on. Let's get you out of here. And find everyone. And everyone's clothing. Let's go home." I petted his chest. But he wasn't looking at me. "Pietr?"

"*Da*," he said finally, shaking his head as if to pull himself out of a daze. "*Da,* we should go."

"Pietr," Marlaena called as we rose and began searching for the best route to get back up to the top. He froze rabbit-still hearing his name on her lips. "Pietr," she repeated. "I'm so sorry. . . ."

Pietr grabbed my hand, yanking me tight to his side. He dragged me after him, fiercely ignoring her voice as it rose and strained to get his attention. To apologize. But all the time I was thinking she didn't mean she was sorry about *me,* but about something else. . . .

Something as new as the thing that sparked in her eyes when they met his.

And that something worried me.

CHAPTER SEVEN

Marlaena

I pulled myself off Gareth's lap, my stomach twisting into knots as my eyes followed Pietr Rusakova and his girlfriend away from the spots we'd all landed.

They picked their way back up the mountain's dangerous side, Pietr occasionally casting glances over his shoulder in our direction. In *my* direction? Did he feel the same sudden, strange and sickening pull I did? The sweeping sense of disorientation?

I stood a moment before doubling over to catch my breath, my hands on my knees, my head low. Gareth was beside me in a moment, his hand hot from the change and pressed into my back, the very definition of comfort.

I winced, twisting away.

"Are you okay?" he asked, his voice thick.

"It's the fall," I said. I held my head, hoping I was right. "Just the fall. It made me queasy."

His fingers roamed across my skull, tentatively feeling for bumps and fractures.

"I'll be fine," I promised. "I just need a little time." I always needed time. "I'll walk it off."

I straightened and looked at Gareth. He swayed in my sight. Or maybe *I* swayed.

He reached out to steady me, but I stumbled back, my ankle twisting and collapsing beneath me, so I flopped against the mountain's side. He nodded, accepting my words but not believing them. "*Fine*. If you say so."

"I say so." I regained my footing, placing a hand against the slope and pushing away from its surface. I peered up the gouged path we'd made coming down. "Too bad we can't just fall back up," I mused. "And too bad you—"

"Need to get pants. You remember that book you got recently? What was it . . . *Eclipse* or something like that?"

"Yeahhh?"

"The werewolves in that tied their clothing around their legs when they shifted so they didn't wind up naked at an inopportune moment. Like this one," he added, catching snow in his hand. "No one wants to get caught out in the cold."

"How did those werewolves . . . ?"

"Beats me. I don't think they could morph a hand once they were furred to actually tie the stuff on, but . . ." He shrugged. "It's fiction, after all. An author shouldn't be expected to think of everything. It's like spoon-feeding readers. Readers aren't idiots. Well, not most of them." He shrugged and peered past me, his lips curling as his eyes roamed. "Besides, a couple loose ends in a story aren't necessarily bad. They make you wonder. If you're bright enough to find them," he concluded. "And bright enough to wonder."

"So."

"I can be better prepared, all thanks to a novel about fictitious werewolves."

"Unlike the many novels about factual werewolves."

"You said it, not me. Things blend all the time in literature." He followed my gaze up the mountain. "I think Pietr and Jessie probably had the right idea. I think they found the right way up."

I rolled my eyes, wanting a different path even more now. "There," I said, pointing. "We can go that way."

He squinted, following the line my finger made. "Okay," he agreed hesitantly. "We can do that. If you want. But I really think their path was better. . . ."

I pretended not to listen. He changed, and the beautiful wolf followed me as we headed up the path I'd chosen for us.

The path less traveled.

By a lot.

Jessie

Stunned from the fall, from seeing Pietr make his change, I made an awkward mountain climber. Knowing it was all over and done with, that the cure was broken like some second-rate magician's spell and now Pietr would die, had stunned me more than any tumble down a ravine could.

At the mountain's top we paused to catch our breath. Pietr found his clothes partway down the hill near Max's shivering form. I froze at the sight of Max, covered in so much red I gulped, imagining a bucket of paint had been dumped on him, trying to lock out the image of Max, a beautiful disaster painted in blood, I said, "Are you . . ."

"I'll be fine," he assured me. "You shoulda seen the other

guy." His mouth quirked up in an uneven smile, his gaze falling to the nearby snow.

I turned to follow his look, but he reached up, catching my face. Gently he turned my head back to face him.

"On second thought, you shouldn't see the other guy." He let me go and stood, stretching and wincing.

My cheek chilled where he'd touched it, and I reached up with a shaking finger to find it damp with blood.

"Where are Alexi and Cat?" I asked, catching Max's shiver at the realization there was a lump leaking red into the little snowbank it seemed to create.

"Clean-up duty," he said.

I swallowed. Pietr's hands rested on my shoulders and he pulled me against him so my shoulder blades were tight to his chest, the curve of my backbone nestled against the muscles of his tight stomach.

"What did you do, Max?" Pietr asked, his voice tremendously level and calm for someone whose heart felt like it would break through his chest and lodge in mine.

He shrugged. "I only continued what she started." He looked at me. "Just proving we aren't starfish."

I gulped. "Gabe?"

Max shrugged again. "He's a little less than he was. He came after me when I was down. I don't respect that," he grumbled. "Let's just say he's not quite so handy now."

"Eww," I said.

Cat returned with a few branches, and Alexi soon followed.

"And why are we not worried about Dmitri?" I wondered aloud, glancing around at the darkening forest that flanked us.

"Pietr's *oborot* again," Alexi stated as if I needed reminding. "Dmitri doesn't have the resources to come after him without additional help. That is why he arranged for Marlaena and Gabriel to be here. He expected more help taking Pietr after he'd changed."

"But he didn't anticipate Gareth's interference."

"Or Marlaena's feelings toward Gareth," Cat concluded.

"And that's the real reason why we're setting fire to Gabriel's hand out in the open and *not* worried about Dmitri raining bullets down on us?" I glanced around, squinting into the trees in the distance, nervous despite their obvious confidence.

"Oh. And I did knock Dmitri out," Cat added matter-of-factly.

"Oh." That was better.

"Of a tree," she continued.

"Ohhh," I said, my eyes widening.

"Onto his head," she concluded.

"Ah."

"That's close to the sound he made," she said with a nod. "That with a dash more pirate to it: Ahhhrrgh."

"Is he—"

"Dead? *Nyet.*"

"But he'll feel like he drank more than one bottle of rotgut vodka when he wakes up," Max said. He shrugged and cupped a handful of snow against his chest and scrubbed at the blood clinging stubbornly there. "I do not know why you did not finish the job," Max muttered as Alexi coaxed the fire to life.

"Go after him while he was down?" Cat asked. "You do not respect that," she concluded with a smirk.

He sighed and leaned over to nudge the hand free of the little snowbank. He threw it onto the fire.

I stared as it sizzled.

"I'm sorry," I said, covering my nose and mouth with my hands. "I can't stand that smell. Can we go?"

"*Da,*" Max said, standing up and brushing his hands off on his jeans. "Good idea."

The others nodded.

It was only Pietr who disagreed. "You go on ahead. I'll stay and watch the fire finish up. I don't want to leave it going."

I pulled out of his arms and looked up at him. The fire was small and far from anything else that might catch. The snow around it made me believe it wouldn't be able to spread beyond the sparse branches they'd fed it with.

But Pietr wanted to stay longer.

"Okay," I said, my eyes on Pietr's face. I glanced at the others, saying, "We'll meet you guys at the car."

"Jess," he said. "You'll freeze if you stay out here much longer. Go on. I'll catch up. Soon," he said.

I hesitated.

"I *promise,*" he said.

I still hesitated a heartbeat, and it was completely telltale.

He looked away and I reached out to take his hand, wrapping my fingers around it.

"I'll see you at the car in a few minutes," I said.

"*Da.*"

We left him to the fire and whatever thoughts were running around in his head. I followed the others, staggering along and trying to edge out my own dark thoughts. Something weird was going on between Pietr and Marlaena and Derek's creepy memories were growing less and less alien.

And that they had pushed through me at just the right time.

Again.

Marlaena

Gabe was bleeding all over the inside of the car and I didn't care. Dmitri and his mini-arsenal was AWOL and I didn't care. Gareth was trying to be gentle and soothing (although I guessed he seethed beneath his calm exterior), touching me with gentle hands every chance he got.

And I didn't care.

Something inside of me had shut down.

And something else was struggling to take its place.

The only thing I cared about was where Pietr Rusakova had gone, who he had gone with and why. I couldn't get him out of my head. His scent lingered just beyond the tip of my nose, making me want to breathe deeper. My fingertips, numb, felt strange and foreign as if they'd only regain sensation by touching *him*.

Gareth reached around and buckled my seat belt for me. "Hello?" he tried.

I blinked. "I'm sorry."

He nodded curtly, stroking a hand down my shoulder and arm to my hand. "Sorry," he muttered, looking into the backseat at Gabriel. "You need to apply more direct pressure," he warned as he backed the car out. "We're all lucky to be alive. You both should be dead—at the hands of the Rusakovas. You're lucky they showed mercy."

"I wouldn't have," Gabriel snarled.

I twisted around to look at him. The expression he meant to be threatening and strong was laced with fear and frustration.

"That's exactly why you're missing a hand now," Gareth retorted. He glanced in the rearview mirror again, shaking his head at Gabriel. "Dude. If you're trying to flip me the bird, use the hand that still exists, genius. Oh. That's right. That's one of the fingers you're missing, isn't it? Funny a brutal fight would manage to force better manners on you."

Gabriel kicked my seat in anger and Gareth pulled the car over. "Don't make me kick you out *here*."

Snow slithered down the windshield before being whisked away by the squealing wipers.

"You wouldn't—"

"Dare?" Gareth asked. "You have no idea what I'd dare given the proper motivation." He looked at me, and I turned to look out the window, knowing he was talking about leaping down the cliff face. Talking about saving me.

No one else would've bothered.

We both knew that.

My stomach was burbling, and I forced myself to look past his reflection in the glass and tried instead to pick out something in the woods beyond to focus on.

"How much money do we still have?"

I shrugged.

"You need to think, 'laena," Gareth urged. "That money determines what options we have. If any."

"I—I'm not sure exactly," I admitted.

"Well, think hard. Because, if you didn't notice, you failed to come through for Dmitri. He may have it bad for Pietr Rusakova, but I have the feeling he'll take anyone who's able to do what he wants without question. Above everything else, he wants a werewolf."

"Give him Gabe," I said through a sneer.

"He wants a whole werewolf. One who follows directions," Gareth added. "Have you noticed how much attention he's been paying Noah?"

I swallowed.

"Let's take the money and run as far and as fast as we can and hope our trail goes cold before Dmitri realizes he's lost us."

I shook my head. "It won't be enough."

Gabe sank into the backseat with a groan.

"Dmitri will be at the motel in the morning—I guarantee you that," Gareth said.

"Not if I kill him tonight."

"Why did you finally agree to come along with me?" I asked Gareth, my fingers wrapped around the steering wheel.

He was quiet for a long time, working out the words to say somewhere between his head, his heart, and his tongue. That was the weakness of Gareth: He always let his heart get caught up in the mix. That was also his strength. "You can't do this alone," he muttered. "You shouldn't have to, either."

"Huh. So when the moment comes, when it's time to actually do the deed—kill the mobster—will you help?"

Again he was silent. "He is a threat to my family. I will do whatever has to be done when the moment comes."

I nodded solemnly and slowed the car down. "That's what I thought," I confirmed a heartbeat before I snapped a hand out, undid his seat belt, and kicked him out of the car and onto the roadside.

He rolled a short distance, shouting my name in surprise.

He was the best of us. The kindest, the most compassionate. If I let him come along—help commit murder—I'd be killing more than some mafia man who had his hooks in my pups. I'd be killing the heart and soul of Gareth.

My Gareth.

My head spun, and I tightened my grip on the steering wheel and nailed the brakes a dozen yards away.

I couldn't let Gareth be destroyed. No matter that I thought without backup Dmitri would get the drop on me.

And end me.

". . . end your sorry existence," Margie had threatened the time I'd forgotten to change the cat litter. I'd hated that cat as much as it had hated me. I'd never realized it knew what I was long before I did—that must've been why it shredded my curtains and peed on my walls. But I'd had my revenge. People say, "Revenge is a dish best eaten cold," but cat, I knew, was best eaten fresh.

And hot. The memory stirred something in my blood. Reminded me of who I was.

I was the alpha.

In the side-view mirror I saw Gareth stop rolling and clamber to his feet.

All the things that came with being the pack's leader— the respect as well as the burdens—were mine to shoulder, to bear. Alone.

Gunning the engine I sped away to find Dmitri and free us of his influence.

Jessie

I was hardly still, tight in the truck waiting for Pietr's return.

"Stop doing that," Max complained, jabbing my knee with his finger.

"Huh—wha-?" I blinked at him.

"You're twitchy."

"Oh. Sorry."

"He'll be back any minute," Cat reassured us, but she was also obsessively looking out the truck's window back the way we'd come. "He knows better than we do what time it is."

I nodded.

Cat began picking at her fingernails.

"Something's going on," I muttered.

"Have you tried calling your father to let him know you are all right?" Alexi asked, adjusting the rearview mirror and trying to find me in the sparse light reflected inside from the snow.

"Oh. No." That was dumb of me.

Alexi passed me his phone.

I switched it on and took a good look. "No good," I countered, handing it back. "No signal." Realizing I really needed to talk to my dad and Annabelle Lee only made me fidget more.

"It won't be long now," Cat said.

I screamed when he popped the door open and I nearly fell out. "Pietr!"

"Were you expecting someone else?" he asked, sliding in beside me.

"Dmitri?" Cat muttered. She rapped the roof of the truck with a fist. "Drive on," she told Alexi.

He snorted and pulled out.

After buckling up, Pietr wrapped an arm around my shoulders, pulling me tight to the inferno that was his torso. He rested his lips on top of my head. "I missed you."

"I've been here the whole time," I said, pressed so close snuggling up to him was easy. I ached all over, but having a somewhat human hot water bottle next to me eased every pain in my body.

He lowered his head so his nose touched mine and with a blink he kissed me, all the power of the wolf burning through his lips to scorch and possess my own.

Max coughed. Then coughed again. I pulled away from Pietr's lips reluctantly. Just long enough to reach out and cuff Max in the back of his head. He laughed and I fell back into Pietr's arms, covering his face with kisses a moment before I confessed, "I missed *you*."

Marlaena

A few blocks from the place where Dmitri was supposedly staying, I parked the car. Unease bubbled in the pit of my stomach. Something was wrong. I slid out of the car, my fingers twitching by my hip.

Hugging the walls, steeped in the shadows of the surrounding buildings, I kept an eye, and a nose, out for any sign of Dmitri. His scent—cigarettes, vodka, and enough cheap cologne to make any werewolf want to claw its nose off—was everywhere, hanging as a thin and sour reminder of his existence.

But his *car*?

It was nowhere in sight.

By the time I slunk beneath his windows and finally reached his door I was cursing. And not under my breath as good girls did. The reek of Dmitri was only a bit fresher here—only a little more recent.

I pulled out Gabe's lock-picking set and went to work. I wasn't nearly as quick at picking as Gabe was—even with werewolf ears there was a quality of hearing and of subtlety to touch I hadn't mastered yet.

And if this didn't work, maybe I'd never get a chance to master the skill.

After three minutes (with no noise from inside) I'd opened the door and was in.

I needed no inside light with my werewolf vision, the trace of a streetlight's glow seeping between the heavy curtains of the room's main window was enough. The smell of Dmitri was so thick I gagged. The air was dank and heavy, all sweat, vodka, desperately cheap cologne, and cigarettes.

Nothing decorated the room. No pictures or mirrors hung, no certificates or awards marked his achievements. It was very unlike anyone's home should be.

Rattling open every drawer and closet, I realized the place had been stripped. Totally empty.

Even if he'd been a minimalist or a man without worldly possessions, still, this room would have held something.

Unless he'd cleared.

Because he'd been warned.

"No!" I shouted, reaching for my cell phone. I pulled up Gareth's number and hit send. "Where are you?"

"Walking home."

"What street?" I slammed the door behind me and raced back to the car.

"Couldn't do it, could you?"

"What street?!"

"Same one I've got road rash from."

"I'm coming to get you. Call the pups. Tell them we're coming home and to keep the doors locked."

I jumped into the car and flew as fast as I could all the way back to Gareth.

Flinging the door open, I nearly knocked him to the ground. "Get in, get in!"

He leaped inside, buckled up, and held on to the handle bolted to the car's ceiling just above the passenger's side door.

He didn't say a word for two merciful blocks, but as we fishtailed to a stop at a sudden red light, he cleared his throat. "You couldn't kill him, could you?"

I snorted. "You're right. You're absolutely right. I couldn't effin' kill him."

He set a hand on my knee. A simple gesture meant to say, "See, I knew you weren't that horrible of a person."

I picked up his hand and set it back on his own leg.

"So why couldn't you do it, 'laena? Why couldn't you kill him?"

I turned his direction just long enough to lock eyes with him so he'd know how truly serious I was.

He swallowed, seeing my expression, and I answered the question I knew he'd regret asking. "Because I couldn't *find* him."

Alexi

She flung open the door and leaped at us so suddenly I jumped back, falling into a defensive position.

Pietr snorted, Cat laughed, and Max just caught her and swung her around so her bright red hair caught every bit of light from the porch's single bulb.

"You're back, you're back, you're back!" Amy sang, giving Max a kiss she surely expected to be quicker than it was.

He pulled her tight against him and worked his mouth across hers like he was trying to suction up a lung. It was far from pretty.

Jessie concluded her call and thrust my phone into my

hand. Her father had surely been as thrilled to hear her voice as Amy was to see Max.

I squeezed the phone and slipped it into my pocket, banishing my impulse to report my own safety to someone overseas. Perhaps I would have viewed their display of affection differently if I still had someone of my own.

Perhaps that was the key to seeing the beauty of another couple's kiss—knowing you had even better yourself.

Amy tugged away from Max, the tension again filling the space between them like a wall, but a wall they were both working to take down in equal increments.

With a grin, Amy pounced on Jessie, dancing around the porch with her before she pulled back away to examine her BFF's face. "Where is the bitch?" she asked, her tone suddenly cold.

"Gabe was the one who took me. He's the one to blame," Jessie explained.

"Yeah," Max said, giving Jessie an odd look. "Marlaena only threw her down a mountainside." He shrugged. "Gabe was definitely the bigger problem."

Jessie rolled her eyes. "I didn't mean it that way. I meant . . ."

Max leaned in, widening his eyes dramatically. "Go ahead. I can't wait to hear what you really meant to say about your willing murderer's innocence."

"Marlaena wasn't going to kill her," Pietr said, stepping forward.

Jessie frowned.

"I think she tried to save me at the last minute—right as Dmitri fired his second shot."

"That did not seem to be your sentiment on the way to rescuing Jessie," I reminded Pietr.

"This is not the sort of conversation to hold on someone's porch," Cat said tersely, shooing us all toward the door. "We can discuss this all inside. Over cups of tea."

I groaned, knowing precisely what my darling sister intended.

Marlaena

We vaulted up the stairs side by side and raced each other to the rooms the pups usually gathered in, slamming our fists on each of the doors and announcing ourselves in our most authoritative voices.

Doors swung wide for us, and Gareth corralled everyone into a single room.

His.

I tried not to stare at his bed in disappointment and focused on the pups, exchanging one frustration for another. "Stop milling around!" I demanded. "I can't count when you're pacing that way!" Worry was clear in their eyes. "Sit!" I barked.

They dropped to the sofa, the bed, and the floor, all cross-legged and wide-eyed, their hands folded in their laps.

And then I called their names out one by one: Jordyn, Londyn, Kyanne, Darby, Beth, Tembe, Debra, Justin, Terra . . . ?" No answer. I scanned their faces again—all so familiar now, even though most of us had hardly been together an entire year. My lips pursed. "Terra?" The pups looked away, each suddenly fascinated by something about the room we'd all gathered in. "Noah." He was also absent. "Oh. Oh, God." I closed my eyes and asked the question my gut had already answered. "Where're Terra and Noah?" But my heart dropped into my stomach the moment the words left my lips. I knew the answer.

"They went with Gabe," Darby volunteered.

Jordyn raised her hand but asked her question before I'd given her permission to speak. "What happened to Gabe's hand—"

Londyn echoed her twin's concern. "Yeah. How'd he get hurt?"

The questions began to fly.

"No, no, no!" I shouted, covering my ears with my hands to try to stop from pulling my own hair out. "Where did Gabe take Noah and Terra?"

They shrugged, frowning.

Londyn said the thing I'd known was inevitable. "They got into Dmitri's car. He said they'd be back as soon as they could."

I fell into a heap on Gareth's bed, cradling my face in my hands.

Gareth slipped an arm beneath me, curling me into his arms. "Shhhh," he soothed. "We'll get them back, Princess. Don't you worry your pretty little head."

The pups fell silent, staring at us both.

I'd finally done it. I'd failed them. By not delivering Pietr—my heart raced at his name—I'd doomed both Noah and Terra.

And destroyed the family I'd been awkwardly building.

"Did they say or do anything else?" I whispered, my voice hoarse.

There were whispers that rose slowly as they conferred with one another. They knew I wasn't holding up well. I sucked a breath through my nose, snot rattling and almost as wet as the tears leaking treacherously from my eyes. Not holding up well? Who was I kidding? I was falling apart.

And no one wanted to be the one to deliver bad news to an alpha on the brink of snapping.

I wiped my face with the backs of my hands and coughed to clear my thickening throat. I was an absolute mess. As my eyes cleared, I noticed Darby had crept over to whisper into Gareth's ear.

His eyebrows rose sharply. "'laena. Your key."

"What?" But I fumbled it out of my pocket and followed as he peeled away from me and strode out the door, muttering to himself. "Gareth?"

He swiped the key through my room's lock and shoved open the door.

In three quick strides he was in front of my dresser, slinging open the bottom drawer. Yanking it free, he flipped it upside down, scattering my socks and underwear across the floor for everyone to see as they crowded behind me, curious.

I knew what he was doing. And I knew why. "Damn him," I said, springing across the room and snatching up the envelope I'd taped to the bottom of the drawer.

The envelope hiding the last of our cash.

I slipped my finger inside it, but it was as empty a gesture as it was an empty envelope.

It was, after all, Gabriel we were dealing with. And if Hell had no fury like a woman scorned . . . well, Gabriel made angry women look like absolute innocents.

And I knew firsthand we never were.

I determined then and there to prove to him that same lesson.

Alexi

Jessie's request for sugar and milk in her tea only elicited a sharp look and a tsk from Cat. In the Rusakova household tea was not truly for drinking—though that was a part of the process—it was a tool for prediction.

Our brief time in Europe not long before we settled in Junction and upturned Jessie's life had brought us into contact with a wide assortment of intriguing characters. While Pietr sulked his way through libraries, museums, and art galleries surrounded by a broad selection of beautiful young women but focused more on the dead than anything as alive as a date, Max used his wiles to get invited to the wildest parties and into the arms of equally wild girls. I visited all of the tourist attractions, imagining how different the trip would have been if Nadezhda had accompanied me, and I sent Nadezhda a postcard daily unless there was more to say and then I used my finest penmanship (which was ragged at best) and wrote her letters spiked with poetry (never of my own invention, as my desire was to impress her, not worry her at my inability to compose a non-rhyming couplet). We all coped with our parents disappearing in different ways, all clinging to different things.

Ekaterina clung to the soothsayers, panhandlers, and gypsy readers who lived on the outskirts of major cities and only came in to tell fortunes, pick pockets, or beg. She was a princess among paupers, and they were as fascinated by her interest in them as she was enamored of their rootless, wandering lifestyle. I joked with her once that, given her behavior, I could only assume she had taken a gypsy lover. She thrust me up against a wall, snarling and spitting, and told me to never say such a thing again.

That was how I knew she had. And how I knew things had ended badly between them.

Still, she frequented their shifting camps and it was there that she learned to read cards of any sort and tea leaves while I taught myself the tricks to reading faces.

"Just drink the tea, Jessie," Cat purred in a most dangerous fashion.

"If you aren't going to let me doctor it up, the least you could do is get a nicely flavored tea. Or, after a day like today, I'd even appreciate chamomile," Jessie muttered.

Pietr glanced at her, sipping obediently.

"It's supposed to calm you and help you sleep," she explained.

"Drink your tea, Jessie," Cat repeated as warning.

"Drinking, drinking," she said, raising one hand in surrender as she raised the cup in the other. She chugged the potent stuff and slapped the cup down on the table at the same time Amy did precisely the same thing with hers.

"For heaven's sake," Cat reprimanded in a way that brutalized the rest of us with a show of class, "you're drinking tea"—she sipped from her cup, her pinky elegantly extended, her face a reflection of serenity—"*not* doing shots."

Both Amy and Jessie stuck their tongues out at her.

She shook her head and tsked again before finishing her tea. Setting down her cup she snatched Amy's up, peered into its bottom, and frowned. "Unremarkable," she claimed.

"What does that mean?" Amy asked, offended.

"Oh, sorry," Cat said, recovering her manners. "I don't see any tremendous danger or anything horribly scandalous in your near future."

"No *tremendous* danger or *horrible* scandal doesn't really qualify as reassuring," Amy said flatly.

Cat shrugged. "Shall we both be realists here and borrow Pietr's Captain Obvious cape for a moment?" She arched an eyebrow at Amy. "You *are* dating a werewolf. And it's *Max*. Danger and scandal are bound to follow. They are simply not of epic proportions. In your near future," she clarified.

"She has a point," Jessie said, winking at Amy.

Max just leaned back in his chair, stretching an arm around Amy's to drag her closer. "Could be worse," he said with a shrug.

"Jessie . . ." Cat palmed her cup and gave it a cursory glance. She set it down quickly and reached for Pietr's.

"Not done," he mumbled, raising it back to his lips.

Leaning across the table, Cat hooked the cup's base with a finger and tilted it up, making Pietr gasp, choke, and spit a moment, his eyes large and indignant as she snatched it away and he wiped at his dripping mouth.

"Done *now*," Cat murmured. She squinted, peering into the bottom of Pietr's cup. She set it down and picked up Jessie's again. "Oh," was all she said before she rose from the table and busied herself with the dishes.

We all looked at one another, equally puzzled.

"What about mine?" Max asked.

From the sink Cat let out an exasperated sigh. "I know what your immediate future is without looking. You do not have enough depth to qualify as complex."

He chuckled. "Call me shallow," he dared behind a smug smile. "People drown in too much depth."

CHAPTER EIGHT

Marlaena

I sent the pups off with Gareth with barely another word. He'd tell them some fascinating story—something with a moral that surely opposed the life I'd forced them all to live—and they'd forget my madness for the moment and fall asleep in comfortable beds.

I paced the room until I was certain I'd wear a path in the cheap shag carpet that somehow smelled like smoke although all the rooms were listed as nonsmoking.

The way my luck had been running, the rooms probably weren't just laced with smoke but had probably been cook stations for meth production.

That was my luck.

Gareth returned, closing the door behind him slowly, a solemn expression on his face. But when wasn't there one?

"Rent's due in a few days," he whispered.

"We'll be out before then," I promised, pointing to the bag I'd already started to pack.

He leaned against the door, his broad shoulders filling the space, his complexion even richer and more mesmerizing against the pale white door. "And where to?"

I shrugged. "We have a car."

"A stolen car," he corrected. "That seats six at best."

I shrugged again.

"What would you do? Split the pack?" He stared at me in disbelief, his expression slowly twisting through a wide range of emotions as he tried to read my face. "Oh," he said finally, crossing the room to wrap his arms tight around me even as I kept my arms crossed over my ribs, forming a cage against his kindness. "You don't know what to do, do you, Princess?"

My spine collapsed, and I fell against him, sobbing.

Jessie

It wasn't long after having the worst tea service ever that Dad and Annabelle Lee showed up in a cab. On the Rusakovas' doorstep he tried squeezing the life out of me with a giant bear hug. "What'd they do to you, Jessie?" he asked, his huge, calloused hands—the reassuring hands of a farmer—on either side of my face as he turned my head back and forth to see its every angle in the porch light.

"Dad," I protested. "Come inside for your inspection, okay?"

Grumbling, he released me, but as soon as we were in the foyer his eyes narrowed and he was examining me all over again. He paused, seeing my wrists bandaged up. His Adam's apple slid in his throat once, twice, as he swallowed his fear and spoke. "You've struggled with depression after your mother's death," he began.

"Crap, Dad," I said, wrapping my arms around him this time. "They taped me up and then tied me up when I cut through the tape. My wrists are bruised and raw and . . . hairless," I admitted, scrunching up my nose.

"It won't grow back darker," Cat called from the kitchen. "Do not worry."

I snorted. "See? Good news all around."

"And everyone else?" Dad asked.

"Far from hairless," Max said with a shrug.

Amy punched his arm. "Smart-ass."

"Language," Cat warned her.

"Nearly normal," I said, seeing the exchange.

"Nearly normal's as normal as it ever gets in this household, huh?" Dad remarked. "Where's my hug from dear daughter number three?"

Silence.

"Where's my hug, Amy?" Dad bellowed.

She flew into his arms, laughing, and he gave her a squeeze and a peck on the forehead.

"You okay, kiddo?"

"Good as can be expected—maybe even a little better," she admitted.

"Better's good," Dad said. "I like better. Why don't you come on home with us tonight, Amy?"

She smiled, but shook her head. "I appreciate the invite, Mr. Gillmansen, but I belong here."

"They treat you good, do they?"

"They treat me better than good, sir."

"Well, I can't argue with that, then." He looked at me. "You ready to go?"

"Sure. Just . . ." Pietr had stolen in on silent feet to watch us and I grabbed him, dragging his head down to where I could plant a quick kiss on him. But my quick kiss took just long enough Dad cleared his throat.

Three times.

"Okay, okay," I mumbled, tearing away from my view of Pietr's gleaming eyes. "Later."

He nodded. "Later," he agreed, handing over the truck's keys, and we headed out the door.

In the truck, Annabelle Lee sat with her nose pressed to the glass, her face pale. The moment she realized I'd seen her, she pulled back, sitting stiffly in her seat, a book open in front of her face.

I climbed in and looked at her as I snapped my seat belt's buckle together. "Hey," I said, as if a return from a kidnapping was as common as heading to the store for milk or bread.

"Hey," she replied as Dad got himself situated and began to ease the truck away from the sidewalk.

"Your eyes go bad since this morning?"

"What?" she asked, not moving the book from where the open pages nearly brushed her cheeks.

"You can't possibly read that way."

Dad spared us a glance, simply saying, "Now girls . . ." But he was driving, and Dad was particular about driving, especially since Mom's death. We all were.

"Annabelle Lee," I whispered.

"Stop it," she hissed. "I'm reading." She sat up even straighter. "And I hate when you call me that."

"Fine," I said, leaning back and folding my arms. "Anna. Please put the book down and look at me."

"No."

"Please?"

"No."

"What are you reading, anyhow?" I asked, leaning in to glimpse the book's back. I snorted. "You are *not* reading that."

"Am too," she defended herself.

"It's my book."

"You weren't reading it. You were gone." Her voice cracked.

"It's not even a genre you like."

She sighed, a slow push of breath that seemed to deflate her. "I don't even think a term of French declension like *genre* should be used when describing this *pulp* you suffer through reading," she said, her voice undulating and thin. She sniffed at the end of her sentence. "It's awful," she said, finally closing the book to sit it on her knee. "I am fiercely determined that the existence of paranormal romance is a sure sign of the fall of civilization." Tears rolled down her cheeks, and she snorted and wiped clumsily at her nose.

"Then for heaven's sake, girl," Dad said, his eyes wide, "quit reading that stuff."

I sneaked an arm around my little sister, my impossibly bright, opinionated, and stubborn little sister.

"You're worried," I commented as she shook free of my half-hug.

"For the fate of the world and the intellect of lovers of great literature everywhere, yes." She rubbed fiercely at her eyes.

"Pffft. You're worried about *me*," I said.

She nodded vehemently. "You read such garbage. . . ."

But I knew what she meant. "You missed me. You would've never picked up one of my books unless you picked my lock and were rummaging through my room because you missed me."

"Picked your lock?" Dad muttered. "Anna . . ."

"Picking your lock doesn't mean I love you. . . ."

"You just said it," I taunted. "You love me, Annabelle Lee. And you were worried about me."

She picked up the novel and slapped it down on my knee. "I *should* be worried about you," she choked. "Your IQ probably dropped the moment you opened this book's cover! I'm probably scarred for life now—no scholarships for me!"

Dad just shook his head.

"Yuuup," I said, grinning at her. "You love me. Deal with it, little sister."

"I will never understand you girls," Dad admitted. "Coming to terms with werewolves and the locality of the Russian Mafia makes more sense than you two do."

"Wouldn't have it any other way, though, would you, Dad?"

Dad's head shook again, slowly, a smile creeping across his face. "Nope. I wouldn't. Anna, hug your sister. Jessie, wipe that smug look off your face."

I did my best, but Anna's task seemed far simpler than mine.

Alexi

He was at the window whenever he wasn't pacing. "What is it, Pietr?" I finally asked from my seat at the dining room table where I spun my cell phone, watching with passive fascination for the position it would end up in when it stopped. Right side up or not.

She loves me, she loves me not.

"Where do you think she is right now?"

I stopped the phone mid-spin and pulled my palm away. She loves me not. "You know this answer. Jessie is home and safe with her family. I expect Gareth has things better under control now."

"I didn't mean . . ."

"What? You didn't mean *Jessie*?" I watched him more carefully now, looking for hints in his body language. He was almost always worried about Jessie and with good reason. "Who did you mean?"

"Never mind," he said, shifting his weight. "It doesn't matter."

"If you insist . . ."

He spun to face me, his lips drawn back from his teeth. "I insist," he said. "Stay out of my business."

I blinked at him. "I did not think . . ."

"That is your problem, brother—not thinking."

My mouth hanging open, I watched him storm from the room and stomp his way upstairs.

How very strange.

I tapped the phone's face and turned it on.

I should not call Nadezhda. I knew that. She was involved with her partner, and I did not deserve to suffer that drama. Or perhaps I did. Perhaps this was some karmic backlash for all the lies I had told. Perhaps the universe was determined to make me pay.

I snorted.

Perhaps I was more like Hazel Feldman than I thought, getting caught up in concepts like karmic retribution. I pressed the button and summoned my courage.

She picked up on the second ring. "Alexi," she said. "I did not expect to hear from you."

"I did not expect to call."

"I am glad you did," she said, her voice softening. "How are the States treating you?"

"I am alive," I said.

She laughed, and I could not help but smile. "There are days I think that is the only thing I can hope for," she admitted.

"Tell me all about it," I suggested, kicking my chair back from the table to rest my shoes on its surface and wait for Cat's scolding response.

But the scolding never came, and we talked until the television show Cat, Max, and Amy were watching in the other room was turned off and the lights flickered out around me. "It is late," I said.

She chuckled. "I disagree. It is early."

"Where are you now, I wonder . . ."

"You know it is best if I do not say."

"*Pravda*. True. Have a good day, Naddy."

She giggled. "Have a good night, Sasha."

Jessie

"Why are you still up?" Dad asked, shuffling back through the kitchen on his way upstairs.

"I should ask you the same thing."

He shrugged. "I don't sleep as well anymore, knowing there are werewolves in the world."

"Huh. I actually sleep better knowing there are werewolves in the world."

He nodded. "It's a matter of perspective, I guess." He looked me over. "School on Monday. How will you . . . ?" He pointed to his own cheek, and I touched mine.

"Looks pretty bad, doesn't it?"

He nodded again. "You should know it's generally accepted that it's only attractive when guys are scarred up."

"Hey! I watched that Mel Gibson flick with you and Mom that time when they got so into showing each other their scars."

His eyes popped wide open. "Don't you get any ideas, young lady." He rolled his eyes, a smile softening his lips as he remembered. "I warned that woman: They're impressionable. That Jessie'll get the wrong ideas. We shouldn't let her see anything other than G-rated movies till she's at least twenty-three."

"Hey!"

We both laughed.

"Wanda called and asked about you."

The laughter died in my throat, remembering what Alexi had accused Wanda of. And it couldn't be disputed. Wanda had at least helped capture the Rusakovas' parents. She may have even pulled the trigger, ending their father's life. "Oh. What did she say?"

"The usual. 'How're the kids? Jessie staying out of trouble?' You know."

"How's she doing?"

"Seems okay. Doesn't talk much about work. Guess she's not supposed to, but it's weird not talking about something."

"When's she coming back?"

"We don't talk about that, either," he said, his mouth opening in a huge yawn.

A huge *fake* yawn.

He didn't want to talk about it, so I wouldn't pursue it. At least not now. Instead I stood up and walked over to him, giving him a big hug. "Good night?"

"Good night," he agreed.

I waited until he had gone to bed to do the same. I slipped out of the clothes that looked and smelled as rough as they felt, thanks to my time in the shed and my less than graceful slide down the mountainside. Sneaking to the shower, I let the trauma of the day slide off my body and disappear in a spiral down the shower's drain along with the filthy water pouring off me. I let the water wear at me, massaging at the knots in my back and shoulders.

My defenses down, Derek returned.

I was in his house again. On the Hill. Reliving the life of a dead teenage boy from behind Derek's eyes. Curled in some-one's lap, my sneakers tucked beneath me. My head rested on someone's soft chest, and I looked up to see the face of Derek's mother as she dozed in a spattering of sunlight that spilled through a tall window in what appeared to be a pri-vate library. It was difficult staying on that lap of hers—it had gotten so small over the last few months. My sneakers kept trying to slide out from under me and spill me onto the rug below.

I just held tighter, listening to the steady beat of Mom-my's heart. My feet felt like they'd peel away from Mommy's lap, the air around me grabbing my waist to steal all of grav-ity's power to let me fly free, unencumbered—free of the troubles and rules of the world, free to do and be whatever I wanted. . . .

Beneath my grasp Mommy trembled and I heard her heart race. I wrapped my arms more tightly around her—as far as my arms would reach since she'd gotten so fat with the baby inside her—and she twitched and gasped, her eyes flying open. They went wide, eyes rimmed with white, her mouth an "o" of horror.

"Ow!" she cried, grabbing at her big, swollen belly, "Owww . . . oh no . . . no, no . . ."

I was floating, loose and free and filled with energy, looking down on the little boy still snuggling into his mother's bosom as, panicking, she tried to push him off her lap. She yelled and cried out in pain and I just hovered there, feeling the strength Derek was bathed in, the strength of his mommy and the baby inside her . . . a strength, I realized with horror, that was beginning to ebb, beginning to fade and soften. . . .

Dr. Jones burst into the room and pulled Derek off his mother's lap, and floating strangely separate from him, I tumbled to the floor for a moment and stood a few feet away before I was pulled back into the odd space behind his eyes.

"Maybe it's not too late," Dr. Jones murmured, trying to calm Mommy as a red stain began to spread across her slacks. "Let's just try and make you comfortable. . . . Calm down," she insisted. "Just calm down." She looked around at us, her eyes narrowing behind the lenses of her stylish glasses. "Leave the room," she commanded as Mommy began to wail.

Her eyes were wide and terrible with hate burning behind them. "Go—get out of my sight, you, you . . . monster," she sobbed.

We tumbled backward at the word and stumbled out the door. *Monster?* Our heart raced and we stood with our back to the wall as Mommy moaned and Jones tried to speak calming words.

"Concentrate on breathing—good, good, slow your heart-beat like I taught you. . . ."

"Derek . . . ," she murmured.

"Stop now—stop. Forget about him. I'll take care of this new development. Don't you worry."

We stayed by the door, standing still as a victim in a horror movie, watching the scene unfold.

"It's okay, it's okay," Dr. Jones repeated, sounding like she was trying to reassure herself as much as Derek's mother. "The worst has passed. Just relax and everything will be fine. . . ."

Even with the water turned all the way to hot, I shivered, and stepping onto the rug to towel off, I realized I wasn't just wiping water away from my face, I was also wiping away tears.

He'd been so young when he'd discovered so much power.

And so young when he died, having only used that power to manipulate others and feed on his friends.

Even more tired than when I'd started my shower, I walked to my room, pulled my door shut, and collapsed on my bed. I wanted answers—that was true. It was the curse of being a reporter or a writer—the need to know.

But I also just wanted to blame Derek. To set his memory on a shelf somewhere to gather dust without understanding his actions. I didn't want to empathize with someone who fed on his friends and killed them to get one last high.

That was one thing I could live without understanding.

If I could just begin to control it . . .

Sleep came quickly, and almost as quickly I was sucked into a dream.

Derek and I stood as one, and still as stone, by a doorway that was only open a crack. As much as I'd known about Derek—or thought I'd known about Derek—I'd never imagined him to be much for eavesdropping. Of course, I'd also never imagined him having been bred for a paranormal purpose, or being used and despised and misunderstood so early on.

He'd been just a kid when his powers started developing. And how could he have possibly known the impact his powers would have at that age?

There was an old Native American proverb I remembered about walking a mile in someone else's shoes before you tried to judge them. Derek might no longer have shoes (or corporeal form) for me to walk a mile in, but the creepy way I now stood and peered out from just behind his eyes . . . that definitely gave me a different view of him and the people who should have loved and protected him.

From himself as much as from them.

Dr. Jones was speaking and we pressed our face into the narrow opening to catch a peek of her as she leaned close to Mommy. "Of course it must be devastating to nearly lose a baby after miscarrying the last one so recently. But our girl's still in there. Still waiting for the right time to be born. So this hasn't been a complete loss."

Mommy shook her head, tears rolling slowly down her face.

I focused, wanting to speed through this. Images moved faster, words sped and began to blur. . . .

"Andconsiderwhatwe'velearned"—too fast . . . I slowed the memory down—". . . about Derek as a result," Dr. Jones said, straightening up to pace before the large picture window with its elegant stained-glass top. "Now we know what happened to the last fetus. We understand why you lost it, and now we can prevent the same thing from happening again."

"I won't let him touch me again," Mommy whispered, her head still moving, loose on her neck. "You can find someone else to train him. . . ."

"No. Oh, no. I don't think that would work. No. Not at all," Dr. Jones said firmly. "While I agree a physical distance must be maintained for the safety of this baby," she said, looking at Mommy's broad belly, "I still think the only one Derek is truly capable of working with is you."

"No."

"You really don't have an option."

"I'll leave the program."

Dr. Jones snorted. "Really? And do what? They are both program babies. I'd rather not push it, but there are ways you might still lose them both. Very quiet and completely legal ways," she said with a sweet smile. "There is a reason we have you sign the documents you do and a reason Derek only knows me as his aunt."

"You would take my children from me?"

"You didn't seriously believe we wouldn't, did you? After all the time, money, and research we invested in both you and your husband. Did you really think you could take some moral stand about family and we'd fold and walk away?"

"Not a moral one," Mommy whispered. "I abandoned my morals and integrity the day I let you convince me this was the right thing to do."

I tried again, speeding the sounds and images and then slowing them again when my head spun.

I could control this.

"Ah, but you *loved* him. And the program was the only way to get your hooks into him, wasn't it? Come now, we're both women of the world. You knew you needed something more than just good social standing to attract Franklin. And let's be honest. Your looks have never been enough to make a man of his caliber stay around past the morning after."

"I sold my *soul*."

I reversed the memory a heartbeat or two. Could I change what she said?

"I sold my *soul*."

No.

I tried to shift Derek—to look somewhere else.

I was stuck unless I pulled out of him, moving like I was stuck in taffy, and let nausea take hold of me.

So much for true control or the ability to change things.

"For a chance at love," Dr. Jones cooed. "Who wouldn't have done the same? Pity it hasn't worked out like the fairy tale you envisioned. Not by a long shot. But you have a lovely house, you are well connected, and women envy you. Though I imagine it must be exhausting trying to keep up with him—trying to figure out who he's seeing on the side."

Mommy looked away.

"There's the pity—you still care. Don't you?" Dr. Jones marveled at Mommy's reaction, the way she folded in on herself, shame plain in her features. "The point is, you both signed papers putting me in a familial position with the ability to not only question your mental and emotional stability and raise significant concerns regarding your capability to raise your children, but you also granted me the ability to invoke power of attorney."

Mommy sobbed openly now.

Dr. Jones rested a hand on her shoulder, giving it a comradely shake. "Don't be so hard on yourself. You were young. I dare say optimistic."

"What must I do?"

"Keep up appearances. Don't allow Derek to be in physical contact with you for long. Not long at all. But continue his training precisely as I prescribe." Dr. Jones handed Mommy a notebook open to a particular page. She tapped the writing with her tip of her fingernail.

"Teach him to *feed?*" Mommy shook her head. "What does that even mean?" She pulled back then, the notebook flopping to the ground, open. "Oh. No. I won't teach him to be a . . . No. *Absolutely* not."

"A what? A *monster?*" Dr. Jones asked, her tone mocking. "It's not something you have to teach him. It's what he already is. What he always has been. We just have to harness it and train him to be the type of monster we want."

The hairs rose on our arms, and my vision bled with black as Derek's world thinned and released me, letting me fall back into my own body, alone. I woke and tugged my heavy blanket up, snuggling as far under it as I could.

But it didn't matter. I couldn't get warm, knowing what I did.

The next days passed much the same way, healing up, seeing the Rusakovas and trying to figure out how to deal with Derek's head stuck in my head, day and night.

CHAPTER NINE

Marlaena

I woke to find Gareth gone. The spot where he'd slept at my side was cold, the sheets rumpled as if he'd made a sudden decision he wasn't ready to tell me about. I fumbled for my phone, but my call went straight to his voice mail.

Pulling back the curtains, I tried to spot the car in the parking lot below, but the angle was wrong. Cursing, I pulled my jeans on over my pj's and stepped outside into winter's biting morning breath.

The car was gone.

Gareth was gone.

I was alone with the last of the pups and no money.

Noah, Terra, and Gabe were still gone. We hadn't felt safe enough to search for them and leave the rest of the pack exposed in case Dmitri had something else planned.

I wandered down the porch, knocking on the pups' doors

as I went. I'd get them dressed, get them packed, and take them down to the motel's lobby to eat a final bowl of cereal and some preservative-rich baked goods the manager always set out as a sort of apology for the fact the toilets often plugged and the cleaning crew was less than perfect. Less than . . .

Less than *average*.

After everyone was packed and fed, we'd . . .

I wrapped my fingers around the banister and stared into the bleak face of winter.

We'd do something. We *had* to do something.

It just sucked not knowing *what*.

And knowing that any action I took in the future depended on the action Gareth was taking right *now*.

Without me.

Alexi

"Shall I grab my gun first or invite you inside for coffee?" I asked, seeing him at the door.

"I'd prefer a beverage to bullets," Gareth admitted, "but I cannot blame you if you do not trust me."

"It is good to know this is one of very few things I will not be blamed for." I unlocked the door and motioned for him to come in. "Coffee is there, by the stove." I motioned to the machine. "Mugs are in the cabinet above."

"You won't even pour it for me?"

"*Nyet*. I want both my eyes on you the entire time," I said, folding my arms across my chest.

I turned away long enough to shout up the stairs, "We have company!" But I no longer needed to shout now the Queen Anne was again a den of wolves.

Max was down the stairs first, scrubbing a hand across his face. He pulled up short when he saw Gareth. "Company?" he snorted. "You should have said *incoming!*"

Gareth examined his coffee and gave the mug a little shake, watching as the contents swirled around inside.

Max rummaged through the fridge, looking for something. With Max, there was never any telling what he might decide was worthy as breakfast.

"Oh." Cat tightened a plush pink robe around herself before joining us in the kitchen. "To what do we owe this distinct . . . pleasure?"

"*Surprise* would be the word," Pietr corrected her, dodging around the other two to stand nearly toe to toe with Gareth. "What are you—" His nostrils flared briefly, and he looked puzzled. But his puzzled expression quickly changed. He took a step back, his gaze running the full length of Gareth as if he was trying to figure something out.

Something that distressed him more than a member of Marlaena's pack standing in our kitchen, drinking our—

"*Coffee?*" Cat said, peering into Gareth's cup a moment before she took it from him and dumped it summarily into the sink. She glared at me.

Gareth was stunned.

"I apologize for my brother's lack of courtesy," Cat said, her smile a touch too saccharine. "We are a somewhat less than proper household, that is true, but we do make it a point of brewing each of our guests a proper cup of tea."

Amy stepped in. "I'll put the kettle on," she said to Cat as she stepped past her.

It was as if they'd rehearsed, as if I were watching some well-planned and well-executed ballet in our kitchen.

"I don't—" Gareth began, warily eyeing the tin Cat opened.

"What?" she asked. "You don't drink tea?" It was clear from her tone that refusal was not an option. Not in this particular Russian-American werewolf household.

Gareth smiled weakly. "I would've been content with coffee. I don't want you put to any trouble." His eyes found mine. "Not any trouble at all."

"Then why have you found yourself on our doorstep this early on a very cold winter morning?" I asked, taking a sip from my own mug. "The coffee is"—I cast a glance toward the sink, then back to Gareth—"was exceptional this morning."

He sighed. "May I sit?"

"*Da*. Yes, of course," I said, pointing to a chair. "Please do tell us what a member of Marlaena's pack is doing in the household of her rival's boyfriend."

Gareth sighed. "Throwing myself at your mercy. To ask for sanctuary."

Jessie

Morning's arrival was bittersweet. I certainly didn't want to risk another dream of Derek's far from savory past, but having had several already, I needed more sleep.

Desperately.

I stumbled into the kitchen bleary eyed and fumbled with the coffeepot.

Annabelle Lee stared at me a moment before putting down the book she'd been reading (my paranormal novel definitely forgotten) and grabbing everything I needed for a low-impact breakfast: bowl, spoon, milk, and cereal. She arranged it all on the table in front of me and pointed to the chair.

"I'm fine," I muttered, flopping into the chair.

"Is it like running a marathon?" she asked. "You really only feel it after it's over?"

I couldn't help it. I smiled. "Comparing a marathon to a kidnapping." I winked at her. "Oddly, yes." I opened the cereal box and dumped some of it into the bowl, covering most of it with milk.

Anna watched me the whole time.

I ate my fill and shoved the bowl out of my way. I glanced at the cereal box, one word jumping out at me and making my eyes fly open in my race to the bathroom.

Vomiting up the cereal I'd barely managed to get down, the word danced in my head: *FEED.*

I needed to talk to Alexi.

Alexi

I sat back in my chair, surprised for the second time that morning. True, the coffee was exceptional this morning, but not nearly strong enough if this was the turn the conversation was destined to take. I set down my mug. *"Sanctuary?"*

"Yes," he insisted, leaning forward. "We've been betrayed."

"No honor in a den of thieves?" Pietr mused.

Cat and Amy just stood, gawking, by the stove as the kettle began to hiss.

"Dmitri and Gabriel have taken our money and two of our young pack members and disappeared. Our rent is due. Without money, there is no place for us to sleep and even if we had money—the motel is no longer safe."

"So what do you expect us to do about it?" Max asked.

The teakettle whistled and everyone jumped.

"I do not expect you to do anything. But I hope you will

exceed my expectations and help us. We need to find Noah
and Terra. And we need a safe place to stay while we figure
out how to do that."

I shook my head. "You want to bring an entire pack—a
pack that has willingly moved as our rivals and put our own
family members at risk—into our home?"

Gareth pressed his lips together and waited.

"*Nye*—"

"Now, brother," Cat cooed, sliding a fresh cup of tea in
front of Gareth, "let us not be hasty with our decisions. Let us
first offer some small bit of hospitality to our guest and hear
him out."

"I've said almost all there is to say," Gareth whispered.

Cat's words were sharp, "Then drink the tea, Gareth."

He tapped the teacup's handle with a tentative finger. "Is
that like 'drink the Kool-Aid'? Because I didn't come here to
die. I came hoping for a chance to keep living."

"Drink the damned tea, Gareth," Cat snarled, and we all
drew back, eyes wide.

Cat did *not* curse.

Not often.

"I will have a cup of tea," I volunteered in hopes of making
him understand Cat's tea was no threat. Not even her cook-
ing was a threat anymore. Much had changed since our arrival in Junction.

But she glared at me and shook her head. "Did I offer to
make you a cup of tea, Sasha?"

"You didn't really *offer* to make *me* a cup . . . ," Gareth
pointed out, but she shot him a look filled with such venom
that he quickly followed his statement us with, "Drinking
the tea . . . drinking the tea . . ." Raising the dainty cup to

his mouth, he sipped and Cat sighed, stepping back to lean against the counter and smile.

The kitchen fell into complete silence except for the sound of Gareth sipping tea and Cat's occasional encouragement of "That's a good boy" and "Just a bit more" and finally, "Finish up."

She retrieved the cup and said over her shoulder, "Please restate the reason you want your pack to come stay with us, Gareth."

"Because they are my family, and although they've made mistakes—big mistakes—they can be redeemed. But if we are kicked out on the street and forced to live on the run, in winter . . ."

Behind Gareth's back Cat showed the cup to Amy, who shrugged at what she saw in its bottom. Cat's smile only grew before she rinsed the leaves into the sink.

"You need not worry, Gareth," she assured, resting a hand on his shoulder and fixing me with a stern look. "Your pack will have a place here with us at least until you've gotten Noah and Terra back."

Gareth rested his head on the table, and I stared at Cat, my jaw hanging open.

Marlaena

He found me in the motel's lobby, sucking icing off an inside-out plastic bag that five minutes earlier had held a cheese-filled Danish. I raised an eyebrow at him and then turned back to the plastic bag, ignoring the simple humans finishing up their breakfasts.

Except for the one female who kept staring at me. I made a face at her, and she busied herself arranging her napkin on her lap.

"We'll be okay," he said, moving past me to get an orange. He peeled it with deft fingers, leaning against the counter beside me and watching me as I crumbled up the Baggie.

"We're always okay," I said, keeping my voice low and looking pointedly at the pups who wandered around the space, chatting, eating, and playing.

He nodded. "Outside?"

I shrugged. "Fine." I snatched a bagel off the counter and tucked an apple into my jacket pocket for later. With the wolf's metabolism burning through me, *later* would be in half an hour.

We stopped just under the edge of the motel's roof, looking for all the world like we were propping up one of its columns with our backs.

"Where'd you go?" I asked in my best *I really don't care, but it's only polite to ask* tone of voice.

"To make a deal. Find us some help."

My stomach churned. "Gabe did the same thing not so long ago, you know? And look where that landed all of us."

"The quality of help I went in search of is much better. And the results—much better."

I crossed my arms over my chest and peered out at him from beneath my eyelashes. "Oh, really? And just who did you broker your deal with, Gareth Wycliff Samuelson?"

He winced at the mention of his middle name.

He didn't know mine, but I'd made it a point to learn the middle names of all my pack members. There was something primitively powerful about invoking someone's full and complete name like their mother might do during a scolding.

"The Rusakovas."

The brief flood of power I'd felt fell away. "No."

"Yes," he assured me. "They were quite reasonable."

"It's impossible." I stepped away from him, shaking my head the whole time, my bangs falling into my eyes. "After what we did to them . . ."

"People can forgive other people," he said, stepping forward to put his hands on my upper arms.

"Not this fast," I whispered, trying to squelch the fear rising in my voice. "What if it's—"

"Stop. Stop it. It's not a trap. And I haven't bargained away anything. They're giving us this as an opportunity. To help the pups."

"I don't believe it."

"Try. Pack the pups and let's get ready to go. We'll stay with them and get Noah and Terra back."

"What did you manage to say to help convince them?"

He shrugged. "I don't think it was really me at all. I think it was Cat."

Alexi

I could not believe Cat. I waited five very respectful minutes after Gareth had left our house before I spoke my mind. "What the hell was that about? Telling him their pack could stay here? With us?"

Cat shrugged and smiled sweetly at me. "I am doing as Fate proscribes."

"Fate?" I smacked my hand on the table. "You are determining our future based on a few tea leaves scattered around the bottom of someone's cup?"

"The tea leaves never lie." She shrugged again, motioned to Amy, and started from the room.

Amy shrugged and turned to follow, but Cat looked over her shoulder at me, adding, "The tea leaves told us about Jessie."

"Ah, yes. Jessie. What do you suppose *she'll* think of housing the girl who may have tried to kill her?"

Cat froze an instant, Amy nearly bumping into her back. "She will realize what you have so often told us—*Keep your friends close and your enemies closer.*"

Jessie

"I think I should be there for this," I said into my cell phone. I had gotten past the *She did what?* and *He agreed to that?* stage of the conversation pretty quickly. Mentally I lingered on the *You let them do this because . . . ?* But I didn't give it the voice it probably deserved.

Pietr's voice was grim. "*Da,* you should be here. It will help make sure she sees that you are firmly a part of the family."

I glanced out the window. Dad was already gone to work. "Can Max—"

"Give you a ride? *Da.* I'll send him. Max—"

"I need to get my license," I complained.

"What good would it do you with having only one vehicle in your family?"

"Good point. But I don't know . . . Don't you think at our age we should have our licenses? I mean, I don't want to be nineteen and just getting my license then. That screams slacker to me."

"Max is on his way."

"With Amy?"

"Of course with Amy."

"I guess that's the only way those two travel."

"They're good for each other." He was quiet a moment, and I wondered if I needed to come up with something to say. He cleared his throat, though, saying, "Do you think I am good for you?"

"*Good* for me?"

"You've been in danger often since knowing me," he pointed out.

"I would have been in even more danger if Derek had gotten control of me," I said.

He was quiet again. "About that . . . Alexi . . ."

"What has Alexi said?" I asked, my throat tightening. I hadn't given Alexi permission to tell Pietr anything regarding what Derek had possibly shoved into my mind during his violent death. Or what seemed to be seeping into my consciousness from the residue Derek had implanted there. . . .

"He is worried about you."

"Is that all he said?"

"*Da.* That is all he said." A long pause followed. "Should *I* be worried about you?"

"No," I whispered. "You saved me, remember? There's nothing to worry about. I'm fine. Great."

"Which is it? Fine or great?"

"Both. I'm so good, it's both. Look, I need to grab my stuff before Max gets here. And tell Annabelle Lee where I'm going. And for how long . . ."

"*Da.* Good idea."

"You don't have to worry about me, Pietr," I repeated, noting the way his tone had changed.

"Fine. I will not worry."

"Great. I love you."

"I love you, too."

I hung up and grabbed my coat, gloves, and scarf and shoved my feet into my boots. I needed to be prepared. What did you say when your enemy—your all-but-mortal enemy—was moving in with your boyfriend and his family? What did you do when someone was quite obviously moving in on your turf? I paused, realizing how possessive I sounded. It wasn't like Pietr was my property. Pietr was . . .

. . . my *everything*. He was who I was willing to lie for, kill and die for. I was terrified of losing that connection.

Lost in my thoughts, I only jumped back into action when I noticed Max starting cautiously up the long driveway. "Anna!" I shouted.

She grunted back, surely reading.

"Going with Max and Amy to Pietr's. Be back for dinner. I think," I added. I pushed through the door and heard it click shut behind me as I bounded off the porch and down the stairs, making a beeline for the car, my thoughts still on the potential battle ahead.

I needed to make sure the Marlaena situation was under control, figure out what power I could wield in this messy situation. . . .

My knees gave way beneath me, my legs failing, and I fell face-first into the snow.

Mommy's voice reached out to me from across the cold and the emptiness, tossing us into familiar territory once again.

I steadied myself in Derek's nonexistent form, glancing down at our shared body. We were older still—fifteen? Sixteen? I couldn't be certain. But from the way we strutted down the hallway of Wanda's mind, I knew we had developed our skills.

And our confidence.

We opened a door.

Wanda's park sprawled out before us, her statues rear-ranged on the other side of the fountain, the gold man top-pled and overgrown with vines that choked it.

Things had gone badly between them.

We skirted the statues and the sky darkened, thunder rolling in the sky above. "I need to hurry. Her defenses have improved since last time."

"Don't worry—just plant the seed and get out."

We dug into our pocket and withdrew a seed the size of a peach pit. Across its surface a word shimmered. *Distrust.* We rolled it over in our palm as we knelt in the soft grass, our fingers digging into the moist and fertile dirt of Wanda's subconscious. And as we dropped it into the hole and sealed it back up, I noticed the word *Betray* glisten across its other side.

We stood, stepped back, and then spread our dirty fingers wide, our hands stretched out above the place where the seed rested.

"Concentrate," Mommy urged.

The ground trembled beneath our feet and we nearly lost our balance as up through the ground a tree sprouted, dark and twisted, gnarled and thorny and covered with leaves that each bore a single word. *Hate. Worry. Fear.* They lined the branches and writhed in the growing wind.

"Now get out," Mommy urged. "The seed is planted and it's taken root. Get out."

We laughed.

And we ran as fast as we could as part of Wanda's world began to fall down around us.

"I've got her." Someone shook my shoulders. "Jessie. Jessie! Wake up or . . . snap out of it . . ." Someone patted my cheek, and I opened my eyes against the glare of sunlight bouncing off snow and ice.

My head throbbed. "Oh. God." I squinted up. Someone stood in the sun's direct path to block it and throw me in merciful shadow. Amy.

"What the hell was that all about?" she demanded.

I grunted. "Did I just make with the drama?"

"Hell, yes." She stomped. "We're driving up here and all of a sudden you flop to the ground like a rag doll. What was that all about?"

I swallowed. "Can we not talk about it right now?" I asked, sliding my gaze to Max as he rose and set me on my feet.

She looked at him, too, and the color that usually filled her face drained away leaving nothing but a scattering of freckles and the barest hint of windburn. "Fine," she whispered. "We'll talk later."

"Great," I muttered. "Let's just get going, okay? I think I'd better have a chat with Alexi."

Max's eyes narrowed, but he nodded, his hand hot on the small of my back as he guided me to the car and watched with particular interest as I buckled my seat belt. "Is there something I should know?" he finally asked as he started the car up and adjusted the mirrors to begin backing down my driveway.

"No," I insisted. Too quickly.

He nodded. "I thought so." He rolled his lips together in thought. "I can handle keeping a secret. I used to keep a pretty big one just to seem normal—just to survive."

"I know. It's nothing," I assured him. "Maybe it's a secret that would do more damage if it gets out and won't be a problem at all if it doesn't."

"Looks like it's a problem already whether you talk about it or not," Max stated.

"Don't you have any secrets now?"

He refocused his gaze. "Fine. I'll leave it alone," he assured me.

But the way he said it, the way he reacted, made me wonder just what secret he was keeping from me, and something twisted in my gut at the thought.

"Are you certain you'll be able to handle this?" Max asked grimly as we pulled into their driveway. The Queen Anne was stark against the gray sky.

"I'm fine," I insisted, pulling my coat tightly around me and adjusting my scarf and hat. "It was nothing."

"Right," he responded dryly. "Collapsing onto the ground all of a sudden is absolutely normal." Max was thinking. Hard.

"No, Max," I said firmly. "No. Absolutely not. I know what you're thinking, and no. You may not tell Pietr what happened."

He grunted.

"Promise me, Max." But my heart sped up. What if a promise didn't mean as much to Max as it did to Pietr? To Pietr, a promise was the ultimate oath. He'd rather die than break a promise. But Max . . . "Promise me."

He waved a hand in my direction, and it did nothing to slow the pace of my heart. "Fine. I promise. I won't tell Pietr what happened."

I examined his words in my head. It seemed like a solid promise. "Thank you," I said with a sigh. "Okay, here we go," I said, opening my door and letting winter tug at me.

Together we headed into the house. Pietr, Cat, and Alexi were there, standing in the foyer. Pietr grabbed me immediately and pulled me into his arms, pressing me snug to his body and pushing his nose to the edge of my ear where my hair was escaping from beneath my knit hat. *"Allo,"* he said, his breath hot and fierce in my ear.

My legs trembled and I locked my knees in defense against my body's immediate betrayal. "Hello, Pietr," I whispered back, stretching up to get my lips closer to his ear.

Max cleared his throat. "Still in the foyer," he pointed out.

I slipped away from Pietr's grasp, blushing.

Pietr glanced at Max, one eyebrow rising in challenge. "We can correct the oversight of our location," he mentioned, glancing from me to the top of the stairs behind him. Toward his room.

Amy snickered.

I peeled off my hat, coat, and scarf and shook my head. "Quit it, you two," I said, handing my things to Pietr to hang for me. "We have things to get ready for."

"Guests," Alexi said.

"And we're putting them—"

"Downstairs," Cat responded. "It will be easy."

"Easy. Right. That's exactly what I was hoping for when I headed here this morning—making things easy on an incoming wolf pack," I muttered.

Pietr grabbed my hand and tugged me back toward him. "Come with me," he said, "while we still have time in a not so very crowded house."

I nodded and let him draw me up the stairs and to the quiet solitude of his room.

The door clicked shut behind us and we tumbled onto the bed together, a knot of arms and legs, kissing each other eagerly.

"I missed you," I admitted, panting as his lips grazed my neck.

"I didn't go anywhere," he whispered back, rolling me beneath him. His hair fell into my face, and I giggled and brushed it back only to watch it fall forward again.

"You did," I argued. "It was like this part of you . . ." I brushed a finger along the heated power of his lips, "was gone. Tucked away."

"I was not myself?" he asked, kissing along my jawline.

"You . . ." But I couldn't agree because of what that meant. If Pietr wasn't himself when he was cured, would he ever take a cure again? "You were still you, just dialed back a bit," I whispered. "Let's not talk about it anymore. *Pocelujte menyah.* Kiss me, Pietr."

He rested his hips on mine, pinning my legs beneath him and kissing me with a heat I'd thought we'd both forgotten. Pietr had his passion back, and Alexi was working with Wondermann—maybe a real cure could still be created. Maybe we could have it all.

We were still in love as much as ever.

His lips on mine, our breath mixing, I was *invincible.*

He rolled away from the wanderings of my eager hands and propped himself up on an elbow, looking at me.

"We should take it easy, shouldn't we?" I asked, scrunching up my nose.

"*Da,*" he answered. "I am not—prepared," he said with a shrug, and I knew he meant he didn't have protection. "And we cannot afford any accidents."

"Yeah. I can't risk getting pregnant," I agreed. "Dad would eventually realize we've had sex."

Pietr chuckled, the noise rising from deep in his stomach,

tumbling past the place his growling accent lived and making everything inside of me quiver.

"Besides," I said, trying to steady my breathing, "I'm *so* not ready for kids. Not yet."

"Not ever," he said firmly.

"Really?" I straightened and pulled myself up to sit there, looking down at him, realizing in my furthest daydreams, those ones that stretched out a decade ahead of us, I'd imagined us married with kids. I hadn't spent much time on those fantasies, especially when it seemed my most important fantasy would be that both of us lived that long. But they'd seemed right. Normal. My parents were married. They'd had two kids and a very happy life together. Until the car crash killed Mom.

"No children. *Ever*?" I clarified.

"*Nyet*. No children. Ever," he confirmed. "Think about it, Jess. If you had a disease—something you knew would kill or cripple someone—would you pass it on?"

"No," I said. "Of course not."

"My life span is incredibly short. What sort of parent would I be to force that—and these changes—on my offspring? What sort of parent would I be knowing I created a child and would leave it early? Abandon it?"

"But, Pietr, our children would be a *mix* of our blood—our DNA. They would have a very good chance at a longer life span," I insisted. "And our children—our *hypothetical* children—" I stressed, "would not be abandoned. They would still have me."

"I would never burden you with a child of my kind."

"A child of your *kind* . . . What exactly does that mean? Beautiful, intelligent, caring? Oh, yeah. What a burden *that* would be."

"An *oborot*. An abomination."

"Holy crap, Pietr. Quit it. You aren't a monster. You're a man—a good one. Yes, you've made mistakes and have some weird genes, but every so often in my dad's family line there's a kid with mismatched eyes, and on Mom's side there's an albino great-aunt. So you bring werewolves into the mix." I climbed off the bed, frustrated. "Stop torturing yourself," I snapped. "There are plenty of people standing in line ready to torture you instead."

I adjusted my top and checked my hair. Slamming the door behind me, I hurried down the stairs.

Cat looked up at me as I entered the kitchen. "Not the best of talks?" she asked mildly.

Horror forced my eyes wide.

"Do not glare at me, Jessie. Can you blame him for taking a hard line about children?"

"Wha—"

"Honestly, you seem so observant most times." She jabbed a spoon toward the ceiling. "Heating grate," she pointed out. "*Allo*, Pietr!" she called.

To which he responded with something very angry sounding. In Russian.

"Language!" she snapped toward the grate.

Pietr stomped in anger.

"You two are a perfect match. Headstrong and teetering just between self-involved and self-sacrificing. If you can both find your balance, you will be wonderful together."

A knock at the door made me jump, and Cat said, "We have guests!"

"Wonderful," I muttered, joining the others in the foyer to watch the door as the rest of the pack members climbed the stairs and approached the house.

Alexi

I decided to greet everyone at the door like a proper host (or an alpha). Marlaena wisely let Gareth take the lead and do the introductions. The pups were gracious and curious, their eyes still wide from seeing the outside of the house. In truth, it was a relatively standard Queen Anne, though I would never claim it to be modest. It was simply the standard home built for its time.

Squeezing into our foyer, one of them closed the door behind them.

"Wait," I said, looking out the lacy curtain that fluttered against the door's window. "Was there not someone else with you?"

The pack members looked at one another and then back to me. "No," Marlaena said. "This is all of us."

"Oh. I thought there was someone else. . . ."

Gareth glanced out the window. "There's no one there now. And we would have smelled the only missing members of our pack."

"Or any other troublemaker," Marlaena added, sharing a nod with Gareth.

I presumed they meant Dmitri, the troublemaker who had landed them in this predicament.

"Where's Pietr?" one of the blond girls asked. Londyn or Jordyn—I could not yet tell them apart.

I stopped myself from saying anything and, instead, looked at Jessie.

She shrugged at me.

"I do not know at the moment," I admitted. "It appears he has thrown us to the wolves." I winked at her.

She rolled her eyes.

Cat slid in between us, her eyes kind but crisp with challenge. "I think it is best if we move all of Amy's things into Max's room and give your pack the basement. It is not the most comfortable location," she said almost apologetically, "but it will allow you all to stay together in one place."

Gareth nodded. "We appreciate that consideration," he said.

Marlaena just eyed Cat. "And no one knows where Pietr is?" she asked.

Cat and I exchanged a glance. Whereas the blond girl's question had seemed offhanded, Marlaena's sounded more calculated.

Jessie asked what we ourselves were wondering in silence. "Why should it matter to you?"

Marlaena raised an eyebrow, as if talking to Jessie was somehow belittling.

Max coughed to draw attention to himself and away from the smackdown that was preparing to happen in our foyer. *Da*, this would be no trouble at all.

"Alphas like to be aware of the locations of other alphas. You wouldn't understand," she said in dismissal.

"Oh, I wouldn't, would I?" Jessie asked, stepping closer.

Marlaena straightened her back.

So did Jessie.

Gareth's hand came down on Marlaena's shoulder, but that didn't turn her attention from Jessie at all. If anything, it focused her intensity to laser hot.

"Here," Pietr called from the top of the stairs, verbally stepping between the girls before they squared off in the foyer below. "I am here." His eyes first found Jessie and he smiled, but his expression changed—subtly, but still a change—and his gaze was drawn as if by magnet to Marlaena.

Jessie

"Excellent," Marlaena responded, shaking free of Gareth's grasp and brushing past my shoulder to better see Pietr as he descended the stairs.

Amy laced one arm through mine and drew me toward the stairs, hooking Pietr with her other.

He moved, joining us as if dazed, pulling his gaze away from Marlaena with a little too much difficulty.

"Max, you too," Amy commanded over her shoulder. "Looks like I'm moving in with you after all."

"I have told you for weeks that is the best option," Max responded with the arrogant flare only he could carry off.

"Yeah, yeah," Amy said with a snort. "Well, then, thank the wolfpack. Because I still wouldn't be doing this if it wasn't for them. You're difficult," she added in his direction.

"Difficult?" he said, his voice rising as we started down the basement stairs.

"Mmmm. Maybe not difficult—more *high maintenance*," she said, as if that label was somehow reassuring in comparison.

"High maintenance," he nearly squeaked. "That is a label for a *girl*. . . ."

Amy stopped us all on the stairs, unlinking her arms with ours and turning in the tight space to look up at Max. "I'm guessing saying you're very pretty wouldn't help, would it?" she laughed, sticking her tongue out.

He snarled. "I am far too masculine to be pretty," he said, raising his chin to accentuate the strong angles of his jaw and showcase his Adam's apple.

Amy just snorted again. "Pretty, pretty," she teased. "Hairy, but pretty."

I laughed, too, and looked to see Pietr's reaction as Amy jogged down the last few steps, fleeing when Max pressed past us, but Pietr was somewhere else—at least mentally. He seemed totally unaware of their antics.

I snapped my fingers in front of him. "Hey."

He blinked at me, smiled, and continued down the stairs with me.

"You faded out right there. Something on your mind?"

He shook his head a little too readily for me to dismiss the look as nothing.

"Really? Nothing worth sharing?"

"*Nyet*, it's nothing," he assured me, his lips slipping into a smile. It was a smile I'd seen frequently on other faces—on Amy's when Max was suddenly too frisky; on Sarah's when she couldn't remember a word she used to toss around so easily; and on my own when I looked into the mirror and tried to convince myself that things were increasingly getting better.

"Okay," I said.

But it wasn't. It most certainly wasn't okay.

Whatever had caught his attention and pulled him away so far and so fast was anything *but* okay.

CHAPTER TEN

Alexi

They had barely moved their negligible belongings in when Max volunteered his services. "I'll go sniff around. See if I can find Noah and Terra."

"We will need Pietr and Gareth, too," I suggested.

"Don't expect me to just sit here while you three try to do search and rescue," Marlaena snapped. "They're two of my pack."

Max shrugged, but Pietr blanched and looked away.

Gareth nodded. "Fine. We'll leave Tembe and Judith with the pups here."

"And what about me?" Jessie piped up. "What's best—me here or there?"

Pietr chewed his lower lip, his gaze again falling on Marlaena. "I want you safe," Pietr said as his eyes slid back to Jessie, and for a moment I wondered which one of them the statement was truly intended for.

"Do not count me out," I insisted.

"This is a scouting mission—if we're lucky, a rescue—not a party," Marlaena snarled.

"It's never a party with you," I responded, holding my ground.

"Alexi comes," Pietr said. "He is a great strategist. Max can drive for us. Jess, you stay here with Amy and Cat and keep an eye on everyone."

"Yeah. We womenfolk'll stay back with the kids," Jessie muttered.

Pietr smiled softly at her. "You know it's not like that." He stood up and walked over to where she stood on the opposite side of the table and slid his arms around her waist.

But there was something stiff and awkward about the way he embraced her, and I noted an odd hesitancy when he lowered his nose into the hair crowning the top of her head.

Jessie leaned into him. "Just come back safe, okay?"

"*Da*," he whispered, nuzzling her forehead and cheek.

"And that goes for you," she said, looking at Max, "and you," she glanced at Gareth, "and you," she said, peering at me. No one missed the fact she wasted no good wishes on Marlaena.

Marlaena leaned back in her chair and propped her feet up on the table's edge.

Cat shook her head, clearing her throat authoritatively, and although Marlaena growled, she put her feet back on the floor. "We want an estimated time of arrival for your return here," Cat announced.

"Yes, some idea of how long we wait until we press the panic button," Jessie said.

"We have no idea how long this will take or even if we'll find them at all," Marlaena muttered, her eyes focused on

Pietr as she looked past Jessie in disgust. "We could be out all night," she added as a little dig.

Jessie twitched in response. "That's unacceptable."

Pietr stepped back so he could look straight into her eyes. "If it means getting Noah and Terra back to their pack safely and breaking ties with Dmitri . . . isn't it worth staying out all night?"

She rested her head on his chest. "Yes, of course it is. Just . . . be careful."

"I will," he insisted.

She stepped into his embrace again and stretched up to whisper something into his ear for him alone. A smile twitched to life on Pietr's sometimes too stoic face and he bent to meet her lips, kissing her gently. She drew back finally, her entire face caught in her smile, and she tapped his hip pocket. "You have a cell phone"—she looked at each of us in turn—"you all do. Make sure you use them. I want to know what's happening every step of the way. Understood?"

"*Da*," Pietr answered, a gleam to his eyes. "Until we are wolf, you will know everything as we do."

"And after they are wolf, you will still know all I do," I reported.

"Good," Jessie said. "Then get to it."

And so we gathered our things and piled into the convertible.

Jessie tapped Max's window.

"*Da?*"

"Drive carefully," she added with a stern look.

"I always do," he replied.

"No. You don't."

He shrugged. "It is a hazard of being me," he said. "And of being Russian. We love to drive quickly."

"Not tonight," she warned. "Things will be dangerous enough without the risk of driving too fast in bad conditions."

I nodded. "You can be very much like a mother hen, you know."

"As long as my little chickies all return safely to my nest, I don't care what you call me," she responded, stepping back from the car.

She stood in the driveway as a few stray snowflakes fluttered down from the tree's branches above, watching the entire time we backed out of the driveway and pulled onto the street, her face full of the worry that no doubt made her heart pound.

Jessie

The pups were all downstairs, their attention firmly on one another as they played an impromptu game of something that required keeping stuff away from another member of the pack, tagging one another at random, and wrestling.

Amy, Cat, and I paused on the steps to watch them. Without Marlaena lording over them, they were much different. More free. They laughed at one another and themselves, the twins falling into shared fits of giggles.

I hated to break it up, but even descending two more steps they noticed us, and froze.

Waiting for a reprimand?

I grinned at them instead.

"We're ordering pizza," I announced. "Anything you want on it?"

Every topping known to man was shouted out from down below and I finally waved my arms, laughing, to get them to quiet down. "Let's try it this way: Anything you *don't* want on the pizza?"

Silence.

Amy snorted. "Got it. I'll call in three trashy pizzas."

"Only three?" Tembe asked.

"Four?" Amy tried.

Londyn and Jordyn both stuck their thumbs up and jabbed skyward.

"Six?" Amy asked, her voice rising slightly.

Cat said from behind her, "Better make it two more," she said, and the pups nodded eagerly.

"Eight pizzas? You're kidding me . . ."

"It's like living in a fraternity house," Cat mused.

"But not as smelly," Amy said. "No. Don't ask how I know, but let's just say large groups of college-age guys should never share the same living space without an established rule regarding room deodorizers and the potential burning of dirty socks and boxers."

Cat's eyebrows shot high on her head, imagining what was surely a horrific scene being painted in her head by Amy's words.

Amy reached up and petted her arm. "Off to your happy place, Cat," she joked. "I'll order eight pizzas and make the pizza joint's evening." She pressed past us and disappeared upstairs.

My cell phone buzzed with a text from Pietr.

Caught a scent. More soon.

I responded with a quick *hugs* and slipped the cell phone back into my pocket.

The pups all watched me, curious.

"So far, so good," I announced. "We were thinking tonight would be a good night for a movie. What do you think?"

"What movie are you suggesting?" Darby asked cautiously.

I smiled. "How about *Red Riding Hood*?"

They wrinkled their noses at me.

"Maybe something where the wolves aren't the bad guys?" one of them suggested.

I mentally ticked off titles on the list in my head. Nothing that didn't in some way vilify werewolves. "Okay, how about no wolves at all?" I tried.

They nodded.

"The Princess Bride?" It was a personal favorite that I'd introduced the Rusakovas to just before Halloween. "It's clever and snarky and has a hot guy and sword fighting in it. . . ."

Some interest, but not as much as I'd hoped.

"An adventure movie," someone shouted out.

"Spies?" Cat asked, her mouth turning up into a sly smile.

They began nodding.

"Excellent," she said, clapping her hands together. "Upstairs to take a vote!" she proclaimed, pointing to the door.

They thundered past, thrilled at one aspect of the evening's homebound adventure. Maybe it was just the fact that they got a vote—that they got a stake in the decision-making process.

Upstairs they gathered around Cat, who held up two Blu-ray cases. The newest in the Bond franchise and the first of the Bourne movies.

"With my father," she explained, remembering as the words came out, "it was always one of the two B's: Bond or Bourne. Which shall we start with tonight?"

They examined each case and took a vote. It was all very democratic. Very civilized.

I went to check on Amy while Cat set up the movie.

She was hanging up the phone. "Do you know how much eight large pizzas cost?"

"I'm guessing the proper answer is *a lot.*"

"Yee-ahhh. I don't know how we'll be able to support feeding them, too. We barely manage to feed ourselves and make the house payments. I mean, I know Alexi has some little nest egg he's still drawing from, but they weren't left with any stash of cash when their parents died, you know? And even the jobs that have been picked up are . . . well, they're just above minimum wage."

"I'm sorry," I murmured. "I guess Marlaena and Gareth and a few of the others will have to go legit. And when the rest of the pups are enrolled in school, surely they'll qualify for the free lunch program. . . ."

We stared at each other.

"Not that we want them accidentally exposed to any additives like the other students at Junction were . . . ," Amy added, her tone low at the thought of it.

"Definitely not."

"Glad Alexi's been on top of that," I remarked.

"Yeah, but what a deal to make, right? Working hand-in-hand with Wondermann to find a permanent cure for werewolves just so Wondermann can reverse engineer it and make the next generation of werewolves irreversible."

"Alexi doesn't seem to be one for doing things only half-assed," I pointed out. My cell phone buzzed again. "New text," I said, reading it. "They think they've found them. The wolves'll be out of contact for a little while now, but Alexi will keep us updated." I put the cell away again. "I hate this."

"Me too. Let's go watch a movie," Amy suggested. "The pizzas will be here soon."

Marlaena

The interior of the convertible bristled with weapons and werewolves. It was good, I thought. Perfect. We were in a sexy car brimming with bullets and bad intentions on our way to rescue Noah and Terra.

Max was at the wheel, leather driving gloves with cutouts to emphasize his knuckles drawing attention to his hands. But with Max driving I guessed girls would have looked at his hands and every other inch of him regardless of sporty gloves.

But Max was not the werewolf on my mind. I pulled the rearview mirror down to peek into the backseat, where Gareth and Pietr acted as bookends to Alexi.

Alexi had been adamant about crowding into the car, even though it meant we'd have to put Terra on someone's lap on the return trip. I guessed Max would've volunteered to suffer through that situation, but, being bulkiest, he was driving. I'd argued with Alexi, but his siblings stood firm. He was the planner. He was their Hannibal (and not the one obsessed with fava beans and that Clarice chick, either).

If their pack was the Scooby Gang, Alexi was Velma minus the skirt and glasses (and plus a good dose of male hormones).

Gareth leaned as hard into the door as he could, trying to give everyone the most room possible. Although we'd been a pack awhile, this concept of such cooperation was new to us. It made me itch.

And so did Pietr's presence.

I blinked, trying to refocus.

But I felt his eyes boring into the back of my headrest.

I sank down in my seat, grabbing hold of anger's heat

instead of the heat Pietr's presence signaled in my body. We were only a few turns away from the location Max and Alexi had traced them to. I needed to be sharp. I imagined my fingers folding around Dmitri's neck . . . because as involved as Gabe was in all this, Dmitri was the catalyst and that meant he needed to be removed from the equation.

Alexi

The fact they had not been hard for us to find only put me further on my guard. "This should not have been so simple," I commented, watching as Max followed the scents as much as the road.

The scents of Dmitri, Gabriel, Noah, and Terra seemed heaviest in this area, now it was merely a matter of narrowing our results. In only a few more minutes we had found their base of operations—a modest house on the far side of Junction. "If they wanted us to never find them they would have gone farther." We drove past it, examining the area for entrance and exit points.

"They would have left Junction," Max added with a slow nod.

"Or they would have masked their scent the way Wanda and Kent did," Pietr interjected. "But they are here. In Junction, with no desire to hide."

"A trap," Max muttered. He turned the car away from the house, beginning to put distance between us and it in increasingly large blocks of real estate. "I want to know what we're getting into so—"

"We know how to get back out," I agreed.

"Go back to the house," Marlaena demanded. "I can't be-lieve you're so paranoid—"

"Cautious," Gareth said.

"It's not a trap. It's just because Dmitri and Gabe are cocky bastards so full of themselves they can't imagine anyone bringing the fight to their doorstep," Marlaena snapped, ad-justing her seat belt. "You give them too much credit."

"You give them too little," I suggested. "Dmitri was mili-tary before he went Mafia. He has a mind for strategy, does he not, brother?"

"*Da,*" Pietr said. "He does."

"I don't have time for this," Marlaena muttered. "We need to get in there, get my pups out, and then—I don't care—blow the place to bits. I just want Noah and Terra out."

"Don't be stupid, 'laena," Gareth urged. "We need to do this together. To cooperate so everyone gets home safely."

"Dammit, Gareth," she snarled. "Alphas don't beta down to anyone—"

"Stop it *now,*" Pietr demanded, leaning forward to lock eyes with her.

Her mouth sealed, and she looked at him wide-eyed.

"You will cooperate for the good of your pack and the safety of my family."

I kept my mouth shut, thinking the whole time, alphas do not beta down to anyone, except each other. That was good enough for me.

At least for now.

Marlaena

Nearly nose to nose with Pietr in the convertible, all the anger drained away from me, and I found my eyes dropping from his intense stare to his firm mouth with its promising lips.

I licked my lips and tore my gaze away, my heart hammering in my chest. I blinked rapidly and tried to regain my place in the conversation. "I will cooperate," I said unsteadily, "for the sake of my pack and because if I don't, you all will blunder around and screw everything up." So why did it suddenly sound like I was pouting?

I was an alpha.

I snarled, promising to myself as well as all of them, "When we get there, I swear I'll—"

Pietr leaned forward between the seats, thrusting a hand up to silence me.

I whipped around in my seat belt. "Don't you—" I warned.

His raised hand just curled and pointed straight ahead out the windshield.

I turned, my gaze following, and before the car had even stopped, I was jumping out of my door and rushing to throw my arms around the boy who was walking in the middle of the road, his head down, looking heartbroken. "Noah!" I shouted.

He struggled in my grip a moment, before realizing it was me, and then he looked up. His eyes were red.

"You're okay now, Noah," I said. A truck whipped past us, blaring its horn. "Let's get out of the road to make sure you stay that way," I said, dragging him to the road's edge.

Max pulled the car over beside us.

"Get in," Pietr ordered, and we pushed into the back together, shoving Pietr out and to the front.

"Where's Gabrrriel?" I asked, the name turning into a growl.

"I'll show you," Noah offered.

"Good kid," I said. "Everyone ready? We still have one rescue to do."

Nods and grunts answered me.

"It won't matter, though," Noah whispered from beside me, his face turned downward.

"What? Why not?"

"Because Terra's not there."

"What? Why isn't Terra there?" I pressed my face to the window briefly, thinking she'd followed him but was walking more slowly for some reason. Packmates and off-and-on girlfriend and boyfriend that they were, I knew spats happened—at the most inopportune times.

"Because this morning Dmitri took her away."

Jessie

"They have Noah!" I shouted, seeing the text.

Suddenly the excitement of car chases, explosions, and good-looking women was not nearly the most important thing as the pups jumped to their feet, shouting, clapping, and hugging one another.

"And Terra?" Darby asked.

My mouth pinched shut. "No, I'm sorry," I said. "No word on Terra yet. But if anyone can find her, it's Pietr, Max, and Alexi."

"And Gareth," Kyanne added.

No one mentioned Marlaena.

Not once.

Marlaena

Noah led us back to the house he'd just escaped from—the same house we'd identified not twenty minutes earlier. He threw open the door, bolder and angrier than I'd ever seen him.

Or ever imagined he could get.

"Those moves Dmitri taught me? They worked on Gabe pretty well. As soon as he helped shove Terra in Dmitri's car, I hit him and left him . . ." He paused at an empty spot on the floor. "Here," he whispered, raising his eyes to mine.

"Grrraarrr!" The wolf burst from the shadows, and limping, knocked me down to the ground and went straight for Pietr.

Pietr fell backward beneath the force of Gabriel's leap, one hand reaching behind to stop himself from hitting the floor as his other slipped out of its human form, tendons popping and bones dissolving to re-form as claws extended. Pietr shoved the wolf back and sprang to his feet again, pushing all his weight forward to pin Gabriel against the nearest wall.

Pietr's huge, clawed hand held the struggling wolf by his throat, Pietr's hips knocking Gabe's aside so the wolf's powerful hind legs had no stomach to kick out against. With a grunt of effort Pietr raised the wolf just far enough that his hind paws scrabbled wildly in an attempt to touch the floor, claws only grazing it.

Gabe twisted and fought to break free of Pietr's unforgiving grasp, but it was no use. The wolf's tongue lolled out, and Gabe gasped for breath. Still Pietr, with hard eyes and pointing teeth, held him suspended.

Gabe's head rolled to the side and I shouted, shoving Pietr

aside with all my strength. He rocked on his feet, and popping his fingers open, let go of Gabe, watching him slide to the floor with a blink.

In the space of a few heartbeats Gabe was no longer wolf but entirely human. He glared at Pietr, his upper lip curling.

Fighting my own cruel intent, I swept down and dragged him up against the wall once more. Only I let him keep his footing and I pressed my forearm across his heaving chest.

"Explain yourself, or, so help me God, I'll end your sorry existence right here and now," I snarled, my fingernails thickening and sharpening into points with a *schnikt*.

His back flat to the wall, Gabriel panted a moment, but his ragged breathing translated into a rough chuckle. "Isn't that what Margie used to claim before she told Phil to get the belt? She was going to *end your sorry existence*?" He tried to look over my shoulder, to where Gareth and Noah watched. "I guess the apple doesn't fall far from the tree." He might make verbal jabs at me, but I shifted my weight to block his view so he'd get no satisfaction tonight.

"Why take the pups?"

"He promised to take me with him," Gabriel whispered, so close I could smell his breath. "If I just brought him Noah and Terra—two wolves for a fresh start. Just what we needed, remember? To separate. To start all over."

"You could have just left. You didn't need to risk the pups. I would have given you money. . . . You didn't have to *take* it. . . ."

"No one gives us anything, 'laena. *No one*. I take what I need. I always have and I always will."

"You're at war with your own pack, Gabriel—don't you see that? You've torn them all apart trying to decide whose side to be on. They're pups. . . ."

"By your definition, so am I," he snarled.

I stepped back. He was right. He was barely eighteen. I forgot that too often as we fought and squabbled over power. We aged so quickly because of the wolf inside and because of the way we tore at each other mercilessly. "Yes," I agreed. "Yes. But I can't compare you to Noah or Terra—don't you see that? You're so . . ."

"Different?" He said it like even forming the word on his tongue left a bitter taste in his mouth.

"Yes."

"That's why we don't work. I'm as different from them as you are. We're both fighters, 'laena."

"And since opposites attract and like forces repel?" I mused.

He shrugged. "Can't you see? We're the same under the skin. We're alphas. We take what we want. Take what we need. We don't answer to anyone." He brushed the remaining fingers of his hand across my face. "And we shouldn't have to."

I pulled away, my guts knotting at the touch of his hand. His scent burned in my nostrils like the acrid smell of fire and ash. "I answer to my pack. That is the definition of being an alpha. That is the definition of leadership. Answering to the needs of those lower down the food chain."

"We must have different dictionaries," he whispered. "A true leader answers to no one but guides his people to where he knows they need to be."

A sigh ghosted out of me. I was making no progress with him. "We have Noah and he's safe. That's one. Let's try this one more time, Gabe," I said. "Tell me where Terra is and I'll forget all about this."

He snorted. "I can't tell you what I don't know."

My eyes closed and I focused on the sound of his breathing, the beat of his heart beneath the iron press of my arm. His heart beat fast, but it held steady and true. Gabe was scared, but he wasn't lying.

"Dammit." I shoved off of him, stepping away and brushing myself off in disgust. I tugged at the hem of my T-shirt, straightening it. "I don't want to see you again, are we clear? I want you gone."

He stared at me passively, his eyes giving no hint of either obedience or rebellion.

I lunged then, knocking him back against the wall hard, my arm across his throat. His eyes went round with shock. "If you don't make yourself gone, I will."

Awkwardly he moved his head up and down just once in a nod of understanding. I peeled back, bolting away, bounding out the door and to the car.

We had Noah back and we'd find Terra somehow.

And, one way or the other, I'd be free of Gabriel.

CHAPTER ELEVEN

Alexi

They tumbled out of the den when they heard us at the door. There were shouts of "Noah!" as the pups pounced him and wrestled their way across the foyer.

"I doubt I could get used to that sort of greeting," I commented, shaking my coat off on the porch before securing the door behind me.

Gareth was already leading them down to the basement to try to stem the inevitable tide of questions regarding Terra. Marlaena watched Pietr.

And Pietr watched Marlaena.

Jessie cleared her throat. "Everyone okay?" she asked, her gaze lingering on Pietr's pale face longer than it seemed she intended.

He nodded.

Max pushed between Pietr and Marlaena and grabbed both Amy and Jessie by the waist, spinning them around. "Everyone is fine," he assured them, giving Amy a quick kiss before he set the exasperated girls down.

I asked the question my brothers were too dense to ask. Or, in Max's case, too self-absorbed to care to ask. "How did everyone do here? I smell pizza."

"Yeah," Amy said, crossing her arms. "You may smell pizza, but you won't get to have any."

I looked at her over my shoulder as I hung my coat up and motioned for Pietr and Marlaena to do the same. Like ice statues thawing, they began to move and followed my suggestion, but their movements were stilted and wooden. I had to look away.

Jessie was not so fortunate.

"The pizza?" I asked, trying to draw everyone's attention from the disaster in the making in our foyer.

"All gone," Amy explained. "Every lick. And I do mean there was licking involved," she muttered. "Of the pizza boxes. But what's a little extra fiber, right?"

I laughed, but the sound came out as false as Pietr's and Marlaena's body language seemed. "So what is there to eat, Jessie?" I asked.

She shrugged. "You look pale," she said to Pietr, stepping forward.

Marlaena stiffened beside him.

"I'm fine," he argued. "Tired maybe. Dmitri was nowhere in sight, and Gabe wasn't much of a challenge."

"Not for you," Marlaena said with a smile that spoke volumes.

"Did you fight him?" Jessie asked as she reached a hand up to Pietr's forehead.

"*Da,*" he muttered, pressing his fingertips over hers to hold her hand on his head. "Marlaena made me stop," he added solemnly.

"Well. Thank you for that, at least," Jessie said in Marlaena's general direction. "Huh. You aren't any hotter than you usually are," Jessie muttered. "And it's not like you could be coming down with something, right?"

Sweeping her hand into his own, he kissed the pads of her fingers.

Marlaena turned away, busying herself with the coat-rack.

"*Nyet*," Pietr assured. "I am fine. Just tired. I'm allowed to be tired, *da?*"

Jessie poked him in the shoulder. "You're allowed to be tired, *da*," she teased. "But not cranky."

"It is good to know," he said.

"Let's find you something to eat, okay?"

"That sounds like a wonderful plan," Pietr confirmed.

Wrapping her arm around his waist, Jessie towed him toward the kitchen, the rest of us following.

Except for Marlaena.

"I'll go check on Gareth," she said, but no one listened because no one cared.

Jessie

"Was it hard—fighting Gabe?" I asked him.

He rolled over to look at me, his eyes clouded with memory. "It was harder to stop." He flopped onto his back, one arm tucked beneath his head as he stared up at his ceiling so he didn't need to meet my eyes.

"But you *did* stop," I reminded him. "You could have . . . killed him?"

"Da." His voice was deep and hoarse. Strained. "I wanted to. He took you from me. He nearly had you killed."

I puffed out a breath. "But don't forget, Marlaena's the one who almost did the killing."

"So what would you have me do?" he asked, his tone going flat and nearly mechanical.

"I don't know," I admitted, setting my hand on his chest so I could feel his heart beat beneath my palm. His heart in my hand . . . I sighed. That's what I wanted. To hold his heart. "Just don't . . ."

He sat up to look at me, pinning my hand to his chest like he was worried it would leave. "Don't what?"

Don't forgive her? Don't look at her that way? Don't . . . don't what? I shook my head. "Just don't let me go," I whispered, sliding my hand free of his so I could lean my head on that space instead.

"Never," he whispered. "Never." He leaned back again, taking me with him, and I dozed off like that, his heart racing in my head.

I woke to Pietr dozing beside me and slipped off the bed, out the door, and down the steps. I headed for Alexi's room, but hearing movement in the dining room I turned that direction instead.

Alexi was at the table, staring at his cell phone and tapping a pack of cigarettes.

He froze when he heard me.

"What's this?" I asked, pointing with my chin.

"Cell phone," he said, holding it up for me to see.

"No, jackass. I meant the cigarettes."

"If you knew they were cigarettes, why ask?"

I pulled out the seat beside him and sat down. "You know what I mean." I poked the cigarettes. "Was it so bad tonight? Fighting Gabe?"

"*Nyet*." He spun the pack, watching it solemnly. "It has nothing to do with Gabriel. Or the fight."

I noticed the phone again. "Oh."

The pack of cigarettes was still unopened, and I certainly didn't want to be the one to ask the question that would make him want to chain-smoke every one of them, but it was a question that needed to be asked. It was the question that was keeping him up at night. "How is Nadezhda?"

"Happier without me."

"Oh. Did you two—"

"Break up? *Nyet*. I never said the words to make us have anything *to* break up. I was such a coward. I never said . . ."

A long sigh escaped me like I had developed a sudden leak. "You never told her you loved her?"

"*Nyet*."

"And how do you know she's not available anymore?"

"She is working with a male partner."

"But—"

"With whom she seems to be on quite familiar terms."

"Oh. Could it be a cover story?"

"It is far more fact than fiction, I am afraid."

"How do you know? Did you ask?"

"Some things you just know."

"Holy crap, Batman. If you didn't ask, then you can't know. You're assuming something's going on. At least ask the question. At least find out if she's available or not. What if all this time she's been waiting on you and you never even take a chance?"

"Our lives are more complicated than that," Alexi said, turning the phone facedown.

"Don't make me call her. I do a lousy impression of you."

The ends of his mouth tipped up in a smile. "I will bear that in mind. Perhaps I will call."

I punched the sky.

"Perhaps. Later."

"You really know how to bring a girl down," I pouted.

"Evidently," he quipped. "You came down the stairs to talk with me already, *da?*"

"*Such* a pain." I tapped a finger on the table. "You know how you told me how I should immediately let you know if I experienced any weirdness after the Derek thing?"

"*Da.* Oddly, I know exactly what you're talking about. Should I wish I had skipped the cigarettes and gone straight to the liquor store instead?" he asked.

"You aren't going to smoke those," I said.

"*Nyet,* I am not," he agreed.

"And you aren't going to start swilling vodka again, either."

"You seem to know me quite well. Have I become so predictable?"

"Not predictable, just . . . more understandable. You can keep your props, but I will rat you out to Cat if I even *suspect* you're about to indulge."

He snorted at me. "I will bear that in mind, too. I remember telling you to immediately report any strange symptoms."

"Well, I didn't follow your instructions."

"And . . ."

"That was not my smartest move," I admitted. "We need to talk."

"So continue."

Alexi

As glad as I was that Derek was dead, hearing Jessie explain what she had been dealing with these past few weeks, with him in her head, made me very aware physical death hadn't even stopped Derek's incredibly awful powers.

"We need to get him out of your head."

"Do you know how to?"

"Not yet. But I will. Has he—"

"What?"

"Has he managed to gain control of you?"

"No. Could he?"

"I do not know. But I need you to be careful. If he's letting you in that close . . . You're blending with what's left of him."

"You can't tell Pietr. Or Max. Not anyone, you understand?"

"As long as you aren't a danger to anyone—yourself included. . . ."

"I can handle it," Jessie promised. "Don't worry. But"—Jessie stared at me with all the ferocity she could muster—"don't tell either."

"That much, I can handle."

She leaned over and gave me a hug and then walked quietly back up the stairs to slip back into Pietr's bed again to wait for morning.

Jessie

Gareth handled the pups' paperwork and they were enrolled in school at Junction High. With so many werewolves roaming the halls I became even more of a nervous wreck. I was only starting to know each of them and guess who might get into trouble and who wanted a real fresh start.

With Gabriel not even daring to sniff around the school grounds and Marlaena too old to be enrolled (and far from having any interest in any form of formal education), the pups were not as difficult as I feared.

In fact, they seemed eager for some guidance.

So I did for them what I had done for Pietr: I toured them around the school and gave them some advice.

And I didn't do to them what I had first done to Pietr: I never tried to slam a door in any of their faces, and I never tried to ditch them at lunch or race them to a classroom.

They would have caught me, anyhow.

I had learned some lessons at least, it seemed.

Alexi

I returned to Wondermann's lab in the city, knowing Jessie, Cat, and Amy had things well in hand back at the Queen Anne. Well, at least Cat and Amy had things well in hand. Jessie's battle with her newest inner demon—Derek—had me worried, but, with any luck and a good bit of skill, I might find a way to exorcise him from all the girls.

"Back on the job, I see," Wondermann said in his snide way.

I paused, pouring a new solution into a thistle tube, and gave him a sideways glance. *"Da.* I had urgent family issues to attend to."

"Aren't all family issues of the urgent variety?" he asked, picking up a beaker.

"Please do not touch that," I asked, taking it out of his hands and returning to the thistle tube.

"I've been thinking about our deal."

I straightened the smallest bit, hearing something like a threat crawling in his tone. "Oh?"

"Yes. Oh. It occurs to me that I have waited on werewolves for most of my life now. And although I am no longer what I would consider a young man, I am by no means old. Although your research and experimentation will surely speed the process, it might be more in my interest to reintroduce the supplement in the children's food."

I set the tube back in its rack and looked at him. "That would be unwise."

"And just why would that be such a problem? It allows me to regain my lab space, get some additional research in the field, and return some of my lab equipment to my other programs."

"We had a deal."

"You sound disappointed. Disillusioned. If you say, 'But you promised,' I will laugh."

"Why now?" I asked, turning to fully face him.

"I'm bored with this. If I thought you were making significant progress, maybe the entertainment value would make this more worth continuing. But . . ." He looked at the assortment of vials and beakers. "You are no closer to a permanent cure than you were when we started this charade, are you?"

I glared at him. "I am closer."

He waved his hand at me. "Your services are no longer needed. Our deal is off. Clean up your things."

He turned and left the room, and I stared at the reaction going on in the test tube. "I *am* close. Damn it."

I stalked through the lab, dropping folders on the floor and kicking cabinets.

"Why? Why now?" I paced. "What has changed?" I raked a hand through my hair and wished I had the pack of cigarettes with me. "I need coffee. Coffee," I muttered, leaving the lab. I went down the hall and turned into the modest room where the coffeemaker perked along most of the day. My hands shaking, I poured myself a cup.

It smelled awful and tasted worse. But I drank it and I thought. Something had changed. A new asset was in play. They had something. Something new. Something that would allow them to make and test a cure without my involvement.

They had a werewolf.

And I needed to find out where Terra was.

Marlaena

Even standing on the back porch in the whistling wind I heard them down the hill in the wood lot behind the Rusakovas' house. Max and Pietr had just begun an early evening run.

They were hunting.

I itched to join them like I'd never wanted to join anyone before.

The pups were all being obedient, either watching a last bit of television, reading some book Jessica's sister had brought over for them, or showering on their way to bed—it was a school night and I was trying to be a positive influence. Gareth, Tembe, and Judith had split to do their running, Gareth keeping his nose to the ground in hopes of catching a whiff of Terra.

He had stood in the foyer, watching me as I watched them head to the back door, and had taken my hand in his own and smiled gently at me, saying, "Come run with me.

The stars are out, the powder is fresh, the moon is bright. It is the perfect night for a hunt."

And it was the perfect night for a hunt. So why was I so torn? So desperate to hunt with a pack that wanted none of me?

Why did I want to race alongside Pietr with my snout sucking down equal amounts of the wind and Pietr's scent?

Gareth had finally left me there, standing in the foyer, planting a quick kiss on my forehead.

I wanted to turn and kiss him back—my brain demanded it. But my heart was beating as if it would explode if I even touched him, so I stood perfectly still, my eyes closed, and I let the moment pass.

Something dark inside me whispered that Gareth wasn't supposed to be mine no matter how much I wanted him to be.

And the *want* I felt for Gareth, the lingering ghost of something that might have been love for the best thing I'd ever stumbled into in my entire pathetic life was eclipsed by a bizarre *need*—like a hunger eating my heart out and making ribbons of my guts—that I felt every time I saw Pietr. Or smelled Pietr.

Or thought about Pietr.

But this thing burning inside me and making the wolf seem cool and distant beside it—this thing was like destiny. Inescapable. And, like destiny, I had no love of this need, either.

Alexi

She had to be here somewhere. Down some hallway, tucked into some room hidden away from most of the employees and yet close enough to the labs to make samples fresh and easy to obtain.

I jogged down hall after hall, waved at the employees and muttered things about coffee getting to my nerves, and kept going. No one stopped me because they were all employees of Wondermann, which by definition meant they had seen far stranger things than a Russian-American scientist jogging off a burst of caffeine.

Down one hall I found it. A small room with a single armed guard standing outside, unlike any other door on any level but the penthouse, where occasionally Wondermann's personal guards strode the area for his own safety.

Before the guard saw me, I got a good look at him and turned back around, making a beeline back to the coffee machine. I returned in a few minutes, holding a cup for myself and one for the man who would become my new best friend.

"*Allo*," I greeted. "Long day, huh?"

He looked at me, examining everything about me. "Decided to take a break from the lab?"

"*Da*, I had to get out of there for a little while. Numbers are swimming in my head. Coffee?" I offered him a cup.

Hesitantly he accepted the cup, though he did not drink but just watched me.

"So. You're the only guard I have noticed here—other than in the lobby or the penthouse. Do you have some fascinating secret you are guarding?"

He snorted. "No secret. Just a punk-ass kid caught sneaking around the offices. CIA told us to hold her until they send someone up from DC."

I froze at the combination of CIA and DC. Either he had misheard or this was the work of the rogue branch. "And they are sending someone soon?"

"Yeah. Some woman."

"Is it not amazing how many women have entered the field recently?" I commented.

"Not as many as you might think. Still pretty rare, from what I've seen."

I nodded. As rare as Wanda? I wondered. What were the odds? "When is the agent arriving?"

"In two days."

"Two days." That wasn't much time at all. "Mind if I take a peek?"

"Be my guest. Kid doesn't do much at all. Just sits there looking miserable."

"Teenager?"

He snorted. "Aren't they the most miserable?"

"*Da*. I have younger brothers," I sympathized.

"A son and two daughters."

I slipped past him and peered in the door's window. I was proud I did not drop my coffee cup when I saw Terra seated inside. "Looks miserable, just as you said. Well, good luck to you," I said, raising the cup to my lips.

"Yeah, you too," he said.

I headed down the hall and away. Terra had not been sneaking around Wondermann's labs—that much I was certain of because she had never been anywhere near New York City.

Junction, yes. But not NYC.

Indeed Terra looked miserable locked in that room, but miserable was far better than dead or being the victim of some experiment.

Dmitri was in league with Wondermann. And Wondermann had set a trap for Wanda, I would stake my life on it. And she was going to take the bait, but for what reason, I could not fathom.

Two days.

I needed to get Terra out of here and make sure Wanda knew it was a trap before she got snared.

Because as much as I wanted her to pay for what she had done by betraying my mother, I wanted even more to be the instrument of her destruction.

I just needed to figure out how to do it.

CHAPTER TWELVE

Jessie

Back at Junction High I'd asked Counselor Harnek for the mother of all scheduling favors. After she'd muttered a bit and glared at her master schedule she was able to make sure most of the pups shared a lunch with Amy, Sophie, Cat, Max, Pietr, and me. Even the wayward Sarah occasionally made an appearance. We filled one and a half of the long tables in the cafeteria and I was able to feel like I still had some semblance of control in my own school.

Except when it came to the sheer volume of homework. Ms. Ashton had given us a new assignment, and it was heavy. We were all supposed to write a novel in a genre we enjoyed.

I thought about the notebook I'd already started filling in during her class. Oh, I'd write her a novel. In a genre I loved. And there'd be only about twenty of us who knew the truth about it:

That it wasn't fiction at all.

That it would be the story of the Rusakovas in Junction.

Pietr was picking at his sandwich, the same pale color in his face he'd had since Marlaena had thrown me off the cliff. Since his change, he'd stayed pale, gotten some of his fire back, stopped needing to wear watches, and started to need to wear his special necklace—what Cat called his collar—again to keep simple human girls at bay.

Except, it seemed, for me and Amy.

"You usually scarf down sandwiches like they're nothing," I mentioned, reaching across to rest my hand on his. "Are you sure you're okay?"

He looked up at me, a strange hollowness holding back the light that usually glowed up from the depths of his eyes. "*Da*. I am fine," he said. "I am just not hungry."

The conversation at the table died down to nothing.

"*You* are not hungry?" Cat asked, her perfect eyebrows sliding close together in surprise. "But, Pietr, you are always hungry."

"I ate my fill last night," he said, referring to the hunt.

"But your metabolism . . ."

He waved a hand at Cat. "It is nothing." He looked at me again, lowering his voice and putting space between each of his words like a warning. "I. Am. Fine."

"Fine," I said, though I believed him less now than ever. "You're fine." I glared at the sandwich. "Then eat your lunch," I challenged him.

He snorted at me and tore a huge bite out of his sandwich, chewing with huge, zealous motions as he stared at me, contempt in his eyes.

Amy just watched him the whole time, putting down her own sandwich before saying softly, "Dick alert."

He shifted his glare to her briefly and then returned its full force on me as he stretched his neck out and swallowed, his Adam's apple sliding.

And then he grew another shade paler.

"Pietr?" I asked as he vaulted away from the table and out into the hall.

I stood to follow, but Amy's fingers snared my wrist. "Don't," she warned.

I shook free of her and followed as fast as I could, but I only saw the bathroom door swing shut as I entered the hall.

I ran to the boys' bathroom and stood there, unsure of what to do next. Yes, Pietr and I had spent quite a lot of time in the boys' bathroom the night of the Homecoming Dance— the night I shared my secret about my mother's death and Sarah's involvement in it—but he'd dragged me inside. It didn't seem right going into it without a male escort.

"The drama that swirls around you constantly . . ."

I spun to see Max approaching, his long strides full of purpose. He wiped at his mouth with his hand, and I heard the rasp of his stubble as clearly as I saw it shadowing his face.

"A guy can't even have a decent meal with his girlfriend around here anymore," he muttered. "Not that my lunch could be called a decent meal. . . . But I wouldn't be blowing my guts out over a sandwich, either." He puffed out a breath and looked at me solemnly. "Stay here. And out of trouble."

I snapped him a salute, and he plowed into the bathroom, grimacing.

Leaning against the wall nearest the door, I tried to hear what was going on inside. I heard their voices—the deep, rich rumble of Max's at his most serious and the slightly higher and more frustrated pitch of Pietr's. I waited impatiently. Toilets flushed. They talked a bit more. I caught one word, *truth,* and then nothing else.

Someone was coming down the hall and I tried my best to look inconspicuous—not an easy task standing outside the guys' bathroom and not being a guy.

The boy paused a few yards away, looking from me to the door of the bathroom and back. Crap. My behavior would seem pretty suspicious.

Inside, they had resumed talking.

I stared at the kid, wishing him away. Couldn't he use another bathroom? One not inhabited by werewolf brothers? But of course not. Hesitantly I reached out and knocked on the bathroom door.

The boy just watched me.

The voices fell silent and in a moment Max stepped out, followed by Pietr.

The boy's eyebrows rose and I shrugged at him, trailing behind two of my favorite werewolves for a short distance— just until I heard the bathroom door swing open and then shut again—and I shoved Max. "So what's going on?"

Pietr stepped between his brother and me and said, "I wasn't hungry. You made me eat. Bad things resulted."

Max glared at his brother. "Don't be a dick. You know that's not the whole story."

"Well then, brrrotherrr," Pietr said, rolling the *r*'s so they sounded like a distant drumroll, "what *is* the whole story?"

"I wish I knew. But something's not right with you. Ever since you snapped through the cure," he said slowly as if he was puzzling bits and pieces together. "You've been pale, you haven't been as hungry—except when you hunt. It's strange. . . ."

"You are imagining things. Perhaps I am pale because the fear of nearly losing Jess still hasn't left me."

I reached out and took his fingers in my own.

"Perhaps I have no consistent appetite because our family is more stressed than ever with nearly a dozen new long-term guests in the house."

Max nodded slowly. "True. It is possible. But you're also being a dick to Jessie."

"I am not—" He shook free of me, tugging his fingers loose from my grasp to point in his brother's face. "I am not being a dick."

I cleared my throat.

"Am I?" he asked, turning on me so fast I hopped back a step.

He looked at me, his eyes scanning the surface of my face and finally landing on my too-wide eyes.

"I am, aren't I?"

"Just a bit," I squeaked. "But"—I reached out for his hand again, drawing it into my own once more—"you're right. About the stress and the worry. It's okay."

"*Nyet*," he whispered, his gaze falling to the floor. "It is not okay for me to treat you that way. Not ever."

"Great," Max proclaimed. "Now that we have that established, can I go back to *my* sandwich? You two can make up on your own, *da?*"

I reached over and patted his arm. "*Da*," I said with a smile. And Max strode off.

I waited a solid minute, glancing down both ends of the hallway before I opened my mouth to speak again. "Just tell me the truth, okay?" I asked him. "If something's wrong, just tell me. If something's changed—be honest with me. We've been through Hell and back. I love you with every bit of my being. But if you don't feel the same . . . just speak the words. I love you so much, I'll let you go and wish you well on your way . . . and I'll be mad at first—royally pissed—but I'll get past it to see you as happy as you've made me."

He looked away, uncomfortable with my honesty. "I do love you, Jess," he said. "I'm just—adjusting."

"To the new pack being around? It is a hell of an adjustment."

He nodded, and I wondered if by speaking too soon I'd given him an easy out—something close to the truth that he could say and I'd cling to.

"Is that all?"

He nodded again and my heart sank. My nervous babbling in this case meant I might never know what he would have said.

Dammit.

"Is there anything I can do to help?"

"*Nyet*. You're fine," he assured me. A heartbeat too quickly.

"What do you *need* from me?" I pressed him even as my brain begged me to shut up. I was fumbling. Something was wrong with Pietr—something was wrong between me and Pietr, and he couldn't define it, so I couldn't fix it.

I felt sick.

"Time," he said. "I need some time."

I swayed on my feet and steadied myself by wrapping my arms tightly around his. Stupid girl, stupid heart. "Time away from me?" I whispered. God, how needy I sounded. It was disgusting. *Focus, Jessica,* I warned myself. *You're stronger than this. Act it.*

"*Nyet* . . ."

I let go of him and took a small step back. "No. It's okay, Pietr. I'll give you all the time that you need. I'll always give you whatever you need. . . ."

"Dammit," he said, reaching out to grab me. He pulled me tight against him, his arms like steel bars caging me to his chest. "I need you. I know that much. But right now," he admitted miserably, "that's all I know."

"I'll take it," I whispered into his chest, knowing that this, too, was going into the book Ms. Ashton was making us write for lit class.

I'd be on top of this assignment and it'd be great therapy.

Alexi

I grabbed some important papers, locked up the lab, went down to the lobby, and signed out early. The guards at the lobby's main desk watched me fill out the sign-out sheet.

"Taking the rest of the day off?"

"I may be taking off a long stretch of days soon," I complained.

"Almost done with the secret project the boss has you workin' on, yeah?"

"If I told you, it would not be so secret, would it?" I returned.

"Ah, he's a clever one, this one, ain't he? Well, you go enjoy your afternoon, you hear? And think of us poor slobs still stuck at work."

Nodding, I spared them a smile, but the whole way to the train and back to the Queen Anne, I struggled to formulate a way this entire mess might still work out.

Luckily, trains were perfect for solving just such types of problems.

Marlaena

It should have been a simple run to the grocery store with Gareth, but the illness began to wash over me the moment I was confined in the car with him. I clutched the door's handle and squeezed my eyes shut, trying to get my vision to stop swimming.

His scent permeated the warm air of the car's interior, spice mixing with leather and the heating metal of a well-tended engine. I loved Gareth's scent—I always had. But now it twisted my guts into knots.

"Are you okay?" he asked, his hand light on my arm.

I shivered under his gentle caress, my body rebelling against my heart.

"Fine," I choked out. "Fine. Just drive."

He drew his hot hand away from me and rested it on the steering wheel. "Okay."

We drove in silence, and not the type of silence I had once enjoyed with Gareth—the kind that grew from understanding, and . . . I nearly gagged . . . love. But it didn't matter now—none of it did. Because part of me was desperate to destroy the best bits of what we had, and I didn't know why.

We got a shopping cart with a wobbly wheel and grabbed the items we needed. I walked alongside the cart as he pushed it and gradually we began to make small talk. About brands, about prices. To anyone watching, we would probably appear to be a normal couple. Not a couple at our happiest moment, certainly, but a couple in a functioning relationship—two people who had known each other long enough to stumble through even the dull moments.

But every time we passed a heater and a puff of air blew

across him and toward me, I had to turn my head away or hold my breath so my knees didn't weaken.

My head ached at the sound of his voice, my eyes blistered at the sight of him, and my heart? My heart was breaking because I still loved him, although my body—my treacherous body—was repulsed by his very existence.

"I—I can't do this," I finally muttered in the frozen foods aisle.

"What?" he asked, but I was already gone, loping down the last bit of the aisle and out of range of all the things I'd grown to love about Gareth.

He met me by the car. He didn't comment about the fact I was still standing outside of the car in the cold when he caught up to me, or the fact I didn't help him load the groceries into the trunk.

He didn't speak to me again until we were nearly back at the house.

"What's really going on between us, 'laena? What's changed?"

I kept my mouth shut and stared straight ahead, letting the road ahead entrance me.

"I thought we were getting closer . . . and then you took Jessie, and Pietr changed, and . . ." His words faded away.

"I . . ."

"Do you want us to be close?"

"Yes," I said. "I do. Of course I do."

"But it's like you can't stand to even be around me sometimes."

"No. It's not you."

"If you say, 'It's not you, it's me,' I'll . . ."

"No. That's not what I was going to say." Dammit, how

did he know what I was going to say? "I was going to just say . . ."

"What? What is it, 'laena? Because you know you can say anything to me. You can bring any of your baggage to my door and I'll deal with it." His knuckles were growing pale as his hands clenched the steering wheel. "Just say whatever you need to say."

"I was just going to say, 'It's not you.' That's all. That's really all I was going to say," I muttered, shaking my head as panic blended with sudden understanding. "Because, Gareth, it's *not* you."

It's Pietr.

He took both Gareth and me aside almost as soon as he returned home. "I have found her."

"What? Who?" Gareth asked, startled.

"Terra," Alexi said mildly. "Wondermann has her."

"Wondermann?" I breathed the name out. "Then Dmitri and Gabriel . . ."

"*Da.* They are all connected somehow. And she needs to be out of there before two days' time is up. Otherwise she will be shipped off or used as bait and then experimented on."

"So take us to her—now," I demanded.

"That is impossible. We cannot afford for this to be traced back to me. It would ruin all my best-laid plans."

"And we wouldn't want that," I sneered. "We wouldn't want to impose upon your plans—even if the life of a pack member depends on it."

"You would not understand," he protested. "You need to track her. Track her all the way to Wondermann. You must infiltrate the building and break her out—*without* my assistance." He paused and drew a quick breath. "And you must do it all within two days, otherwise you will have lost your opportunity—and your packmate."

"We'll take Pietr and Max," I said stubbornly.

"You cannot. For this, you are on your own again. Your pack rescuing your packmate. Is that not how you have always preferred it?"

Gareth nodded and laid a hand on my shoulder, the warmth of his touch sinking into me and making my head fuzzy with nausea.

"And how do we know this is not a trap for us?" I asked him, realizing the danger.

"You must simply trust that it is not" was all he'd say.

Alexi

I called Jessie next. "You must warn her," I said firmly. "I do not care what else you talk about or how you get Wanda on the phone. But you must warn her that Wondermann has baited a trap for her by using a werewolf and that the werewolf in question is being removed from play this evening."

"What about when she gets all untrusting, the way Wanda always does?"

"Assure her she has a friend on the inside."

I could hear the smile on Jessie's face when she next spoke. "I'll pass it along. And, Alexi? I'm so glad you've moved past the . . . the *past*," she said. "I'm so glad you've forgiven her for whatever happened then."

I grunted into the phone. "I try to learn something from every situation," I assured her before hanging up. I did not mention that what I had learned was that by delivering this single message, I rebuilt trust in Wanda, made Jessie believe all was well, and would probably make Wanda more anxious to get back at Wondermann.

And that all those things rolled together beautifully to set the stage for Wanda's undoing.

Marlaena

We rode in on one of the last trains of the evening, Gareth's eyes fascinated by the world blurring into indistinct smudges of night punctuated by bursts of speckled light—towns and small cities.

"Not a trap," I whispered.

Gareth looked at me, his eyebrows raised. "Not a trap," he agreed. "Alexi wouldn't betray us. He does not strike me as the type to betray another."

I snorted. "Doesn't he?" I wondered aloud. "He strikes me as the exact opposite—the most efficient and clever of traitors."

"I'll just hope you are wrong, then," Gareth muttered, a smile dimpling at the edge of his generous lips.

"I'll hope that, too," I admitted, but my stomach still twisted—this time at more than Gareth's proximity to me.

Our train arrived at the station, and we stumbled out of the car and onto the dimly lit platform, following a meager trail of people as they headed out. We stumbled up and onto the street, getting our bearings.

"Can you smell her?" I asked, my own nostrils flaring to drink in the flavor of the city's night. I caught the scents of steel, concrete, and glass—smells as cold as ice and freshly fallen snow. Too near the vents in the sidewalk or the steaming manhole covers and my nose was filled with scents far warmer and fouler.

"No, not yet. There are so many trails by so many people," Gareth murmured, scuffing his shoes across a soft dusting of snow. "The city must be the best place to disappear."

"I've considered it myself," I returned, looking at the lights that soared up from the sidewalks and macadam, lights stretching and glaring along the silhouettes of sleek buildings. "Here. It's this way."

We blended with a slow-moving crowd focused on the occasional nightspots that cropped up in small groups. We stopped near the footprint of Wondermann's building and glanced at each other.

"Remember our plan?" I asked, but I knew he did. Gareth was sharp and had no problem remembering.

"Around back, in and up to fifteen. A fight, then down, out, and away."

I nodded. "Let's do it."

Jessie

I had already written three more chapters in my lit assignment and made additional notes in another notebook about what I needed to add later. I was reviewing some homework with the pups when I finally had to say something about Pietr's twitching. "What's wrong? You can't sit still for all of five minutes, it seems."

He refocused on his own schoolwork, but three minutes later he was looking toward the foyer. Toward the door.

"What's going on, Pietr?" I asked, dismissing the last of Marlaena's pack from the table.

I pulled out the chair to sit beside him and rested my hand on his arm. "Tell me what's wrong."

"It's nothing. I just can't focus on this." He shoved his papers away, dropping the pencil on top of them.

"What's on your mind?"

"Nothing," he said. Quickly.

"You're worried about something. You keep watching the door."

His eyes widened the barest bit before he regained control of his expression. "I was just wondering what's going on right now in Wondermann's building. Is she okay or should we have gone, too?"

"I'm sure Terra's going to be fine."

"Right," he said. "Terra and Gareth. And Marlaena."

I blinked. Shoving away from the table, I stood. "Right. I'm sure they're all fine, Pietr. Even Marlaena." And then I walked away from the table as fast as I could so I didn't start yelling.

Or crying.

It wasn't long before I pulled out my lit notebook and started writing again.

Because writing was so much cheaper than therapy.

Marlaena

I tugged the can of spray paint out of my coat pocket and loped around the side of the building, Gareth going the opposite way. We had agreed we'd split up if we had to—whatever it took to get Terra out of Wondermann's grasp. We knew where we'd meet up afterward in case things didn't go well and we knew at what point to abandon hope of the other ever returning and to just get out of the city.

Slinking along the very edge of the building I saw there was only one camera whose eye I had to blacken, and then it was just slip around to the area they used as a loading dock and . . . there he was.

Gareth stood on the steps, his foot in a door, though from the rug that was wedged to hold it open, it didn't seem an entirely necessary move. He glanced down at the ground, which was littered with cigarette butts. "The place for the guards' smoke break," he said. He pointed to the nearest stretch of observable sidewalk with his chin. "Alarm's disabled," he added. "See the food cart?"

I took a look. "Yeah?"

"It serves gyros and drinks. Two-handed food. And no one wants to fight with their food *and* an alarmed door when they're getting ready to enjoy a break."

"Noted," I said, slipping into the doorway.

"Ready for some cardio?" he asked with a smile.

"It's the key to escaping zombies, so yeah," I returned with a grin.

"Up, up, and away," he said, starting up floor after floor of stairs.

We were barely even winded when we reached the fifteenth floor.

"In and take the first left. The guard marks the spot," Gareth reminded.

We carefully opened the door and jogged down the hallway, peeking around the first left to get a glimpse of the guard. He stood stiff and straight at his post and looked bored beyond belief. I cracked my knuckles and spotted the place on his belt where the keys hung.

Right beside his holster.

He yawned and rubbed his face with a slow hand, not knowing how we intended to liven things up for him.

Alexi

It was awkward, watching them. Pietr drifted further from Jess unwittingly, his eyes never resting on her for long unless he truly forced himself to focus, and yet, when I'd seen him watching Marlaena, everything about his attitude intensified. He straightened his back, threw back his shoulders, and raised his chin, a swagger in his walk. With Jess, he was gutless and guilty—tired beyond recognition, and pale.

Jessie clung to him, watched him more closely, and kept her hands on him as much as she could.

After the pups had finished their homework, and Cat, Amy, and Jessie had figured out dinner, Jessie grabbed me to go outside and spar.

We fought and we stumbled around each other, practicing both our best and worst moves. When we had exhausted ourselves and she had spilled out her frustration all across my rib cage, we sat in the windbreak the porch's corner provided and talked—me rubbing warmth back into her hands.

"Something's wrong. He's sick. I can tell," she whispered, blowing on our joined hands. "He's sick. But it doesn't make any sense. He's *oborot* again now."

I nodded.

"He shouldn't be capable of getting sick, right?"

"*Da.*"

"So why is this happening, then? How can he be sick if he can't *get* sick? And Marlaena—it's like she's caught some bug, too. She looks pale and weak, but there's this fever to her eyes. . . ."

I looked away from Jessie then, my heart pounding angrily in my chest. "A fever in her eyes? What do you mean?"

"Her eyes go this crazy purple and then flare red when we're nearby. I mean, I know she hates me, but . . ."

It was so unfair.

"Maybe there's something going around . . . ," she suggested. "Something only alpha werewolves are susceptible to . . ."

I nodded, but the motion was halfhearted. "*Da*. Perhaps that is it," I agreed. "Perhaps there is some new ailment—something brought in by the new pack and only triggered for some reason here and now. There is so much about the *oboroten* that we do not yet understand. . . ." I rose and extended a hand, pulling her to her feet.

"Good point. They are relatively new, I guess. . . . Lots to still understand. . . ."

"*Da*," I muttered. *Like imprinting. And how to overcome it.*

I held the door open for her, still avoiding her eyes.

"Maybe you should get back in the lab—figure this all out," she suggested, searching out my eyes.

I nodded again. "*Da*. I will head back to the lab as soon as I can, but there are other circumstances now."

"You need to wait on Wondermann."

"*Da*."

"How close were you to the cure? The real, point-of-no-return cure?"

"Closer than ever before, but not quite close enough. I will get it, Jessie. There must be a solution."

Jessie threw her arms around me, hugging me tightly. "Thank you, Sasha," she whispered into my neck. "Thank you for helping me fix whatever this is." Then she released me and disappeared into the house.

I wanted a cigarette. Desperately. How could I possibly fix this, now that I knew what *this* was? This was designed to *not* be fixable. To simply be an imperative above all others.

For the good of the species, not for the good of anyone in particular and certainly not for the good of any notion like love. When the *oboroten* were designed, love was clearly the last thing on anyone's mind.

Marlaena

There was no point in trying to sneak up on the one guard in the hallway, but there was every reason to surprise him quickly and make sure he couldn't radio for help.

We sprinted down the hall, Gareth bowling the guard over as he reached for his radio and gun and I played keep away with those two very important items.

I slung the radio down the hall, pocketed the gun, and Gareth shoved a gag in the guard's mouth as I pulled out my roll of duct tape. "Sorry about this brief intermission in your otherwise dull day, but we need what you're keeping stashed away and we followed her trail to here."

He struggled and mumbled into the gag, thrashing against the duct tape I'd just lashed around his ankles and wrists.

"I wouldn't do that if I were you," I warned, but he struggled a bit more—just enough to lose his balance and fall to the floor, an embarrassed and writhing mess of tangled humanity.

I snagged the keys from his belt and fumbled with the lock.

A little distance down the hall, his radio made a noise and Gareth and I exchanged a startled look.

"Repeat," the radio called. "Hourly check-in." I wrenched the door open, cursing our timing. "Repeat," the radio announced again. "Hourly check-in. You better not have nodded off, Johnson."

The guard thrashed around, but I didn't care because we were inside.

"Holy crap!" Terra shouted as she jumped to her feet and threw her arms around Gareth. She nearly hugged me, too, but thought better of it, instead saying a modest, "Thanks."

"Yeah, yeah," I mumbled. "Let's get out of here."

We burst back through the door and hopped over the guard, hearing the promise of the building's other guards crackle across the discarded radio. "On our way . . ."

"So are we," I said as I raced down the hall and shoved open the door. Pausing a moment on the landing, I listened for the incoming guards. "They're coming up. I want us to avoid contact if we can, got it?"

Terra nodded. "No contact."

We pounded our way down the stairs until the men were at the base of a flight we were at the top of. Leading the others, I grabbed the metal underpinning of the stairs leading up, holding the metal ribs that made up its gut, and swung myself over the banister and down onto the other staircase and then repeated the sweeping motion, swinging myself onto another lower flight of steps.

Two flights beneath the guards with Terra and Gareth at my back we raced down another flight while our moves registered in the minds of our enemies and they turned to follow us down the stairs they'd just begun coming up. Footsteps pounded on the steps above us as they gathered speed, descending. Radios crackled again and doors popped open below us. "Again," I urged Terra and Gareth, my hands sore from grabbing the poorly painted metal, but we did it again and this time I switched my handhold, twisting in midair, the soles of my shoes hitting the banister so that I slid down the flight on its railing.

Guards stared at us as we slid by surfing the banisters and then leaping down, snatching at the next staircase's underbelly and doing it all again until we were nearly at the exit, guards' mouths gaping as we vaulted for the door.

With a squeal, the door bent back on its hinges and we rushed into the cold air, feeling it snatch our breath from our mouths. We flew out of the building and down the last steps and spun to the right and back down the alley with the blacked-out camera.

The soles of our sneakers slapped the sidewalk in a rapid staccato rhythm, and we turned down two more side streets and then an alley and stopped there, stooping over our shoes to catch our breath, the cold air burning with a crueler intensity down our superheated throats.

I listened to much more than the rapid breaths we took or the way the blood rushed in my ears. I listened for the sounds of men following us or sirens coming—would they call the police to help them find us, or would that be putting them in an awkward spot?

They couldn't have been holding Terra in any way that would be considered legal. . . .

No sound came to me beyond the normal noises of the city at night. I sighed and looked at them both, but found my vision swimming with vertigo when I lingered on Gareth, the exertion from our run up and down the stairs causing his scent to deepen and strengthen through his sweat, and I pulled my attention away from him to lock my gaze on Terra.

It was 9:15 at night—I knew it as well as I knew we were werewolves. And that meant we had just thirty minutes to make it back to the train station if we had any hope of catching the last train running back to Junction. But with thirty minutes we could walk swiftly—not break into a frantic run that might be spotted by anyone looking for us—and in that way blend into the crowd that still wandered the streets and sidewalks of the Big Apple at night.

Jessie

They called from the train, Gareth for Alexi. From Alexi's expression I could tell things had gone better than expected and that they were on their way home again. Pausing, I wondered if that's how they viewed the Queen Anne—as *home*.

"I guess I better head to the station," Max said, pulling on his coat.

"*Nyet*." Alexi stopped him, tugging his own coat from the foyer's coatrack instead. "I will get them. You need rest. You have school and work tomorrow."

Max growled, but shrugged back out of his coat.

Alexi glanced at me. "I had better take you home before I go to the station."

"Oh." I looked at Pietr. He would be here without me when Marlaena returned, high on her success. My stomach rebelled at the thought. She'd already made excuses to be around him. . . . "Maybe I could . . ." I fumbled for my phone, calling Dad.

"Sorry, Jessie," he said, his voice oddly low and sounding

more tired than it had in a long while. "I think I need you to be here with family tonight."

I blew out a sigh. "Okay, Dad. I love you." Hanging up, I reached for Pietr. "I have to go now. Maybe you should turn in early," I suggested. It was thinly veiled at best.

But he looked at me with his sweetest expression and said, "That sounds like a brilliant idea." And then he kissed me as only Pietr could, and for a moment I forgot all about Marlaena and our awkward rivalry.

But, pulling away, I saw how his skin had blanched and a strange pain floated behind his eyes.

"Are you—"

"I'll be fine," he whispered. "Go now."

"I love you," I said, but he stumbled into the kitchen and never replied. I just clutched the bookbag holding my lit assignment's notebooks even tighter, knowing I'd be filling more pages tonight.

Back home I was greeted by my dogs, Hunter and Maggie, and was summarily sniffed and licked. Pushing past their curious and probing noses, I closed the door and gave Dad a hug before crossing the kitchen floor to poke Annabelle Lee in the arm as she read at the breakfast nook. She grumbled and raised the book in front of her, but not before I saw her smile and fight to wipe it from her face. My little sister loved me and she was trying to cope with that fact.

"Gonna head to the barn," I said to Dad.

"I was just out there. Everything's fine," he said, worry etching his brow as clearly as if he'd verbally pointed out that bad things happened to people in our barn.

I wanted to change that. A horse barn should be a happy

place that smelled of hay, feed, leather, and horses, and I was determined to see it get back to that. "Rio and I could use some time."

He nodded, oddly unwilling to fight tonight, and I briefly wondered about his eyes being as red as they were. Allergies? But I didn't dwell on it because if Dad had *just* been in the barn, odds were good the barn was safe. I raced up to my room and changed into my riding clothes and tugged a case out from under my bed.

By the time I'd gotten back to the front door, most of the lights were out in our house and Dad and Annabelle Lee were in their rooms.

I jogged to the barn, my dogs flanking me, Maggie bouncing as much as running. That was the crazy thing about Labs. *One* of the crazy things about Labs, I thought, watching how she sprang straight up in the air only to land on all four feet and repeat the move as I struggled to open the barn door. Hunter (the resident what's it) just whined. Everything about him was crazy.

I flipped on the lights in the barn and sucked in a deep breath. The hay smelled sweet tonight, heavy with the scents of timothy and clover, and closing the door behind me, I could almost imagine spring waited outside.

I set the case on a nearby hay bale and popped its clasps open to look at the gun inside. I wasn't going to be a victim anymore—not on my parents' property. I'd thought about this a lot since Gabe's attack. It was fine—even good—to improvise when attacked by a werewolf, but it was even better to be prepared to remove the threat.

I tucked the gun case behind a stack of hay bales in the barn. Attacked twice here was twice too often. If something or someone came for me again, I'd be prepared.

Rio whickered for my attention.

"Be there in a minute," I called. I glanced at our tool wall. Rakes, hoes, pitchforks, and shovels lined one wall in the barn and kept the place organized and neat. And, as I knew, some simple tools like those made potent weapons, but you had to get your hands on them first. So I grabbed a couple things and moved them to other walls, making sure none of them was in the way or inconvenient to the barn's function.

Standing in the wide aisle that ran between the horse stalls, I did a slow spin, observing my handiwork. Yes. This could work.

Rio stomped her hoof, impatient.

Laughing, I grabbed a brush and stepped inside her stall to spend a little time being kind and gentle with her before we went for our ride.

CHAPTER THIRTEEN

Alexi

I decided several things that night as Marlaena, Gareth, and Terra rode the train back to Junction. First: Pietr and Marlaena had imprinted regardless of how they actually felt about each other. Second: I could not sit idly by and watch my grandfather's success with genetic tampering ruin Jessie and Pietr's relationship. Third: I had no time to wait for Wondermann to summon me back to his lair. Fourth: I was going to need someone else who had experience with Grandfather's research. And, finally, fifth: I was going to add Rolaids into my daily diet whether I wanted to or not the way my gut burned as I made my mental list.

So, after seeing the werewolves off to school the next morning, I drove over to Golden Oaks and only hesitated for the length of Autumn Fire's song "Empty Sorrow" before I summoned my courage, locked the convertible's doors, and walked inside.

The nurse recognized me from my earlier visit and smiled, sliding the sign-in folder to me.

I signed, I dated it, I explained the purpose of my visit in vague and friendly terms, and then I walked the short distance to Hazel Feldman's room.

Jessie had tried once to get me to refer to Feldman as Mom, but I made sure she knew her attempt should be short-lived if she wished to live any longer herself.

Granted, Hazel was a pleasant enough woman (for someone who had handed over her only child to be raised by werewolves and trained to make his own brothers and sister believe he was truly one of them). She was cordial and welcoming and witty, but she was not the woman I could ever imagine calling my mother.

My mother was Pietr, Max, and Cat's mother. Her name was Tatiana, and she was dead.

"Good morning, Feldman," I said, striding in like I—how did Amy say it?—*owned the place*. I fell into the nearest chair, crossing my legs and folding my hands over my knee with some smattering of Max's natural drama.

She smiled and opened her mouth to reply, but I continued. She had not taught me manners, she had no right to expect me to use any on her. "Let us cut to the chase. Pietr was pushed past the cure. He has imprinted."

"Oh."

"Not with Jessie."

"Ohhh." She fumbled with the pleats of her skirt. "But imprinting was designed to—"

"Strengthen the breed—not to allow for choice. Or free will."

"Or love," she added as realization dawned. "The one Pietr imprinted with . . . ?"

"The leader of a rival pack. They have traveled quite a distance, slowly gathering wolves and living by their own cultlike
standards—embracing every aspect of their *oborot* nature."

"Every aspect?"

I nodded. "They are dangerous because they know their
lives are short. So they strive to *suck out all the marrow of life.*"

"Should we not all do the same?"

"Perhaps, but not using the methods they tend to embrace.
Theft and violence among them."

"What would Thoreau have thought of them?" she mused,
recognizing part of one of his better known quotes.

"He wouldn't have been able to doubt that by their deaths
they've certainly learned whether they lived or not. But the
way they sometimes discover living is by getting themselves
killed," I clarified. "They continuously spout 'the Wolf Is the
Way' and such things."

"I had not anticipated this, and I doubt your grandfather
would have, either." She plucked at her pleats in satisfaction.
"Fascinating."

"Dangerous and deadly," I corrected.

"Are they—?"

"The ones from the recent news? The group the police
have mistaken as a gang?"

She nodded, and I mimicked the movement in reply.

"How many are there?"

"Thirteen including the female alpha. Though one is"—I
coughed—"somewhat less."

"Twelve led by the one who imprinted with Pietr. And
how is Pietr?"

"The phrase 'sick as a dog' springs to mind. He cannot
sleep and barely eats. If I did not know better, I would have
thought he was lovesick." I shook my head. "But love has

nothing to do with this. It is cruel, really—letting biology lead. So what do we do?"

She shrugged.

"What can you tell me?"

"Without a lab at my disposal? Nothing. You have the journals. That is all the knowledge I can provide without performing significant experiments of my own. I may have strayed from my father's lifestyle, but the lessons learned in his lab will stay with me until my death."

The way her wrinkles deepened and her mouth turned down gave me the distinct impression more lessons than the use of chemicals and equations and periodic charts had been taught in Grandfather's lab. "What do you need?"

"In a lab?" She sat up straight and looked at me more sharply, once again appraising me with her eyes. "Significant equipment to do things correctly. We're talking about genetic manipulation at a very specific level. This cannot be accomplished with a child's chemistry set."

I looked at my hands, clasped tightly in my lap, my knuckles whitening. "Perhaps my association with you may yet prove to be fortuitous. There is a lab at my disposal. There is an open account for supplies. But there are also significant risks."

She sat up straighter, her eyes sparkling as she reached for her ever-present deck of tarot cards. "Did I tell you to stop talking?" she asked, a grin slanting on her pale lips. "The only risks around here are that someone might sprain something playing bridge. As I am not yet dead, I have no aversion to doing something that might make me feel more alive."

"We will need to leave now."

"Excellent." She swung her legs over the bed, and putting the cards down, reached for her cane. She clutched it, straightening once it was in her grasp.

She took an unsteady step forward. Then another. I just watched, my arms crossed, while she made her plodding progress forward.

What good was she going to be in a crisis situation? I sighed. Was bringing Hazel Feldman into this an even bigger mistake than blindly proceeding without her help?

"Do you need . . ."

"What?" She peered at me like a hawk spying its next meal far below. She chuckled. "You were going to ask if I needed any medications, weren't you?" The chuckle grew into a belly laugh.

I shrugged. "You live *here*."

"You do understand that making an assumption makes an ass out of you—"

"And me," I completed.

She snorted. "No. Just you. I do not live here because I require ongoing care, but because when you reach my age—which is not so very great in the overall scheme of life—you are faced with certain choices. You can work as a greeter at Walmart if you're short on funds; travel the world if you're far from being short on funds; if you have a good number of active friends you might wander the local mall and gather for lunch in assorted fast-food restaurants (which will surely shorten your life span), or you can come to a place like this a bit prematurely in hopes of meeting new friends, hearing about their travels, and never needing to be a greeter at a super-center."

I nodded but withheld the grin pushing at my lips. "So?"

"No medications unless you think you will continue to be a pain in the ass, in which case, aspirin, please."

I snorted. "Are you ready then?"

"One moment." She drew a card from her deck. "Oh. That

is disappointing and exciting all at once. Grab my purse, will you? I need to make sure I have my medical insurance card."

I blinked at her.

"And, in my bathroom, grab a gauze pad and some Band-Aids. Stop looking so worried. We're on a schedule, are we not?"

I nodded and did as she instructed.

She shoved everything unceremoniously into her purse. "There's a good boy," she said. "Off we go."

She shooed me out of her room and back to the nurses' station.

I cleared my throat to get the nurse's attention. "Signing Ms. Feldman out," I explained.

Feldman snorted. "Sign yourself out. I am quite capable of taking responsibility for my own actions. Now at least," she added, eyeing me. She snatched the folder and filled in the required spaces, under "Reason for Travel," scrawling, "Because I'm not dead yet."

"My son is taking me into the city to spend the day," she announced proudly, her head high.

"Your son?" the nurse replied with a startled blink, looking me over. "Why, I had no idea. . . ." She jotted something down on her clipboard.

"Yes, yes, it's quite the tale," Feldman intimated.

"It is too bad she does not have the time to hear it," I said, removing Feldman's hand from my shoulder and placing it on the counter.

I was not impressed by her willingness to act proud. Or tender. The woman had lied for decades. Perhaps she thought nothing of lying even more now—to me even as we were in such close contact.

"I apologize—just a bit more paperwork to fill out before you go anywhere. . . ."

"It is no problem," I assured her.

"After decades apart we have been reunited." She leaned forward on the counter to give the girl more information.

I barely kept from glaring at the way she romanticized our reunion. As if we hadn't been within two hours' flight of each other for years—though the direction of the flight shifted frequently while I was growing up and moving around. Moving around? More aptly on the run.

"Well, I think it's wonderful that you two found each other after all these years," the nurse said, her smile so wide it verged on looking pained.

"*Da,*" I agreed. "After all these *years.*"

Feldman's knobby fingers reclaimed my arm, nails biting into it like a predator's claws, and my mouth clamped shut.

"Last one," the nurse said, retrieving the papers. "You two have fun."

"*Da,*" I replied. "I am certain it will at least be memorable."

The nurse just smiled.

In the car, Feldman immediately went to adjust the radio station and I stopped her. "*Nyet.* This is my car—"

"And what a beaut it is—" she said, admiring the interior.

I ignored her and turned out of the parking lot.

"Have some respect. Do not adjust the radio station."

She shrugged. "Shall we discuss our plans, or make it up as we go along?"

"We can discuss them now," I agreed. "The train might be crowded."

"And you worry someone might overhear? Do you trust no one?"

"I trust few enough. I have learned to not trust too freely."

"I am sorry about that," she said, turning to look out the window.

I winced. "You have the right to take credit for *that* as much as you have the right to take credit for anything else in my life—not at all."

She sighed and folded her cane, resting it in her lap. "Fine."

I asked the question that had been gnawing at me since the moment I had realized we were now fighting an imprint. "How much time do we have?"

"Until?"

"Until Pietr dies?"

"He will continue to deny the imprint?"

"*Da*," I said, certain of nothing more than I was certain of my youngest brother's stubbornness.

"A month or perhaps a little more. But you must make him eat." She tilted her head, observing me keenly. "But that is not the question you should be asking," she warned.

"What should I ask?"

"You should ask when he will finally lose his mind. Because it will happen if he denies the imprint. And then death will seem a mercy."

I swallowed hard. "Insanity?"

"Yes. Three weeks from the onset of the imprint. Do you know exactly when . . . ?"

"*Da*," I confirmed. "He wanted to die that day."

"Before this is done, I suspect he'll feel that way again," she said softly. "You must act quickly, Alexi."

"Tell me what to do. I will do anything to save Pietr. He is my brother in all but blood."

Feldman nodded. "First then, I believe we must make a plan."

Jessie

My cell phone buzzed in my jeans pocket and I carefully slid it out. Sarah's eager smile showed on the screen, and I pulled up her text message.

> Something big's happening. Perlson's on the move.
>
> On the move? Where to?
>
> Not sure. Had some phone calls today. Called someone "boss."
>
> Great.
>
> Sarcastic great or great great?
>
> Both. Thanks.
>
> He's leaving office now. Headed toward science wing.
>
> Going there now . . .
>
> Good luck.
>
> Thanks.

I stood up and headed for the hall pass, scrawling *bathroom* into the notebook. I would head toward a bathroom, just not the nearest one. I needed to check out the one in the science wing.

Pietr glanced up at me, quirking an eyebrow in question. I just shrugged and dodged out the door.

I made good progress with nearly no one in the hallways until I spotted Perlson up ahead. I heard someone else approaching.

Someone in heels.

Ms. Harnek saw me the moment I saw her and luckily she was levelheaded enough to blink and tilt her head in just the perfect way that signaled me to go into hiding while still displaying her standard terse expression to Perlson as he walked toward her in the hallway.

I slid into the alcove surrounding one of Junction's less-than-perfect water fountains and tried to hear whatever they were saying over the cycling of the water in the fountain's rumbling tank.

"And to what do I owe the pleasure of this meeting?" Harnek asked.

"I wanted to pass along some information that should cheer you up tremendously."

"Go," Harnek challenged.

"Precisely."

"What?"

"I will be going soon. Leaving Junction behind for greater educational opportunities and a sunnier climate."

"And again I say: What?"

"I put in for a transfer."

"In the district."

"In a way. The company has some worthwhile connections in the educational industry."

"Is that all this is, really? An industry? Like a factory pumping out docile and decently educated citizens?"

"There is no better type of industry to be involved in if the product is a more properly educated American," Perlson declared.

"So where will your transfer take you?"

"I am being promoted."

"That seems to happen with the incompetents," I thought

I heard Harnek mutter, but the water fountain started to rattle its way through part of its standard cycle. I leaned against the wall and pressed my knee and shin into the fountain's side, shifting its tone slightly.

"What have you been promoted to?" Harnek asked finally.

"Principal of a lovely middle school."

There was a lengthy silence. At least it felt lengthy considering the strange position I'd gotten myself into.

A boy walked down the hall, on a direct course for the water fountain. I barely stopped from groaning in recognition. He paused briefly when he saw me and cocked his head. He was the same kid who had needed to use the bathroom where Max and Pietr were sequestered while having their recent talk. While I stood guard outside like a total dork. What timing this kid had. I pushed my lips together and jerked my head at him in what I hoped was a distinct *come over here* gesture. I pressed a finger to my lips for good measure.

He ambled over, staring at me the whole time he took the longest water-fountain drink imaginable. I waved a hand at him to finally shoo him away, and he staggered back in surprise and then flipped me off before jogging away.

If I was the strangest thing he'd seen in Junction, he should count himself lucky.

I adjusted my position and refocused on the conversation.

"You'll just take this madness there," Harnek was saying, her tone clearly disapproving.

"It's *already* there—and things are progressing at an amazing rate."

"An alarming rate is probably what everyone else thinks."

"You would not feel that way if we had seen the same level of success with our students here as they are witnessing in

California. I hypothesize it's because the food is being inserted into their diets at such an important stage of their adolescent development."

"So you'll go there, take the reins, and do what?"

"Whatever the company asks me to do."

This was *so* going into my supposedly fictitious novel. . . .

"And what happens here? Who is transferring in?"

"I have no idea. No one wants a school like Junction with so many headaches and such a history of violence."

"Well. I don't quite know what to say. *Good luck* because it seems like my good luck finally kicked in by seeing you gone, or *break a leg* because you're putting on quite an act and I really hope you break a leg?"

"Always a pleasure, Ms. Harnek."

"Bite me."

Alexi

I returned to Wondermann's headquarters with the cover story of concluding the cleaning of my lab. I was paralyzed by frustration at my lack of boxes and the complete accumulation of stuff when I noticed Feldman getting underfoot. "Stop," I insisted, waving her away from a box she had begun to empty. "I am packing that."

"Not as efficiently as you could," she said, carefully reconfiguring the items and puzzling them back together so that the box held nearly twice its previous contents.

Marveling, I admitted I would not have thought of that arrangement and let her do the same with the next box. And the next. As one person I was quite capable, but with another person of differing skills and experiences perhaps . . . "Do you suppose . . ." But my train of thought was interrupted when a guard entered the lab.

Not a guard from the lobby and not Terra's guard. A guard clearly from Mr. Wondermann's office, complete with black suit and tie, earpiece, holster, and a look that made vultures appear cuddly.

"Mr. Wondermann requests your presence in the penthouse."

"I am quite busy," I said, not giving him a second look as I returned to my collection of boxes.

"Mr. Wondermann is requesting . . ."

"And my son said no," Hazel snapped.

"Your son?" He turned away, pressing his earpiece and muttering.

Not good. Not good at all.

"When I said *requesting,* I meant: You will come with me now or we will have an altercation." He patted the bulge at his side, smiling.

I looked at Feldman and shrugged.

"I've never seen a penthouse. I'll check it off my bucket list."

I nodded, sidling up to her as we followed the guard to the elevator. "It may be the last thing you check off your bucket list," I whispered.

"Oh. I need my purse," she said, turning around.

But the guard stuck out a hand and stopped her. "This will be quick, I promise."

"Fine," she said with a glare.

We rode the elegant elevator in silence and obediently followed the guard's directions out of it and into the jungle-inspired splendor of Wondermann's penthouse. Feldman kept quiet, but I could tell by how rapt her attention was that she found the surroundings to be exquisite. The guard stepped away from us, motioning us to wait there.

In a moment Wondermann was with us, utterly professional and businesslike and completely cold. He and I shared one desire that morning: the desire to skip the small talk. "I believe you are to blame for the loss of my experiment's subject."

"What have you lost? A rat, a monkey?"

"A werewolf."

"Really? What would lead you to that conclusion?" I asked, keeping my tone far more even than my racing pulse.

"She was freed by two young people."

"So you are taking the 'birds of a feather flock together' theory as your proof?"

"A little research shows the two who rescued my subject—"

"She is not a subject. She is a girl. She has rights."

"*You* would believe that. Try proving her need for human rights in a courtroom once she's changed." He opened and closed his hands at his sides, the very picture of menace. "The two who rescued her have been spotted in Junction. Where the Rusakovas reside."

"For a small American town, Junction is quite well populated. Geographic location is no proof of personal acquaintance and certainly not a measure of friendship. Is there something else about your missing girl that is bothering you?"

His nostrils flared. He was holding back.

He had been using Terra as bait for Wanda, as I'd suspected. He wanted her to pay for the damage she'd done to his facility in Junction.

I wanted her to pay for destroying the only family I'd ever known.

"You will return to your lab. You will resume work on the cure and you will not leave my facility until you have success."

"*Nyet*. You see, I am nearly done packing my things. And unpacking is always such a headache. As you yourself once pointed out, you have waited decades for werewolves—what is a little more time?"

He twitched. There was more to this story.

The newspaper article.

What brilliant timing.

"I noticed your stocks have suddenly gone up because of a much anticipated military contract. But the details are all quite sketchy. The most in-depth report I could find mentioned 'changing the face of war forever.'"

The vein near his temple rose.

"Do you envision the face of war as somewhat furrier, per-haps? You have promised them werewolves, have you not? And now you find yourself clearly without any werewolves to give or use so you can learn to make more—better wolves for a better tomorrow, perhaps? Everyone has failed you. Your hunters, Dmitri . . ."

"Do what I say or I'll shoot her."

"*Nyet*," I said. "I do not think so. I think you will do what *I* say."

"I mean it, Rusakova. You return to your lab and you give me what I want or I'll renege on every one of my promises—*after* I shoot your mother."

"I do not recall this being part of any previous plan," Feld-man griped, glaring at me.

I shrugged.

Wondermann changed tactics. "And you, Hazel, wouldn't you like to live out the rest of your life in some beautiful place fit for a princess? Just for giving me the help I want?"

"I blew past my princess years long ago. And I only have a few years left at best. I've had a full life. If it ends here and now, it was still a grand adventure. And that, my dear, is a hell of a sight better than most people can claim."

"Don't think I won't do it."

"Go ahead," I said. "Shoot her."

Wondermann blinked, but tipped his head at the man with the gun.

The bullet grazed Feldman's shoulder. "You son of a bitch!" she snapped at Wondermann. "Grow a pair of balls and order a kill shot. No wonder your father's gone blind in his old age. He can't stand to see the pansy you wound up being!" She sucked on her lower lip and glowered at her arm. "That stings," she muttered before letting loose with another string of curses.

I did not even flinch.

Wondermann's eyes flicked from Feldman to me and back again several times. "I could kill her. . . ."

"Oh, no *you* couldn't," she griped. "You had to hire some dumb ass just to graze me—you probably can't even pull a trigger without wetting yourself. Men today! Why, in my day . . ."

I was starting to understand why Jessie liked the old woman. She had guts.

I looked at him and shrugged again. "All she does is complain."

"She's your *mother*. . . ."

"Are you really so naïve as to think biology ties into affection?" she retorted, looking him up and down. "Well, perhaps you would be. But he"—she pointed to me with a jab of her bony chin—"couldn't give a rat's ass if I lived or died. I may be his mother, but I gave him up—handed him over to live a series of lies. He's screwed up. Damaged goods. He knows it. And he knows I'm the reason."

Wondermann stood there staring at both of us, dumbfounded.

"I think it is time we discuss my terms. You want werewolves and need a good and proper cure to reverse engineer in order to make sure they are always werewolves. I want a good and proper cure for any member of my family—my pack—that desires it. But time is short. . . ." My mouth was about to outrun my brain. What did I want in order to get to the cure before losing Pietr to insanity or an absolute death? What did I need?

"In order to make everything work, we require the following things," Feldman announced, stepping forward awkwardly, one hand pressed to her slowly bleeding arm.

Amazing.

"You will continue to uphold your previous agreement. Every supply we ask for hand delivered immediately as top priority. Two adjoining rooms, or a suite with separate bedrooms and baths at one of the four-star hotels on Times Square with a view of Times Square."

I gawked at her.

"You will find it simply inspiring," she assured me. "I'd suggest the Marriott—absolutely lovely. We require all the imagined amenities, including meals and laundry service as well as transport to and from the hotel by private car."

I kept blinking at her. I would have never thought of any of those things, I realized.

"We require a daily stipend of two thousand dollars each for—let's call it *incidentals*. Oh, don't look so pained," she said to Wondermann in her most soothing tone. "It is a small price to pay knowing you will be able to deliver on your military contract. I'm certain the price the United States military is willing to pay for a new breed of nearly indestructible soldiers is a pretty penny. If there's one thing the U.S. enjoys investing in, it's the tools of war."

"Defense," he whispered. "It is a defense contract."

"Tomayto, tahmahto," Feldman declared. She turned, bringing her hand down to cup the other on the top of her cane, peering at me like some wrinkled and wizened little witch from a child's fairy tale. "And you, Alexi, is there anything else you want?"

"*Da*," I whispered, realizing what it was. My entire life I had been trained to keep secrets, to trust no one with the family's business or my grandfather's knowledge. And listening to Feldman suggest things I would never have thought to ask for, seeing her push the envelope so many amazing ways, I knew it was time to make a break with old habits. If I was going to perfect the cure before losing my little brother, I needed as much help as I could get.

If two heads were better than one, how fast might we succeed if there were five or six of us working together to solve the problem?

"I want help. Your four finest scientists here by nine a.m. tomorrow. I do not care how they get here, but they simply must, for us to succeed."

Wondermann pursed his lips. "No."

"What?" Feldman and I asked in unison.

"You heard me. No. I will not answer to your terms."

My vision grew hazy. We had been so close to getting everything we could possibly need and want. . . .

"Then we have reached an impasse," Feldman said.

"*Nyet*," I whispered. "There must be something . . ."

"There is only one other thing I want, beyond the were-wolves," Wondermann said, turning his back to us.

My head spun. Think, Sasha, think . . .

What was a man like Wondermann still lacking? What had eluded him? I wanted to pace and give my brain a chance to determine the right course of action. But I did not dare. It would be too easy for him to see he had me up against a wall. So I stood still, regulated my breathing, and thought as fast as I could. What did he want that he couldn't have just by writing a check? Who—besides my family—had cost him something? Who had betrayed him?

"There was a woman in your employ. A woman who betrayed the company and allowed us to get inside the bunker with armed men and destroy all your precious research—all your files, computers . . . everything."

"Wanda McGregor. Yes. I know of her." He tapped his fingers on his desk. "Is she not a family friend?"

Feldman stood still as death, deliberating.

"She betrayed my mother. There is no friendship there to be had."

"Interesting."

"What if I told you I could give you her? What would you be willing to do then if I handed over your traitor?"

"I would not treat her kindly," he clarified.

"I would not expect you to. She has not treated others kindly, either. What mercy does she deserve in return for granting none?"

He spun on his heel, the look on his face both criminal and angelic in its absolute joy. "I thought I might come to like you eventually. We have a deal then. Deliver me Wanda McGregor by the month's end or you lose . . . everything."

———

Back in the lab I grabbed Feldman's purse, understanding now why she had wanted it.

"Thank you," she muttered, unzipping it and pulling out an assortment of Band-Aids and gauze. "I'll regret this momentarily, but do you have a little rubbing alcohol to swab it with?"

I dug through the supplies and found some and carefully rolled up her sleeve to wipe the graze clean.

She sucked her lips and said some truly uncomplimentary things about Wondermann's heritage while I bandaged her wound and thought, all the time I did it, that she was actually quite remarkable for an old woman who had abandoned her only child.

CHAPTER FOURTEEN

Jessie

"So what are you going to do about them, Jessie?" Sophie asked me as I stood in Junction High's hallway gawking at the milling members of Marlaena's pack.

Only the adults and Gabriel were notably absent from the school hallway.

"What do you mean?"

"Well, I thought I should be prepared for whatever game plan you have in mind."

"I don't—"

"Yes, you do. You always do. You'll get involved somehow. No doubt about it."

Wide-eyed, I looked at Cat, Max, Pietr, and Amy for support.

Max shrugged. "Sophia's right."

"Thanks ever so much," I snapped. But I turned back to face

the gaggle of pups. Here they were without Marlaena's steady influence. Here they might be influenced by someone else. . . .

"So what's the plan?" Max asked, unfurling his devilish grin.

"How many specialists do we still have in the boiler room?" I asked Sophie.

"It's like they speak some freaky code," Max grumbled to Amy. "Annoying."

"Except I speak it, too," she said with a grin of her own.

"We're down to eleven since the food vendor changed and the additive disappeared."

"So if we added maybe eight pups . . ."

"No. Absolutely not. Things are volatile as it is. . . ." Sophie crossed her arms and glared at me.

"Please?"

"No."

"Imagine how awesome it'd be if we could turn them—I mean, *encourage* them to be better than what Marlaena is forcing them into. It'd be like rescuing kittens. . . ."

She rolled her eyes at me. "Those *kittens* are way more fiercely fanged than any kittens I've ever dealt with."

"Aw, come on, Soph. You've made such a difference to the specialists already . . . why not add some other kids who need guidance into the mix?"

"Jessie has an interesting point. Why not give the pups a little love and kindness and see where it leads? They've been on the run awhile—maybe all they need are some roots," Max suggested, leaning in.

Sophia looked flustered by being the focus of his attention. "I can't believe I'm even considering this."

Frankly, I couldn't either.

Marlaena

"Shhh," Gareth whispered, running the damp cloth along my fevered forehead to sop up my sweat and cool me. "It'll be all right."

Not long ago all I would have wanted from Gareth was his gentle touch and his focus and attention directed at me. But now? I grabbed his wrist and held his hand above my face. "Stop." My eyes fluttered shut, and I tried to regain control of my breathing. "Just, stop . . ."

He rocked back on his heels, pulling away from the bedside. "Whatever you say, Princess."

My eyes opened again, and I tried to focus on him—on the smoky-colored man with haunting eyes I'd wanted for so long. . . . But my brain took his every feature apart and lessened them by mathematical increments and threw Pietr's design into the mix—showing just how short Gareth fell in comparison. I was going to be sick.

Again.

He had the trash can beside me before I even flopped over the bed's edge, and as I emptied my guts into the can he stroked my hair and whispered kind and gentle things.

And I hated myself. I had wanted Gareth forever. I loved Gareth, well, as much as I could love anyone, but the fascination—no, *fixation*—with Pietr overwhelmed all that.

This strange chemical thing was crushing something beautiful. . . . maybe something I was simply not worthy of having. Did he know how his every touch only made me hungrier for Pietr's imagined ministrations? Could he fathom how frequently my mind went from the real and beautiful existence of him to the fantasy of Pietr? A fantasy I was desperate to strike from my mind?

I spit out the last of the bile that burned in my mouth, and
Gareth handed me a glass of water that I hadn't even noticed
him bring in.

Jessie

Pietr was quiet in school that morning, staying a few feet away
from me most of the time. We attended classes together,
spoke to each other at a distance, sat together at lunch, and
that was where disaster once again struck.

He was nibbling tentatively on a beef jerky strip when
the cafeteria doors were opened from the small courtyard
and a puff of cold wind blew across my back, picking up my
hair and waving it out ahead of me in the space between
Pietr and me. I swatted it down and pulled it back behind
my neck, but Pietr's pale skin tone greened slightly and he
launched himself toward the hallway and the nearest bathroom.

"I swear I deodorized," I said, trying to make light of the
strange way Pietr was acting. I grabbed my lit notebook and
jotted that line down. I could use that in my novel assignment, too.

Amy smiled weakly at me.

"Max?" I said, closing my notebook, but he was already
wiping his mouth and getting to his feet.

"I'll go check on him."

"Maybe you should just take him home," I suggested.
"He's obviously too sick to be here. Maybe call Alexi . . ."

He nodded. "See you at home," he said to Amy, leaning
down to kiss her.

Stretching up in her seat she kissed a smile back onto his

face and I was instantly jealous. Not of Amy kissing Max, but of the fact that any recent action like that on my part would have left Pietr puking up a lung.

Considering I was dating one of the hottest guys at Junction, the current situation was far from good for my self-esteem.

The rest of the lunch period was relatively uneventful, and I used my special all-purpose-Harnek-pass to skip out on science and head to the boiler room to check on the "specialists" as Sophie and I had taken to calling them.

There were fewer now that Wondermann's company was no longer providing the food that had been dosed with a triggering agent, and a few of the remaining ones had lost nearly all their powers—as well as their sense of what made them special.

High school was weird that way. Most of the time you just wanted to fit in, but sometimes you were desperate to know how different you were from the rest of the crowd.

Sophia looked up when she heard me on the stairs and then made a point of looking behind me. "I didn't bring them," I announced, realizing she expected the pups. "You haven't said I can yet."

"Yet," she said with a smile. "Still an optimist." She closed the book she was flipping through and signaled me over. "Maybe you should. It's all Island of Misfit Toys down here anyhow. How much more misfit can you get than a cult of teenage werewolves on the run?"

I grinned. "That's the spirit."

"Don't say spirit," she requested, and I laughed.

"Next time then."

Marlaena

They were only a few yards ahead when I found them, Pietr and Max, hunting. They ran as smoothly as water over the snowy path, focused intently on the deer that couldn't be far beyond my sight since it smelled so strongly of musk and fear. I saw it a heartbeat before Max went for its belly and Pietr its throat, and in the space of the next three heartbeats the deer's heart had beat its last.

They tore into it, not even noticing me until I clicked my teeth together, and they turned, faces smeared with bright and beautiful blood, mouths dripping gore and drool. Beautiful beasts, they glared at me, their eyes as red as my own.

But before they decided whether to invite me to dinner or chase me away, a branch broke on the other side of the thicket and we knew we were not alone.

A bullet cut into my shoulder, and I yelped as I rolled to face the direction it'd come from.

Not the direction of the broken branch.

Another shot ruffled Max's fur and he turned that way, snarling and backing up so his haunch hit mine. I whined, trying to see one of our opponents, and another gun fired, the bullet ripping through the leafless undergrowth. There was a clatter like a gun had hit the ground and someone cursed.

Someone else exclaimed something in Russian, and suddenly the woods were alive with three angry voices. We lowered ourselves to our bellies and prepared to spring, my heart pounding through me as my shoulder throbbed. I nipped at it.

Over our heads someone shouted at the others, "Drop your weapons and I will let you live." Dmitri?

"You drop your weapon and we'll let you live," someone shouted back—a woman, by the pitch of her voice.

"Do it!" another man shouted.

Dmitri snarled something in Russian again and opened fire on them both.

For a few moments the air above us was alive with bullets and the fur along my back buzzed with shots that came too close.

And then there was only ragged breathing, from me and . . . from the bushes surrounding us.

And then it was only mine.

Cautiously we rose to our full canine heights and prowled the underbrush, our ears our first line of defense. There were no more words from the shooters, no more sounds of breathing, and when I found the first one, a young man in hunting gear, I realized there was no more life to them, either. I stalked to the other bodies, Dmitri's and the woman's, and I paused and tilted my head, recognizing her.

I had seen her before at the motel. I had even made a face at her while I finished my breakfast. I pressed my nose to her throat, taking in a deep breath of her scent, and I hopped back. Like bad luck, her scent had been nearby ever since Chicago.

I raced back to the young man and took a long sniff of him as well. Also familiar! The hunters who had chased us— the ones who had taken Harmony and dogged our steps all the way to Junction—lay dead around the Rusakovas' fresh venison. Forgetting the pain in my shoulder I sat back and I howled out my joy.

Suddenly I was human and shivering, and Pietr, naked and bloodstained from the deer, his fingers trembling, dug the bullet out of my shoulder as the wound began to close.

In that moment, between the stars and the snow, was the closest I'd come to perfection. I grabbed him and kissed him hard.

And he kissed me back.

Jessie

Pietr came to my bedroom window that night, spattered and smeared with blood. I pulled him inside and watched him tumble to my bedroom floor, his feet tangling and his body shaking like he had the worst case of the flu ever. "What's wrong, Pietr?" I whispered, pulling him close.

He was cold—so cold, and that was definitely not in his nature. "Dmitri is dead. And hunters. They shot each other fighting over who got the glory of killing the three of us."

"Are Max and Cat okay?" I asked, scrambling up to look out the window onto the lawn.

"*Da,*" he whispered. Max and . . . Cat are fine. But I . . ."

"You're a wreck. I need to get you home."

"*Nyet, nyet,*" he moaned. "Not home . . ." He rubbed at his eyes so hard I pulled his hand away. "There is something I must tell you," he said, his voice hoarse and breaking. He sucked down a deep breath. "Since I broke through the cure, something is different. . . . Something is wrong with me. Something in me has broken," he whispered. "*Puhzhalsta,* please . . . you must help me."

I wrapped my arms around him, and he shuddered in my grasp. "I will, I'll do whatever I can to make this better," I promised.

"Say it again," he begged. "Promise me that whatever it takes, you'll help me make this better." He grabbed my head, holding my face in his hands and staring at me with desperate eyes.

"Of course . . ."

"Promise."

"I promise I'll do whatever it takes to make this better."

"Thank you, thank you, Jess," he whispered, right before he grabbed my trash can and heaved his guts into it.

I called Max. "He's acting really weird."

Silence.

"Max?"

"*Da*, I know this, Jessie. I just don't know why. What is he doing now?"

"Sleeping—well, shivering in his sleep. He feels cold. That's not normal, is it?"

"*Nyet*. I'll come get him."

"Come get us both. I'll leave a note for Annabelle Lee. She'll cover for me." I hoped.

He did not fight us when we loaded him into the car to take him home, and alone in his room, he finally told me what he needed me to do. "Cure me again, Jess."

"It didn't hold—it's not permanent."

"But it helped. I need that help now," he said, his eyes roaming the room.

"Fine. I'll cure you in the morning."

"No," he whispered, grabbing my arm. "You must do it now."

Seeing him so scared, I could not deny him. So I gathered the necessary items, cut myself, and mixed the cure for Pietr.

And, for the sake of my own remaining sanity, I stepped out of his room while he went through his final change.

Again.

CHAPTER FIFTEEN

Marlaena

Since we'd shared that kiss the night Dmitri and the hunters ended one another, Pietr Rusakova had become a fire in my brain—a simmering sensation that slipped into the space between my skull and flesh and seethed there at a slow and steady boil. But I loved Gareth, not Pietr Rusakova and his lean body with sleek muscles and slightly slanting eyes that gave him a mysterious eastern air. . . . My stomach dropped and my knees loosened. . . .

Damn it!

With a sweep of my arms I cleared the nearest table and for a moment the sizzling in my skull lessened.

But Pietr's image assaulted me again, and I bit back a scream of frustration.

I didn't love Pietr. He didn't love me. This horrible chain between us—this strangely unbreakable bond—was driving me crazy.

And I knew he wasn't doing any better.

We watched each other—absorbed every detail of the other—like addicts taking their next hit. It was embarrassing at best. But it was more than that. It was crippling.

I fell to my knees, scrambling to pick up the stray items I'd knocked down, praying that by keeping busy I'd lock my brain down. Get my emotions back under control.

But I picked up a photo and saw Jessica and Pietr. Together. My teeth lengthened and sharpened into fangs, and my body buzzed realizing I wanted to tear her apart with my teeth—shred her just to hear her scream—just to know she'd never touch Pietr again.

I jumped up, the photo falling from my fingers, and swinging around I cracked my hand into the table's edge.

"Owww!" I cried out, thrusting my fingers into my mouth to suck on them as I paced the room, mad at myself for being so stupid.

And for a solid three minutes I thought of nothing but my pain.

My head snapped up at the sound of someone in the doorway. Gareth asked, "You okay?"

I felt woozy just looking at him, but I steadied myself. "Yeah. Yeah, I think so."

He nodded and got ready to go.

"Wait."

He turned back to face me quickly. "What do you need?"

That was Gareth. Wanting to satisfy my needs. "The thing people do to try and block an idea or habit from their mind. . . . It's a therapy, I think . . ."

"What sort of therapy?"

I shrugged noncommittally, but the idea had stuck in my head now and I was determined to see it through. "Something where they . . . I don't know . . . pinch themselves or poke themselves or . . ."

"A therapy where someone hurts themselves?"

"Kind of . . . It makes them associate the pain with the habit they want to break."

His eyes were impossibly kind. "Don't," he whispered. "Don't hurt yourself over this, 'laena."

"I'm already hurting *you* over this."

He looked away.

"Aren't I?"

"This is difficult on everyone."

"What is *this*?" I countered. "Maybe if I know . . ." I shook my head. "Whatever it is, it's making me do things I don't understand—things I don't want to do. . . ."

"You don't know what this is that's making you act this way with him?"

"No," I admitted, my stomach curling in on itself in fear. "Do you know?"

"I think so," he whispered. "And I don't think aversion therapy is going to help. I think you've imprinted with Pietr Rusakova."

I sat down. It was crazy. Imprinting was something that only happened in novels or movies. It wasn't real. It couldn't be.

I coughed out a laugh. "Yeah. Right. Imprinting. Like in *Twilight*? I swear I won't get any more books."

"Not just *Twilight*—there've been other books and graphic novels that suggest it. And the possibility . . . I overheard some things while Dmitri was around. It's more than possible. I'm sorry, 'laena, but that's the only real explanation. Unless you've fallen for him."

"No. No. I do not have *any* feelings for Pietr Rusakova. Except the occasional annoyance. Okay. More than occasional."

"Then it's an imprint."

I shook my head again, but it only made his image swim in my sight as his scent finally reached me.

"You look pale. I need to go, don't I?"

"I'm sorry."

"Me too, 'laena. Me too."

I couldn't stay there, not in that house surrounded by aspects of Pietr and coddled by Gareth's kindness. I sneaked out the door as soon as I heard Gareth head up the stairs to the bathroom, and pulling my hood up, I did my best to disappear into Junction.

I found a small diner somewhere between the Rusakovas' Queen Anne and the motel we'd left, and fighting a creeping nausea, I took a seat and emptied my pockets. Seven dollars.

I ordered dry toast and water and bravely nibbled and sipped. My stomach turned in rebellion, and I shoved the plate aside.

His arrival made me jump. He'd looked much better when he'd run with my pack. But now Gabriel's hair was oily, the edges of his jacket's sleeves were tinged with dirt, and although no one else seemed to notice, he smelled.

"You need to go," I whispered, leaning across the table. "I told you I never wanted to see you again."

"You don't look so good, 'laena," he said. He reached for my hand, and I pulled it away just before his remaining fingers brushed mine. "Look what Pietr Rusakova has done to you just by existing."

I swallowed hard, not wanting to know how he'd figured it out when it seemed Pietr and I were the last to know. "You're as guilty as he is—guiltier," I muttered. "If you hadn't kidnapped Jessica, then Pietr wouldn't have broken past the cure and maybe we would have never known. Maybe we could have just gone on. Left Junction. Been happy . . ." I lowered my head to the table's cool surface and shuddered when a chill raced down my backbone. "Sometimes it's best never to know something. Look what knowing's done. Look how it's destroying—things . . ." I barely stopped from saying *us*, seeing a very worried-looking Gareth open the diner's door.

He sat down in the next booth.

How could there be any "us" when all I could focus on was the *him* of Pietr Rusakova? He was like a drug in my blood, coursing through me with every pump of my heart, poisoning my thoughts and controlling my actions. . . .

Gabe's hand rested on mine, and I realized the water glass in my grasp was rattling. "You're shaking," he said as an apology, pulling his hand away.

"Thank you, Captain Obv . . ." The word strangled in my throat. Captain Obvious. One of the pet names Jessica used for Pietr.

Pietr with the strong shoulders and lean build and smug smile . . . Damn it. I raised my head just to let it hit the table with a solid *thunk*. Pietr, whose very biological existence threatened any hope of happiness I might ever have with Gareth.

"Things don't have to be this way," Gabe said, his eyes intense and determined. "You didn't know before. What if there was a way to erase the imprint?"

"There isn't," I hissed. "Once you imprint, it'll haunt you both for life."

"For life," Gabe agreed. "But if it could be undone . . . if you could be freed, would you want to be?"

"God, yes. I'd give anything to have this gone—"

He was out the door before I could even finish my sentence, and something dropped like lead into the pit of my stomach.

Once Gabe was gone, Gareth raised his chin and sniffed, checking the direction the air flowed before he sat down next to me at my booth. "Sorry, Princess. I make you sick—trying to take a few precautions. Are you okay?"

Hold it together, I urged myself. Just keep it together. He's here trying to do what he thinks is the right thing. He had no idea how much the right thing hurt.

My stomach squirmed in my gut, threatening to toss up even the small bites of toast I'd choked down not fifteen minutes earlier.

"Sorry," I gasped as I shoved him out of the booth and onto the floor in my headlong rush for the bathroom.

Embracing the toilet with no thought of germs, I wondered just how far I could go fighting the imprint. And what was the worst that'd happen if I just gave in?

But I remembered the look on Gareth's face as I'd burst past him, and shaking with dry heaves, decided I could go at least a little longer for his sake.

Jessie

"Why do I feel I'm going to absolutely regret this?" Sophie asked me as we led the pups to the door of the boiler room.

"Because taking a leap of faith can be difficult?"

"Maybe because working with werewolves is even more nerve-wracking than working with exploding citrus," she griped.

"You know I love you, right?"

She snorted. "That and five bucks might get me a decent coffee."

I held the door for them and watched as they all quietly trudged down the stairs, Harnek's special Guidance passes clutched in every hand.

Only one was missing from the group, and it was a planned exclusion: Gabriel. He'd made himself scarce since his major falling-out with Marlaena's pack, and frankly, I hoped to never see him again. He was nothing but trouble. A devil in a wolf pelt.

"So here we are, kids. Nirvana for the paranormal underground," Sophie announced.

The pipes rumbled and the pups looked up, frightened.

"Nirvana has many unrealized charms," I reassured them.

"And just why should we be coming down here?" Londyn asked, an eyebrow raised and her body language doubtful at best.

"Because pack or not, more friends are better to have than less. At least if they're good friends," I said. "Specialists, meet your new friends."

Neither group looked impressed.

"Yeah?" Sam, the group's firestarter, asked, "what makes them so special?"

"They can teach you—"

But Terra morphed her head into that of the wolf like the pro she'd already become.

After the screaming stopped, Terra changed back.

Fabulous.

Sam got his jaw working long enough to say, "That's hot." Coming from a pyro, that was a big deal.

"Yeahhh. To clarify, they can't teach you that. What I was

going to say was they can teach you how they survived with their own strange powers so that you can, too."

And so we began. Awkwardly, but that's the way some of the best friendships start. And when I finally had a minute to get Sophie to myself, we talked long enough to know Derek wasn't just my problem. And if he still had a hold on Soph, I could bet he still had his hooks in Sarah.

So I gathered two of my girlfriends together and arranged to do what every teenage girl with a boy stuck in her head needs to do: get some control.

I slipped up the stairs on quiet feet—nowhere near as soft-footed as an *oborot,* but I'd grown stealthy through my association with them. And because of the danger we'd seemed to be in nearly constantly.

At Pietr's door I paused, standing in the opening, just taking it all in.

The room was filled with built-in bookcases. From floor to ceiling every space was occupied by books: whether a classic of foreign literature, a modern-day novel, or a book on philosophy or religion. Different colors, fonts, and languages covered the room like the most well-educated wallpaper imaginable. The only place without a shelf was the spot where a single circular window peered out over the yard like the wide and staring eye of a cyclops.

Pietr was stooped over his homework, absolutely enthralled with math. Or science. At this stage in high school it seemed they blended so well, they were frequently taught together.

The hair he'd been so often sweeping back out of his eyes had fallen down to obscure them, and occasionally he blew out a frustrated puff of breath to try to send the shock back to its desired place.

He was so focused—one hand scribbling away in pencil at an amazing speed while the other tapped on his keypad, his eyes darting between the two as he checked and transcribed some sort of equation.

I stepped into the room and dropped my bookbag on his bed.

He startled in his seat, spinning to face me. "Jess," he said with a sigh that sounded like it held the very definition of relief.

"A little jumpy today?"

A faint smile slanted across his face.

Something was off. Something was wrong.

I sat down on the bed to study him. "You okay?"

He nodded. Too quickly.

"Come here," I commanded, patting the mattress. "Sit with me."

He rose slowly—hesitating—and set down his pencil. For a moment my heart pounded at the way he looked back at his stack of homework—as if it would win over me.

Again.

But sandwiching his papers into his book, he closed it and came to sit down beside me. My heart sped up, and I leaned against him only to draw back in surprise.

"You're burning up," I whispered, not caring that his arm slid off my shoulders as I turned to face him more fully. I placed my hands on his strong shoulders and bent forward, pressing my lips to his forehead.

He was hot—and not in the way my amazingly sexy boyfriend usually was, but in the way that made the breath come boiling out of him and made me worry sweat would simply sizzle across his skin. "What's wrong? Is this because of round two of the cure?"

But it couldn't be.

He shook his head slowly, leaning into me.

"Talk to me, Pietr."

He rested his forehead against my collarbone, and I moved back against the wall to keep us both upright.

"I need to talk to Alexi," he said softly. "He'll know what to do."

"What to do . . . ?"

But he was getting up, leaving the comfort of my arms and the bed, and not looking at me.

"Know what to do about what?" I asked, but the door shut behind him and soon all I heard was the sound of his footsteps on the stairs and the thumping of my anxious heart as it rattled against my rib cage.

Alexi

"I am working on a special project," Nadezhda said softly. "Something big. It may well be the project that defines my career as an agent."

"Or do you mean the project that defines you as a woman? You as yourself."

I could hear her smile into the receiver. "Perhaps that as well," she admitted. "There is a company that has, shall we say, 'nested' in the United States. A very immoral company that is doing experimentation."

"What sort of experimentation?"

"A type you are quite familiar with, it would seem. Personally familiar with, if surveillance tapes are to be believed."

I sat straight up, my spine tingling as a shiver raced along its length. "What are you talking about, Nadezhda?"

"Are you in league with the Devil, Sasha? Or would it be better if I asked if perhaps I might know precisely *which* devil you are in league with this time?"

I stayed quiet, thinking as fast as I could. "I have been working at a particular facility. . . ."

"How involved are you in said facility?"

"Tell me why it matters."

"Perhaps I am looking out for you."

"Perhaps I am there because I am looking out for someone myself," I returned.

"Answer my question, Sasha."

"*Nyet.* I owe you no answers."

Now she was the one who grew silent. Speculative. "*Pravda.* True. You owe me no answers. You owe me nothing. But I also owe you nothing. And yet, here we are, still connected. Still speaking, and this is me—trying to connect us as well as I can."

"Perhaps the distance is too great," I suggested.

"You are not speaking of physical distance." Not a question, she was simply stating the fact.

"I am working for a Mr. Wondermann," I conceded.

"*Da.* I know that much."

"On research of a scientific—of an experimental—sort."

"I suspected. And is the nature of the experiment legal?"

"Does Interpol want to arrest me?" I chided.

"Do not be an ass. I want you to understand that the corporation employing you—"

"They do not employ me. I volunteer."

She was stunned to silence. "Did you get her out? Were you the one who called in the other wolves to free her?"

I held my breath.

"It took me weeks to arrange to get her there and set all the snares I had to . . ."

"What?!"

"She was being held illegally by someone outside of the government. By having Wanda retrieve her, we might have shut his operation down even earlier. By providing the werewolf, I hoped he would have finished with you—erased your entire involvement with his corporation before we sprang the trap on him. I was trying to protect you."

"By trying to protect me, you nearly ruined everything." No Wondermann meant no cure, which meant no Pietr.

"Perhaps you are no longer the person I should be speaking to. Perhaps . . ."

"Perhaps what? Perhaps we are enemies now?"

Her lingering silence was answer enough.

"We are not enemies. I do not think I could ever be your enemy. I am volunteering under duress."

"Then that is not truly volunteering."

"We are on the same side, Nadezhda. We are still on the same side. We seem to even *switch* sides together."

"So will you help me now?"

"Help you do what exactly?"

"Gather information to bring down Wondermann's company. All very legally."

"How will you do it?"

"All you need to know is that, with your help, we will bring them to justice—slow, grinding justice."

"Is there any other kind in America?"

She laughed.

So did I. "What do you need from me, Nadezhda?"

"Paperwork. A trail that shows the Wondermann Corporation is guilty of tax evasion. We are close, but a man inside . . ."

"Fine." I waited, but knew she'd tell me details when she was ready. "Does he make you happy?"

"What? Oh. Alexi. He and I . . . we are no longer together. It did not—it would not—work."

"Just like us."

She sighed so heavily into the phone that it sounded like a gust of wind pushing straight into my ear. "Alexi . . ."

"*Nyet*," I insisted. "I will do this thing for you. I only need to make sure my plan is completed before yours goes fully into action."

"Do not take too long, Alexi," she said. "This must be done soon or many more will suffer at the hands of this corporation."

"I will be as quick as I can possibly be. I am doing this for a most important reason."

"So it is for *you*? Because *you* used to always be your most important reason for any course of action."

"Perhaps you did not ever know me as well as you thought."

"Perhaps not," she agreed.

"Because *you* used to be the most important thing in my world."

She hung up the phone, and I was left with my cell at my ear and nothing but silence coming back to me.

Jessie

Pietr came to help me with the horses, his fondness for them growing as he got to know each of them. We didn't board and train as many as we had when Mom was alive, but the barn was always full of personality, and of stalls that needed mucking out. And Pietr was not afraid of lifting a shovel. I had to imagine he'd lifted one frequently getting rid of Dmitri and the hunters' bodies.

Pushing the thought from my head, I returned to grooming Snap while Pietr checked the water buckets.

My attention shifted from my work to Pietr when I heard a bucket hit the floor, water sloshing everywhere. "What the—"

Gabriel was in the barn, the door to the outside shut, my dogs going crazy as Gabe took Pietr to the ground and started pounding on him.

No longer wolf, Pietr wasn't even able to defend himself.

"Gabriel! Get off of him!" I eyed the stack of hay bales I'd stashed the gun case in and did a quick visual tally of the tools I'd decided earlier could be used as weapons.

They'd all been neatly rearranged in their normal rack on the far wall. Dad had decided to be helpful and clean up after his highly distractible daughter.

Awesome.

I dove for the gun case and popped it open, slipping the clip into the gun's butt until it clicked and then I stood. "Stop! Stop it!" I ordered.

"Or you'll do what?" Gabriel yelled, his awkward fist twisted in Pietr's hair, keeping his neck at an evil angle, ready to smash his face into the ground again or snap his neck.

Shoot to wound. *Show mercy,* I willed myself. Give him the chance you'd want someone to give you. "I'll shoot you." I steadied my hands, making it clear I'd follow through.

He laughed and focused on Pietr once more.

I pulled the trigger. *Squeeze, don't jerk.*

Blood burst from Gabe's shoulder, and he flew backward with the impact of the shot.

Pietr's head flopped forward, and his sides heaved with a convulsing breath.

Blood covered his face, smeared and black with dirt and stuck with bits of hay. "Pietr . . ."

He struggled forward—toward me—his eyes peeping through the mess of his face and focusing on me.

Gabe was cursing up a storm.

"Stay where you are," I warned him as I headed toward Pietr.

But Gabe wasn't one to take orders. He lunged for Pietr again even as the blood wept from his shoulder and grew in a bright stain across his shirt. Murder lit his eyes even more brightly than the red of the wolf.

And then my vision got furry around the edges and I felt the tremble in my brain that announced another lesson from Derek. I spread my feet for balance and locked my knees.

I would not go down.

Like a transparent screen laid across the very real and bloody world I lived in, I saw the ghost image of Derek tag Jack and stand him on the railroad tracks, unblinking, the same grin on his face as I'd seen when I'd opened the make-shift bodybag at Pecan Place, the asylum.

I felt a slowly building power ease into my veins, and my head began to feel light. . . . "Damn it!" I shouted.

On the wavering railroad tracks Jack just smiled vacantly and waited for death, and Derek, standing in the trees not far away, caught the surge of Jack's energy like the best adrenaline rush ever. Two words circled in my brain, chasing each other in a slow spiral.

Regret.

No.

Regret.

No.

Beneath the shadowy train track murder scene Pietr and Gabe fumbled back into focus, Derek superimposed on Gabriel. *No.* He—they—had Pietr and this time there would be no mercy. *Regret.*

No regret.

My body buzzing, my eyes wide with horror, I took my shot, screaming, "I don't want this lesson!"

Gabe's head exploded in bits of bone, blood, and gray matter and I fell to my knees, feeling something rip away from my brain like a whirlwind bursting loose and evaporating in the cold winter air.

I dropped the gun, sick at what I had done.

What he *made* me do.

What *they* made me do.

I vomited into the hay, and my body quaking with the heaves, I dragged myself to Pietr and the awkward mess that was the remnants of Gabriel. Shoving the corpse aside, I rolled Pietr over and tugged at my sleeve so I could wipe the grossness away from his eyes.

"Pietr," I whispered. "It's over, Pietr." I said it with such certainty. I knew it was true. There was no more voice of Derek in my head. And there was certainly no more Gabriel. I squeezed my eyes shut, unable to look. I'd taken his life. I would have a multitude of regrets. "I'm here."

"Jess," he groaned, one hand reaching clumsily for me. He pawed my cheek and then fell back to the dusty and blood-stained floor.

He groaned more than breathed, his body convulsing.

"We need to get you inside. Get you patched up. Get rid

of . . . the body." I didn't want to attach a name—a nearly human identity—to *it* anymore.

But before I could reach down to help him to his feet, he began to change.

Again.

CHAPTER SIXTEEN

Alexi

Finding the information Nadezhda required was not as difficult as I had feared once I set Feldman to work. She looked every bit the part of the doddering and harmless grandmother, happily telling the employees their future from her silly deck of cards if they just told her an interesting fact about the company.

The company that never paid them quite enough to maintain their full loyalty.

Feldman had an amazingly sympathetic ear, and the employees loved every moment she spent with them. Somehow she did not short me in her devotion to completing the cure, either, and I wondered how she worked so much so tirelessly.

When she handed me a file she had managed to sneak out of an office when the employee had gone to warm her coffee, I asked her how she did it all. Did she not get tired?

She shrugged. "My time is short. I choose to spend as much of it making up for my past mistakes to you as I can."

After that I didn't send her out on additional errands but kept her at my side in the lab, where I could make sure she did not exhaust herself.

Jessie

It was when Alexi had returned home briefly from the city to collect tissue samples and additional DNA swabs that I overheard his plan. The moment he set down the phone, I was in his face.

"Alexi—no, you can't do it. You can't just sacrifice Wanda."

"The hell I can't. . . . That woman betrayed my parents. Killed my father . . ."

"You don't know that she pulled the trigger."

"She did as good as pull it. That woman, that woman your father loves, betrayed my parents, brought about their deaths either directly or indirectly. She broke our family and ruined my life."

"Bullshit."

"What?"

"Bullshit," I repeated, folding my arms before me. "She didn't ruin your life—no one's ruined your life, and no one can. Except you. Besides, your life's just begun. You have plenty of time to ruin it all by yourself. Several times over."

"Shut up, Jessie," he urged, scrubbing his hand across his forehead. "Just shut up. The decision is mine—was mine," he stuttered. "And frankly, there was not much of a decision to be made. Pietr's life, Max's life, and Cat's life for her life. Do you understand? *Pietr's* life, Jessie."

My knees turned to water, and I squeezed my eyes shut. "I understand your motivation, Sasha," I said, grating the words out. "I do. I want the cure for them—maybe more than they want it for themselves right now. But there has to be some other way. You can't bargain with Wanda's life."

"Give me one reason why. Why I cannot barter away a traitor to save my siblings."

"Because she wasn't the traitor. She was manipulated."

"Manip—"

"Manipulated."

"Impossible. Utterly inconceivable."

"I have proof."

"Proof? *Nyet*. It's inconceivable."

"You keep using that word," I chided. "I do not think it means what you—"

He growled and scooped up the nearby lamp, hurling it against the wall so that it shattered. "There is no one alive who is capable of that sort of mental manipulation . . ."

I nodded. "You're absolutely correct. There is no one—"

"*Alive,*" he concluded, staring at my head as if he could peer directly into my skull. "Oh. Oh, no."

Alexi

"I've called Sarah and Sophia. There's something you need to know before you hand Wanda over to the big bad," Jessie said, powering up her cell phone and making her calls.

"I cannot imagine what you could possibly show me that might change my mind."

"Just quit arguing and sit down, Sasha."

I did as I was told, sitting on the love seat. Sarah and Sophie sat on either side of me, our legs touching on the small couch.

"After you see this you'll know Wanda didn't want to hurt your mother, or your father. She was friends with your mom." Jessie knelt in front of me, her hands out for Soph and Sarah.

"When Derek shot all his memories into us, we were all touching." She nodded at the other two girls and they set their free hands on my shoulders.

"Nice manicure," I told Sarah.

She beamed.

Jessie rolled her eyes at me and continued. "I think if we do this right, you'll be able to see what I see. . . ."

"And what if I do not want to see?" I asked.

"You'll want to see," she assured me, closing her eyes. "And don't worry, we've tried this before."

Sarah snorted. "Once."

"Once *successfully*," Jessie clarified. "Twice, if you count the time our heads wanted to split. . . ."

"As promising as this all sounds . . . The wheels are already turning, Jessie. What if this is destiny?"

She snorted at me, opening one eye. "You don't believe in destiny, remember? And wheels can always be stopped. Close your eyes," she ordered.

I obeyed.

"Sarah and Sophie, think of Derek. . . ."

I gasped when I felt something slide inside my head. Images flickered there just behind my eyelids like a stuttering reel of black-and-white film. Things stabilized; the black and white bled into sepia and then other colors, the images moving.

We stood in a long hallway, our hands linked.

"This is Wanda's head." Jessie's voice came to me through a thickness clouding my ears. "This is the way her brain lays out. Each door is a gateway to a memory or potential future. Hold on, let me get our guide. . . ."

A filmy figure slowly gained substance in the hallway before us and became a blond boy in his mid-teens.

It took me only a moment to recognize him.

"Derek," Jessie confirmed. "Only a few years ago. Back when your mom would go for her daily jogs. Just before she disappeared. Take a minute and absorb the setting. We're not staying here long, just long enough for you to glimpse the before."

I examined the space before us as only someone with my interest in body language might. Everything was angular here, everything neat and orderly and unremarkable, with a look of military efficiency and a simplicity that a Spartan would aspire to. There were no frills here, no elements of design, nothing that marked Wanda as anything but the result of a government agency.

It was as remarkable as it was terrifying.

Jessie turned to nod at me, and the walls fell down around us, slipping away into the floor so that we were standing on a narrow throw rug of stark design, floating in a great dark space. I nearly lost my footing except that Sarah and Sophie held on to me. "Sorry about that," Jessie apologized. "It only takes a moment, but . . . You might want to close your eyes. It can be disorienting."

"Are my eyes not already closed?"

"In one place and time, yes, but in the library of Derek's memories they are as big as saucers. Hold on," she warned.

I squeezed my eyes shut and felt the floor beneath us tremble.

"And now . . . after," Jessie announced. "You can open your eyes."

Derek again oozed into existence before me like a slick creeping across a damaged ocean, and then, complete, he froze.

"This is what she was feeling immediately after she turned over your parents. . . ." Jessie motioned all along the length of the hall. "Go ahead. If you ever doubted how Wanda felt about what she did—what she was *forced* to do—take a good, hard look. We have a few minutes before the memory folds."

The doors were there, as were the rug and the walls and simple tile ceiling, but now crucifixes hung almost everywhere. Filling most of the spaces between each in the long bank of doors. But, upon closer inspection I noticed there was something wrong with them. I balked at the realization. Hanging from each crucifix was not the Christian Savior Jesus, but Wanda.

Wanda crucified in her own mind.

Sarah snorted. "Even that weird painting by Klimt that all the college girls hang in their dorm rooms is cooler than that."

Sophie batted at her arm.

Past door after door and crucifix after crucifix I went, my steps faster as I neared the end of the hall and a huge painting.

Before me, in the world of Wanda's brain, da Vinci's *Last Supper* hung.

But, like the crucifixes, the painting was somehow wrong, too, and it pulled me up short as I stared at it to try to determine the difference.

There. In the place of Judas Iscariot, the man who had betrayed Jesus with a kiss, was Wanda.

A traitor in her own mind. And not just any traitor, the biggest traitor of them all.

"Take me out of here," I told Jessie, grabbing Sophie's and Sarah's hands and squeezing my eyes shut. "Take me out of here *now*."

The sense of disorientation only magnified when I was hurled back into my body, my consciousness slamming into my skull.

Sarah let go of me and stood, stretching, and Sophie set her hand in her lap. "It's like a roller-coaster ride at the end."

"Roller coaster from Hell," I hissed, gagging as I vaulted to the bathroom. But Jessie's show-and-tell had done the trick and as soon as I had rinsed my mouth out thoroughly with mouthwash I called Nadezhda to change the timing of the raid on Wondermann and to pull Wanda back from the frontline position she would want to take.

Jessie

I heard the pounding before I saw what was making the noise, and I took the steps to the Rusakovas' basement—and Amy's makeshift bedroom (before it was the pack's make-shift lodging)—two at a time, my curiosity getting the better of me.

At the stairs' base, I pulled up short, cocking my head as if a different view would explain what I was seeing.

"What's all this?" I asked, seeing sawdust and an assortment of nails, boards, and hammers. "What are you building?"

Max set down a two-by-four and looked at Alexi.

Alexi in a workbelt.

"Am I losing my mind?" I asked, looking at them both.

Their gazes still locked on each other, they both swallowed, simultaneously.

What had I said?

"Okay. Let's try this again, this time without you shutting me out." I cleared my throat. "You two, doing construction? Why?"

I examined the structure they were creating in the basement. They were thickening the walls. "Are you trying to increase the R-value of the insulation?" I asked, instantly regretting supplying them with a viable excuse.

Max began to slowly nod his head.

But Alexi shook his. "*Nyet,*" he said, setting down his hammer.

I scanned the rest of the room. Yes, there was wood, but there were also sheets of metal—steel? "What are you really doing down here? What are you building?"

"Jessie," Alexi said, slipping his hand around my upper arm and steering me away from the impromptu construction site. "Pietr is . . . not doing well. You have noticed some changes in his behavior, *da?*"

"Yes," I said, nodding my head. "Of course. Ever since Gabriel . . ." I looked away. "Since Gabriel nearly killed him and forced Pietr past the cure again." And since I'd killed Gabriel to save Pietr. "Yes, he's been different." Forgetting things. But I was trying to forget things, too. Running with the pack more. But I was clinging more tightly to my friends and family, too. "We both are."

Alexi's eyes closed a moment, and I knew he was thinking.

"It is more than that. Think about it, Jessie. Even if you do not want to. You have noticed, *da*? Both Pietr and Marlaena . . ."

I tugged my gaze to the ceiling, hearing their names linked like that. "Yes. They're acting weird. Sick again, too. But it's just some illness, right? You said it might be something brought in by the new pack—like a werewolf flu."

"I had hoped so," Alexi said.

It was the closest he could come to admitting he was wrong about something—admitting he'd hoped it was a different way than it was.

"But if it's not some bug . . ."

Alexi's eyes were huge and soft. Sad.

Max was watching me, too. He licked his lips. Nervous.

"But what could it . . . ?"

Images spun out of control in my head. Pietr staring at Marlaena, her absorbing every aspect of him even across a crowded room. Marlaena joining Max and Pietr on their hunts even after Max had firmly told her no—like she couldn't help herself. Gareth looking so utterly heartbroken and watching me like we were kindred spirits. . . . Pietr getting sicker by the day and sickest around me, but rallying every time Marlaena walked into the room. . . .

Max had me by the arm, lowering me to sit on the floor almost as soon as my knees gave way in realization.

"Oh, God," I whispered. "They've imprinted."

Alexi

"Jessie. Jessie," I called, kneeling before her to tap her cheek. "She fainted. Did you ever expect she would faint?" I asked

Max as he slipped to the floor and tugged her limp body across his to give her support.

"There is much about this I never expected," he replied darkly. "What do we do now, brother? How do we fix things?"

Jessie roused in his arms, her head lolling to one side. She groaned. "You start by telling me everything. Every little detail. Both of you." She straightened. "I need to know and understand it all so I can help."

She caught us looking at each other over her head.

"Oh, no. Absolutely not," she said, placing a hand on my chest and shoving me back. "Don't you dare hold any bit back because you think you're protecting me. Not now. This particular school reporter is totally against censorship, so don't even try."

I struggled to think of the best way to handle this.

"They've imprinted, right?"

I hesitated.

"Say the words, Sasha. Give me the truth."

"*Da*. They have imprinted."

She let out a long sigh. Confirmation was not what she had hoped. "And imprinting is just like . . . like a chemical thing. An addiction. They need to be around each other." She swallowed. "They need to be with each other."

I stood. "I do not see how this is helping matters."

"Don't you dare try to shut down my questions because you don't know where I'm going. Don't. Dare."

I shrugged. "*Da*. It is chemical."

"So it's not emotional. He doesn't love her. She doesn't love him."

"*Nyet*," Max rumbled. "He does not love her. I doubt he even likes her. And she . . . well, she hates him even more because—"

"Because it's like he's controlling her. And Marlaena's not big on being controlled," Jessie concluded.

"*Da.*" Max unwrapped himself from around her and slowly stood, taking her hand to help her to her feet.

She wobbled at first, but quickly regained her self-control.

"So they don't want this—it's a desperate need. That is only stopped by . . ."

"Knocking her up," Max said.

I punched him in the gut and immediately regretted the action, trying to rub the pain out of my hand as I bit my lips. "There are better ways of expressing the situation," I complained.

Jessie's eyebrows were as high as I'd ever seen them. "He has to get her pregnant?" She raised a hand to us both, palm out as she turned her face away. "Sitting down again," she warned, and sank to the floor.

We both kneeled beside her.

"Isn't there any other way? He doesn't even want kids, ever. There has to be some way," she repeated, adamant. "Some way that . . . I dunno . . . keeps them from . . . *that.*"

I shook my head. "I am so sorry. The imprint is activated so that the next generation is stronger. Their genetic codes complement each other perfectly, and their heightened *oborot* senses have recognized that fact, throwing their bodies into this state of heightened awareness. I am afraid it must run its natural course. Like a virus."

"The imprint is like a virus. Something that can't be stopped? You either get past it, or . . . or you don't. I'm sorry, Sasha. I can't accept that." She picked at the concrete of the basement floor. "You said their heightened *oborot* senses recognized each other. That was what kicked this all into gear, wasn't it?"

"*Da.*"

"That's why he was so determined to have me cure him again. But it wasn't strong enough, was it? It couldn't mask all the symptoms anymore. Our cure is like antibiotics, isn't it?"

I just watched her, unclear.

"You take the medicine hoping it'll wipe out your illness, but your body—or the illness itself—can build up a tolerance, right?"

"It is entirely possible."

"Marlaena never took the cure before. What if she takes it now? If she took it and her body believed it was simply human again, wouldn't Pietr's also? Wouldn't his body forget the imprint?"

I only managed to squeak out "I" before Max jumped in.

"Marlaena won't wash out the wolf. She won't take the cure. It's the opposite of her whole 'the Wolf is the Way' thing," Max said.

"Even though it's tearing Gareth up?" Jessie wondered aloud.

We both shrugged.

"Gawwd," Jessie said, stretching the monosyllable so it was much more. "She's such a selfish bitch."

"She's confused," Max muttered. "We're all confused."

"Sasha." Jessie said my name as if it were an oath. "Sasha—a permanent cure. Isn't that what you're working on?"

"Nonstop," I confirmed.

"Not if you're here, building this . . ." She pointed to the reinforcement we had only just started on the wall. "You need to get back to the lab. Let me deal with construction. I'm a farmer's daughter, I know my way around a site. And I'll bring in Dad and we'll get this done. I want you back in the city at work first thing tomorrow morning," she ordered, her eyes fierce, sparks of gold glittering dangerously in the brown most people probably thought was simply average.

I nodded my compliance.

"So wait—why the construction? You're reinforcing this room, aren't you?" She stood and turned in a slow circle, taking it all in. "This isn't some love nest you're building. This is . . ."

"A prison," I confirmed. "Pietr will not give in to his baser instincts, and it is destroying him. And shortly before the imprint kills him because he has denied its orders and is therefore irreparably flawed, it will drive him insane."

She nodded, taking it all much better than I might have hoped. "Interesting. And how much time do we have?"

"Two weeks at most, before insanity takes control. Then another week until denying the imprint kills him. And sane or not, he will deny it."

She nodded again, then headed for the stairs. Clutching the banister, she turned to face us once more. "Thank you. Thank you for your honesty. I'm sure we can make this work." Then she climbed the stairs, her head held high.

Jessie Gillmansen was a trooper. If anyone could get through this, I knew she could.

Jessie

The forgetfulness. The obsession. The short temper. Pietr was going mad. I made it all the way up the stairs and out of the basement-turned-cage-construction site and into the kitchen before I fell against the counter and slid to the floor, sobbing. I couldn't do this. This was too much. Every time I thought I had a victory, it just slipped away. Pietr was dying and the only way to let him live was to let him be with Marlaena?

Curling in on myself, I tucked my knees to my chest and just cried until Gareth found me there.

He knelt down beside me, sliding his arms around me and letting me sniffle all over his neck, and briefly, I thought I heard him crying, too.

CHAPTER SEVENTEEN

Marlaena

We ran like wolves made of wind, speed our drug, our tongues lolling, the long hair of our shoulders brushing as we raced down the deer trail side by side. The air bit our noses and stung our eyes, crystals of snow flying up from the ground as we spun in the hairpin turns and followed the musky scent of our quarry.

I laughed, the sound trilling out of my furred throat and past my lolling tongue like the most natural of unnatural sounds.

I had never felt more alive than I was, leading our combined pack on the hunt with Pietr.

Or more angry.

Max dove between us, his width shoving me into the brush at the path's side and pushing me behind both he and Pietr.

Gareth kept pace with me then, and as much as my mind

whispered it was Gareth I loved and Gareth I wanted, every cell in my body ached with the need and hunger for Pietr Rusakova.

With a grunt I stretched my legs even farther, slipping back between Max and his younger brother, wedging myself there. With a thrust and a kick, I shouldered Max into the bushes.

With an outraged growl he gave chase and my ears tucked tight to my body, my tail low and long. Part of me wanted to outrun him—to be safe. And part of me—the part that still held tight to the hope that was Gareth—wanted him to kill me.

To end me.

To end every bit of the madness that was making me hurt the only person I'd ever dared trust.

Ever dared *love*.

He caught up to me, and turning whip fast, I faced him down, all teeth and claws, hate and daring. He came for my throat, and I welcomed his snapping teeth and his steaming breath with a snarl of my own. We tumbled to the ground together, and I felt his mouth on my throat and saw Gareth's shocked expression as the last thing filling my fading vision.

Jessie

"What the hell . . ." Amy's startled voice made me turn toward the back door. Cat set her cards down and looked at me.

We heard the popcorn bowl hit the floor, falling from Amy's fingers in the hallway, and we bolted from the dining room table, rushing in her direction.

There was blood everywhere. Rich and bright red, flowing and fresh. For a long, frightening moment I couldn't tell who the blood belonged to. I just knew it was spread nearly equally between Pietr and Max.

Pietr shoved Max, the force of them nearly equal and making them land against the walls on either side of the hall, standing as two tall and powerful, bloody, and equally savage and sweet warriors.

Then I understood.

Because between them came Gareth.

Carrying the limp body of Marlaena.

She was coated in blood—her own, I realized—seeing how it crusted thickest along her slender neck. Her head rolled loose on her neck and her eyelashes fluttered, the pulse in her neck pounding and then all but disappearing before it started its violent rhythm again.

Gareth brought her to the sitting room and before Cat could even shout about getting sheets or towels, he'd draped her body across the love seat.

Her chest still rose and fell. She still breathed and lived, but it was an ugly and awkward life at best.

"Bandages," I whispered, hearing Max race up the stairs to the bathroom and the first-aid supplies kept there.

"And I repeat," Amy said, "what the hell?"

"Max pushed her," Pietr said, his tone flat and his eyes unfocused.

Amy's eyes narrowed. "That's more than a push," she said. "I know what it looks like when a girl's been pushed."

His eyes cleared a moment, and he stepped back with a curt nod.

Everyone in the Rusakova household knew Amy, of all

people, understood what it looked like, and felt like, to be pushed around.

"What happened, Pietr?" she tried, her voice fraying in frustration.

Max blew past with bandages and gauze pads. "I gave her a little push and she attacked me."

"You pushed a girl?" Amy asked.

"Not like that," he muttered, realization slow to dawn in his eyes. "No. No—not ever like that. . . ."

"Then what was it like?" Amy whispered, staring him down.

"I was trying to run with Pietr. I came up between them and—"

"Pushed her into the underbrush," Pietr concluded.

"Underbrush doesn't try and tear out your throat," I said, watching as Max turned back to help Gareth apply pressure to Marlaena's seeping wound.

"She attacked me. Baited me. Came at me when I was wolf," Max snarled, glaring at the girl his hands tried to help.

Gareth sighed. "He is correct. She came at him like a rabid animal."

"Is it the—" I fell silent, seeing Pietr.

"The *what*, Jess?" he asked, blinking, his eyes cleared.

"Nothing," I insisted.

Did you dare tell a crazy person they were crazy? Was there any one advisable course of action? Alexi would know what to do. He always knew what to do, or at least was able to bluff his way through a situation convincingly enough that people believed he knew what to do.

"What?" Pietr stepped closer to me, and catching my scent, his eyes rolled.

"Nothing," I soothed, reaching out to touch his hand. But he pulled back.

"Don't lie to me. You lie to everyone else. Don't start lying to me, too."

"I'm not . . ." But as I stepped forward to reassure him, he jumped back like a frightened animal, and turning, dashed out the back door.

Amy took the single step required to stand beside me. "He's not himself," she said, leaning in to rest her head against mine. "Remember that, Jessie. That's not your Pietr."

"I know. I know. But that Pietr . . . he may be the only Pietr I have left."

"Don't give up on Sasha yet. There's still some time."

"What if it's not enough time?"

But instead of answering, she just held me close in a hug because we both knew too well there was never enough time with the Rusakovas—until we had a real cure.

Back home the next day a knock at the door made me freeze, seeing Gareth standing on its other side. His thick dread-locks were pulled back into a modified ponytail, and his eyes were red. But not the red of a man on the verge of changing into a wolf, instead, the red of someone not getting enough sleep. I understood. My own eyes looked eerily like his and burned like I'd forgotten to blink for days.

"Come in," I muttered once I was certain Marlaena had not somehow healed up and managed to join him.

He slipped in with the grace of the beast that was always just a breath away and waited for me to show him the way to the couch.

He fiddled a moment with a coaster on the coffee table,

waiting for me to clear my throat or maybe waiting to find the right words. I could relate to that.

"We share a common problem, you and I," he whispered, not meeting my eyes.

"Yeah. She's redheaded and bitchy and named Marlaena." I flopped into Dad's easy chair, tucking my legs underneath me. I played with the edge of the armrest cover, waiting for him to bark at me.

He didn't. "They've imprinted."

"I'm aware of that fact."

"You see what it's doing to them both," he added.

"And you know what it's doing to *us*."

He nodded. "But what it does to us and what it does to them is incomparable. This might break our hearts. But it will kill them. And that would break our hearts, too."

I stopped touching the dustcover and stared at him. "It sounds like you have an idea."

"I do."

"Go."

"Wait. It requires a very open mind and some truly liberal thinking."

I straightened in the chair. Already I didn't like where this seemed to be heading. "I said go."

"The imprint is designed to attract the best mate for passing on superior genetics to the next generation, that's it. Once the female's impregnated, the imprint should drop because the deed's been done."

"Whoa. What are you suggesting?"

"Let them embrace the imprint."

"You mean embrace each other."

He paused, searching my face. "They are fighting the imprint so hard they are dying."

"But maybe they're winning. We don't know."

"How late are you willing to wait to know for sure? Are we going to watch them suffer when we could just let nature take its course and move on?"

"You're talking about letting them—*encouraging* them—to have sex together."

"It's only sex."

I jumped to my feet. "Only sex? *Only?* Sex is a pretty big thing, where I come from—it means something. It's an act of love and is usually a commitment."

"I told you this requires extremely liberal thinking."

"Yeah." I puffed out a breath. "I may be liberal enough to date a werewolf whose family comes from a country my own once considered our enemy, but I have my limits." I wrapped a strand of hair around my finger just to pull on it. "I think you'd better go."

Gareth rose to his feet. "If you think this idea sits well with me . . ." He shook his head. "They are killing themselves, Jessie. And we're encouraging them to do it. What are you willing to sacrifice to save your love's life?"

Mute with frustration, I pointed toward the door.

The slamming of it proved he'd gone, and I sank into the chair and cried. But only long enough to regain control of myself so I could sound sane on the phone with Alexi.

"I need you to do something for me," I told him, the quiver nearly out of my voice.

"*Da,*" Alexi said. In the background I heard the clinking of glass and the hum of machinery. "What is it, Jessie?"

"I need you to tell me how to cure Pietr. How to break the imprint."

"If I knew . . ."

"No. Not 'if I knew.' Go over all the ways to break the imprint with me again, Sasha. Now. I need to think."

"He gets her pregnant. I find a chemical antidote. Or one of them dies."

"Gareth was just here pushing plan A. How close are you to plan B?"

"Not as close as you want me to be, but closer every minute."

"Keep working on it, Sasha. You can figure this out. I know it."

"But it may take time I do not have. . . ."

"Just keep pushing forward."

He sighed. "I will, Jessie. You have to know that I will."

I hung up the phone and all I could think about was not plan A or B but the very existence of a plan C. Gareth wanted to know what I was willing to sacrifice to save my love's life? What if the answer was simply one word—a name? Marlaena.

Alexi

"Red again!" I shouted, hurling the beaker against the lab's wall. It shattered, the formula splashing and leaving a bright stain on the otherwise unremarkable paint job.

I was at an impasse. The cure was stubbornly turning red each time I dripped the catalyst into it. Red was not what we wanted. Red proved that some ingredient in the cure's formula was in the wrong amount. Or some ingredient was simply the wrong ingredient altogether. . . .

I reached for another beaker, but Hazel's hand came down on my own, stopping me.

She shook her head and removed my hand from the lab table's surface. "How does this help us? Now someone needs to take time away from their research and experimentation to clean up your mess."

"Ironic, is it not?"

"What is ironic?" she asked, the wrinkles around her eyes rearranging.

"That you are complaining about cleaning up one of my messes when, in fact, we are both struggling to clean up your father's mess. If he had never encouraged this line of research—if he had decided his laboratory would research something else for the good of Mother Russia . . ."

"Then Wondermann would have developed the *oboroten* on his own and we would have no chance of undoing the damage he still would have seen done."

I snorted. "You make it sound as if it is destiny, the two of us working to fix werewolves in America."

"And what if it is? What if life and history combines in one frightening juggernaut barreling toward its own conclusion, with very few ways we might adjust or avoid its path?" she asked. "What if most things are fixed and perhaps foretold and we only have rare moments to shift the way destiny weaves together? What if *this* is such a moment?"

I shook my head, a thousand ways to disagree with her musings sliding around in my brain. "I deny the existence of destiny," I said, "but that does not mean I do not understand the stupidity of wasting our time. What determines our future is not some destiny written in the stars but rather our own sense of perseverance. Back to work."

Jessie

Dad had joined the construction effort and brought Anna-belle Lee, who insisted on reading aloud to us. Suggesting Anna save her voice and let his old boom box work some magic, Dad just grumbled when she responded that the only magic it might ever work was finding a clear radio station, and certainly not a good one, she added with a sniff. She had begun reading the third chapter of *Little Women* when I dropped the nail I'd been holding.

It never hit the floor, coming back up to my eye level and resting in Gareth's palm.

"Thanks."

He shrugged and held it for me as I pulled the hammer back. "I want to help. The pups do, too."

Out of the corner of my eye I saw them standing by obe-diently, dressed in work clothes—most of what the pups had gotten so recently as a result of Dmitri's association was start-ing to look more like work clothes, anyhow.

Everything and everyone seemed to have lost their shine over the past few weeks.

"The pups need to focus on their homework," I pointed out as I hammered in the nail.

I was greeted by a chorus of "Done," "Done," and "So very done."

"And is it all right?" I prodded, striking the nail one last time so it was flush with the wood.

Gareth leaned in so I could see his face plainly. "I've checked all of it. I think they're set." Then, more softly, he said, "Let us help you, Jessie. We all want this to be taken care of."

I spun to face them, Annabelle Lee's reading dropping

away to silence. "We'll gladly accept all the help we can get, but I don't want anyone screwing up their grades because they're spread too thin."

Dad coughed. "Pot calling the kettle black," he announced.

"I don't have a choice," I said.

He shrugged and went back to work.

Annabelle Lee continued her reading.

"Can you tell them what to do?" I asked Gareth. "And then go and . . ."

He nodded. "Keep an eye on trouble?"

"Yeah," I agreed, hating the fact we couldn't trust Pietr and Marlaena in the same house. With Alexi back in the city working desperately long hours, Cat was stuck watching them now, but I knew Gareth was much-needed backup.

That night, as Cat watched Marlaena and Pietr, I returned to the basement. Time was nearly up.

Amy and Max soon found me, and not saying a word, picked up tools and began to help. Then Gareth and the pups tumbled out of their beds and joined in.

And by the time the sun had come up, we had holding tanks for two rabid werewolves.

Luring a werewolf into a place you want to trap it, with decidedly few escape routes for you, is a stupid, stupid thing to do, I realized as I called Marlaena every dirty word I'd ever heard (and a few I took significant liberties with).

Luring two werewolves into a place you intend to trap them with decidedly few escape routes for you is simply and utterly insane. But then, I had spent time in the local asylum, Pecan Place.

And actually it was easier than I expected to make both Marlaena and Pietr angry enough to chase me into the basement. But getting them locked in and getting myself back out alive?

That required Max.

"Set and *spike!*" he shouted as he barreled into Marlaena, shoving her into the first cage. Well, not so much a cage as a panic room. But smaller. A panic *cell?* Max locked the door, pulling a heavy bar across it to keep her inside.

A standard deadlock wasn't going to do it. We had to go medieval on their asses.

Pietr shifted his attention from me to his brother and this was one moment I was glad *not* to be the center of his attention.

"Come now, brotherrr," Max growled, putting his hands up. "Be reasonable about this. You have lost your ever-loving mind and we are trying to save you. So . . ."

Pietr lunged at him, but Max dodged and wiggled his fingers as an obnoxious invitation to Pietr to try again.

Outraged, Pietr did.

And like the most amazing of bullfighters, Max stepped aside and let Pietr rush straight into his cell. The door slammed shut, the bar came down, and I ran straight into Max's arms, thanking him again and again.

And then crying like *I* needed to be locked up, too.

His arm around me, Max led me up the stairs and shut the basement door, lowering a newly installed bar there, too.

"I think you should go home tonight. Take Amy with you," he said.

She was already waiting in the foyer, a bag in her hand.

I nodded and let them take me home.

Alexi

"I wanted to call you first," I said to Jessie as Feldman and I boarded the train, all our belongings in an awkward combination of suitcases and duffel bags and one very precious briefcase. "We are coming home, Hazel and I."

There was a lengthy silence as she processed what my words truly meant. "You mean . . . you have it?"

"*Da.*"

"You have the cure?"

"*Da.* Enough for everyone."

She screamed so loudly I moved the phone away from my ear. It was a moment before I dared to move it back.

"You are happy now, *da?*" I teased.

"I'll be over the moon if you're on your way here now," she confessed.

"Then ready your rocketship, Jessie Gillmansen, because we will be arriving at the station at two."

She shrieked again, and I hung up.

"She seems pleased," I said, setting the phone on my lap. But try as I might to remain cool, I grinned like an idiot at the thought of, after so many years on the opposite side, truly being a hero.

My next two calls were brief. "Wanda," I said. "Listen to me. No matter what happens next, you must not go near the Wondermann Corporation. You must not join Interpol on the raid."

"Don't you tell me what I can do, Alexi Rusakova . . ."

"I am not telling you what you *can* do, I am merely making a friendly suggestion. Wondermann wants you dead. His best men will be watching for you."

"I'm already headed to the city," she griped.

"Excellent. It is not much farther from the Big Apple to the best of small-town America. And there are people here who I know are desperate to see you."

She grumbled a bit. "If I go . . ."

"You will most certainly be targeted the moment you are identified. Make the smart choice. Come home to Junction."

"Crap," she muttered, and I knew I had convinced her, so I concluded the call.

"One more," I said. I punched in Nadezhda's number. "Naddie, we are out. I have everything I require. Take your men in, but be careful," I said, disgusted at how soft my voice went.

"And when I am finished, you will take me for a celebration drink?"

"I am leaving the city now," I said.

"Oh. That is unfortunate. Well, I have a raid to organize." And then she was gone.

It was the longest train ride to Junction ever. And it was strangely longer back to the city after I deposited Feldman, our luggage, and specific instructions for administering the cure (perhaps too cruelly specific, I mused in retrospect) to Max.

I arrived at Wondermann Corp. minutes before they led Mr. Wondermann out in handcuffs, Nadezhda holding him firmly by the arm. Never had a woman looked so absolutely alluring in jackboots and a flak jacket.

Seeing me, she shoved him into someone else's arms. "Load him into the car," she said as she headed in my direction.

"You nearly missed me," she said.

"I thought I had a little longer."

"I thought you were leaving the city."

"I did, but the train tracks run both directions."

"Amazing, is it not?" She holstered her gun and reached into her pocket. "I guess I arranged this for nothing, then. . . ." She held out a slip of paper with a series of numbers and letters scrawled across it.

"A confirmation number?"

"Yes. I have arranged for a much-needed vacation and I am supposed to pick up my ticket in an hour."

My heart dropped. Nadezhda would be winging away from me too soon again. "To where?"

"Some small town in the back end of the American no-where. They call the place Junction."

"*Pravda?* It so happens I am also returning to Junction this evening. And, if you are quick gathering your things, we might still have time to catch that drink you requested."

Jessie

Feldman carried the briefcase and opened it once every bit of luggage and everyone was inside the Queen Anne.

"Alexi was very specific about where the needle needs to go in," Max explained, handing syringes to Cat and Gareth. "The cure will fix the life-span issue and break the imprinting code, but it will still allow transformation."

"Best of both worlds," Gareth whispered. "And where must we administer the shot?"

"If you guard the door, I will demonstrate," Max said, open-ing the basement door.

Downstairs, the cells fairly shook with the angry beasts

contained inside. Gareth set down his needle and followed Max down the steps.

"Ready?" Max asked.

Gareth nodded, lifted the bar on Pietr's cell, and yanked open the door.

Alexi

"So I told him precisely where he should stick it."

"Wait, wait," Nadezhda said, laughing over a pretty drink with an umbrella in it. Our train was due to arrive in fifteen minutes, but right then and there, with her, time meant little. "You told Max the cure had to be stuck in a certain part of their anatomy in order to work?" She blinked back tears. "Oh, Sasha . . ."

"What?" I shrugged. "For years they have been a pain in my ass. Why not briefly be a pain in theirs?"

Jessie

Max fell on Pietr like the shot he held was a harpoon, not a syringe, and he hit the plunger the moment the needle met the flesh of his backside. Pietr howled and thrashed, his teeth long and wicked, his only thought to rend and rip and destroy, and then he collapsed.

He twitched and coughed, and Max rolled off him, satisfied with his success and crouching a little distance away, his eyes intent.

"It has to be a shot to the ass," Max said.

"Looks like it feels like a kick to it, too . . . ," Gareth added.

The wild red bled out of Pietr's eyes, and his teeth returned to their normal length and pointiness, and between fierce shudders, he seemed to catch his breath. He rolled into a seated position and rubbed his head, jamming the heels of his hands into his eye sockets like he was trying to clear them of memories as much as clear his vision. "What did I do?" he whispered.

He raised his head, his eyes meeting mine. "Oh, god, Jess . . . what did I do to us? To you?"

He was my Pietr again—beautiful, headstrong, guilt-ridden, and melodramatic. And I still loved him.

I cleared my throat and stepped into the small, dark room. "You were a complete and utter ass to me," I said boldly. "You redefined *dick*."

"I know," he whispered, getting to his feet.

"Pants," I said, reaching out to provide a new pair.

"And you're going to make up every bit of it to me," I added as he slipped into his jeans. "For as long as it takes."

He straightened and nodded at me, his face strained and solemn. And he said the only two words I needed to hear from him, the two words that set Pietr Rusakova apart from any other teenage guy in Junction, werewolf or not. "I promise."

Marlaena

Something inside of me had died, my heart no longer beat as fast or as strong, and I rolled onto my side, emptying my guts on the floor, a deep sorrow settling in my bones. I had lost something precious, I knew it. My memories of the last two days were a blur. I remembered the gunfight in the forest, the taste of Pietr's lips . . .

I was going to be sick again.

I reached out to the only one who mattered to me. "Gareth," I whispered.

Jessie

Gareth slowly helped Marlaena to her feet, wrapping an arm around her waist to steady her.

She wiped at her face, and he held out a washcloth for her. I wondered if she had any idea how often he had stood at the top of the basement steps, listening to the beasts rage below and waiting for a time he could soothe and care for her again.

"Come," Gareth said so softly the word nearly escaped my simple human ears. " *'Come live with me and be my love, / And we shall all the pleasures prove,'* " he cooed, holding the syringe out before him like it was not a needle but a single red rose he was presenting to her.

Everyone else had taken the cure. Every eligible Rusakova and every member of the pack.

Except Marlaena, who preached "the Wolf is the Way."

Her gaze flitted from the syringe to his gentle eyes and back. Again and again. Her lower lip quivered. "I can't . . ." She shook her head, red hair flying around her face.

"Come," he pleaded. "Grow old with me."

"Nooo." The word came out like a whine. "I never . . . I never imagined . . ."

"Imagine it now," he soothed, reaching out with his left

hand to smooth a strand of her hair back and lovingly tuck it behind her ear.

She was trembling.

"You and me, sitting on some big, beautiful porch down south. Cracking jokes and sipping tea. Hand in hand," he promised. "Imagine seeing our pups have pups. They'd be ferociously beautiful. . . ."

"Your smile," she agreed, her finger reaching out to touch his lips so tentatively it made my heart hurt.

"Your eyes," he conceded solemnly. "Our spirit." He took a step closer, and she stepped into his arms. "You can see it, can't you? You and me—together forever."

"For as long as our forever is," she said in a way that made me think she'd often said the phrase.

"Yes. For as long as our forever is. So you'll still love me as an old man?" He chuckled.

But the air between them chilled, and she blinked at him as if coming out from under a magician's spell.

"Will you still love me as an old man?" he asked again, this time his voice low, dark with doubt.

"We'll never know," she croaked, looking away.

"What? Marlaena . . ." He reached for her cheek, but she dodged back, holding the recovered syringe in her hand like some prize from battle.

"We'll never know if I could love you as an old man," she said levelly. "Because by the time you are that old man, I'll be long in the ground."

"Don't say that," he begged. "Just imagine it with *me*. . . ."

"No. I never could imagine growing old before, and now . . ." She tilted her head and looked at him so sadly. A tear flashed down her face and was gone—wiped away by her own angry hand. "Some things are too hard—too cruel to imagine, Gareth. You . . . with gray in your hair and wrinkles around your eyes, your skin ashy, your movements slow and clumsy . . ." She blanched and shook her head again. "I cannot. No," she corrected herself. "I *will* not."

"*Please.*"

"Our forever just won't be as long," she consoled him. "We can still have this . . . but this is how we're meant to be. This is how we were designed."

"By a man's hand," he clarified. "Not some god's. He was a *man*. A treacherous, self-serving *man*. We can fix his error. Now. Use the syringe."

"No. Treacherous. Yes. Self-serving. Yes. But he was our creator, and what better defines a god than that? I will not go against my creator's design."

"Damn it!" he roared. "I didn't want to have to—" He lunged at her, grabbed her, and knocked her to the ground, retrieving the syringe.

She struggled beneath him and I stepped forward, but Pietr's hand gripped my arm and he tugged me back.

"I want a long life with you," Gareth growled. "As difficult and thickheaded as you can be, I want you to live. . . ."

She thrashed beneath him, more wildcat than wolf. "I won't have it—I can't!" she shrieked.

He readied the needle.

And then she said it, soft as a breath. "Please. Please," she said. "I don't want this. Shouldn't it be my choice?"

He trembled above her, the needle poised to deliver the cure. The tremble was part rage and part love and part sorrow. He nodded then, just one fast jerk of his chin, and his eyes stormy, he rocked back onto his heels and stood.

He looked down at her as she lay between his feet, all at once utterly vulnerable and fierce in her resolve. And then he turned the needle away and extended his hand, helping her to her feet once more. "You are right," he whispered. "It must be your choice."

He handed her the needle.

"Yes. It must." And she crushed the syringe in her bare hand and let the cure dribble out between her fingers with the bits of glass.

Marlaena packed her bag and left that night as the news hit the television that Mr. Wondermann, and all of his computers and documents, had been seized and locked up on tax evasion charges.

It seemed like good news on top of good news.

But losing Marlaena was strangely like shooting Gabriel. She'd been an outcast from society before and now she'd make herself an outcast a second time by choosing to live (and die) as the untamed wolf. She couldn't be forced to change and she certainly didn't care to try to change. As much as I didn't like her I still felt bad for her. She'd only found her place and a group who would love and support her a little while before rejecting them.

I wondered if it had been a preemptive strike. Reject us so she didn't have to risk being rejected herself. But I'd have years to ponder it, if I really wanted to. Now I had a few more things to clean up before I could feel good about collapsing into a heap.

Alexi

As stunned as I was by the news of Marlaena's choice, I still recognized it as her own and I had to respect it as such. *Da*, she had crushed the last syringe of the cure, but Hazel and I knew how to create more as easily as if it were now in our nature. We had persevered and we had won the day.

And, later that night, back at home, I wrapped my arm around Nadezhda as we sat cuddled together on the aptly named love seat, resting well in the knowledge that if more *oboroten* came looking for a cure, they could make their own choice about taking it.

Jessie

I found Wanda at the horse farm late that night after I'd tucked Pietr into bed and called Dad to bring me home. Amy insisted on coming along, and I welcomed the company. And Dad needed dear daughter number three, from the worn look on his face.

Wanda was in the kitchen, poking at a cooling pizza that looked as loaded as the ones we'd ordered for the pups. Dad and Amy made themselves scarce, and I sat down across the table from her.

I opened with small talk, but she wasn't buying it, so, knowing I'd regret it, I began to eat a piece of the pizza to give me a legitimate reason to be there. Between bites, I talked about Dad and Annabelle Lee and the farm. Nice, normal things.

She shoved her chair back from the table and gave me such a look, I swallowed prematurely and choked a moment.

"Look, I understand what you're trying to do, Jessie, and I respect it," Wanda said. "But it won't work between your dad and me. Some things just aren't meant to be," she explained, reaching out to pat my shoulder. "Your dad needs someone nice and loving—"

"Do you love him?"

Her mouth hung open a moment, empty of words. "Yes. Very much. More than anything. But he deserves someone nice and loving. I'm a fighter," she said, rising and reaching for her coat. "It's all I ever wanted and all I ever dreamed of."

"No. No, it's not. Not all," I said firmly, taking the coat that now hung in her hand. "Don't you remember ever wanting something else? Something like you just described? Nice and loving?"

She blew out an exasperated breath. "Sure. Everyone wants to be a firefighter, an artist, or a writer at some point—pipe dreams. That doesn't matter when you start to grow up and get real."

"What if I told you I know you wanted to be something else when you grew up and someone took that away from you?"

"Aw, crap, Jessie. In any place and talking to any other kid, I'd say you're full of it. But we're still in Junction, aren't we?"

"Very much so."

She shook her head, her ponytail snapping. "You know what? It really doesn't matter. The past is the past. I don't even remember any other plan or dream."

"When was the last time you meditated?"

She snorted at me.

"Prayed?"

"Have you forgotten who you're talking to?"

"Fine. When was the last time you did a visualization exercise?"

"Yesterday, before heading to the range for practice."

"Awesome. Go sit on the couch. You're not the only one doing some practice here or there."

She sat, and I tossed the coat down beside her.

"I want you to visualize an office space about as wide as my arms and three times as long. Fill it with things—tell me what they are."

Her eyes closed, and she whispered, "A desk with some potted plants on it, a couple tall bookcases . . ."

I smiled. Even if she didn't realize it, the room in her head was coming into view again.

". . . there's a whiteboard . . ."

"Good! Is there anything written on the whiteboard?"

She gasped, and I knew her eyes had opened. I flicked her shoulder. "Close your eyes again. Breathe."

The sound of her breathing slowed again.

I lowered the pitch of my voice and steadied its rhythm, working to lull her into the space inside her head. "Enter the room. Slide your hand along the cool surface of the desk. Lean over to smell the moist scent of the soil in the potted plants."

I heard her inhale.

"Now make your way to the whiteboard. Tell me what's written on it."

Her voice was slow, thickened by a state neighboring a true trance. "My goal of joining the CIA. Weird . . ."

"What's weird about it?"

"It's not my handwriting," she said, her voice plodding along.

"That's because someone else wrote it. That's not your dream, is it?"

Silence.

"Remember, Wanda. Remember your dream. You can still have it."

She sighed.

"Do you see an eraser?"

"Yeah, but no markers . . ."

I remembered Derek stuffing them in his pockets right before he left. "Doesn't matter. Erase the board."

There was a moment's silence. "There's something underneath," she said, her tone bordering on reverent.

"Let it bleed out," I said, my voice slow and steady. "Let it reveal itself."

"Oh," she whispered. "Is that it? It looks like it . . ."

"What does it say?" I asked, my brain sticky from the stress of the last few days, the effect of late-night pizza, and trying to lead a visualization for a woman who was everything she'd never wanted to become.

"Kindergarten teacher."

The spell broken, I heard her flop back into the couch, and I opened my eyes to see her face—a tumult of emotion. "Kindergarten teacher," she repeated, stunned. "I—I remember now . . ."

Her eyes were bright with moisture. "I wanted to teach. How did I . . . ?" A deep breath escaped her. "Why do I get the feeling you just opened up a whole can of worms in my head and the label reads, *Derek?*"

I moved over to sit beside her, dropping an arm over her shoulders. "We always need good teachers. Always. Probably more than we need any profession."

"I've lost years," she whispered, realizing.

I grabbed her hands as they started to tremble. "But you still have years. Maybe it's even more important now to spend whatever you have left on the right track. The track you wanted to be on originally." I reached up to her head. "Let's start small. Loosen up," I instructed, pulling the band out of her hair so a curtain of blond strands hung loose around her shoulders like it had the first time I'd seen her in Derek's memories. When she was still innocent and hopeful.

"This is a lot to take in, a lot to change," she said, playing with her hair.

I stood, smiling. "Then I guess it's a good thing our species is so very adaptable." *Adapt to survive.* I wobbled on my feet a moment, remembering Derek's first lesson for me.

"You okay?" she asked.

"Yeah. I'll be fine. I'm just a little tired. I think I'll say good night, do a little writing for my lit assignment, and head to bed. I have a great ending for the book I'm supposed to write for class now."

"Congrats," she said. And then, standing, she folded her arms around me and gave me a hug. "And thank you for everything."

CHAPTER EIGHTEEN

Jessie

I woke to someone calling my name, my head still thick with the fog of dream images swirled away, evaporating into the dim light of early morning.

"Jessie!" the voice called again, and I sat bolt upright, the blankets falling away from me as the chill of early morning snatched at my face and arms. Squinting, I focused on the sound of the voice, its timbre and tone, and my heart sped in my chest, rattling against my ribs. Could it be? I swung my feet off the mattress and drummed them on the carpet.

"Mom?" I whispered.

Damn it for being so dark.

But if that was Mom's voice, then . . .

I steadied myself, clutching my pillow with knuckles that ached. My brain was full of spiderwebs, pictures sticking and stuttering in the sticky gossamer mess. If that was Mom, then . . . there'd been no accident. No death. No depression, no struggle with forgiving Sarah, no dating Derek, no Russian Mafia, no Alexi, Max, and Cat, no . . .

No Pietr.

No.

My hand released the pillow to touch instead the stack of notebooks on my nightstand. My writing assignment . . . fiction and fantasy meeting nonfiction. Real life plus werewolves . . .

No Pietr?

I gasped.

Could it all have been a combination of my dreams and homework? Dear god. Had I eaten pizza last night right before bed?

"Jessie." The door opened, and Amy stepped into my room. "Can I steal a blanket?"

I shuddered.

"Jesus. I don't look that bad this early, do I?"

Not my mother then. Amy. *Jessie*, she'd said—not *Jess*.

So . . .

"You don't look so good yourself," Amy commented, heading straight for me.

"Why are you here?" I whispered, searching her face for answers to the questions I wasn't sure I really wanted to ask.

"Umm." She pursed her lips and tilted her head. "Blanket?" she said. Very slowly.

"No. I mean—why are you sleeping here?"

"You weren't feeling really great last night after pizza—"

Damn the pizza. My eyes struggled to focus on the notebooks. Could that be what it all was? My writing assignment and a pizza-induced dream?

It all seemed so real.

The way he looked, the way he smelled and tasted, the way he touched me—loved me . . .

Holy crap. I hoped I'd managed to write all that down as convincingly as I'd imagined it—that'd get me an A plus for sure. . . .

But reaching out for the notebooks I stopped and struggled to swallow the lump in my throat.

I was *never* eating pizza before bedtime again.

It all seemed so real.

He seemed so real.

Even as a werewolf.

My chest ached and I tried to take slow, deep breaths. Tried to get a handle on the new surge of loss that threatened to sweep me under and drown me . . .

But if he was just a character I'd devised . . . I hadn't lost him, really—I'd never had him. He was just a construct of my imagination.

A really undeniably hot and troublesome construct of my imagination.

Maybe I needed to see a counselor after all.

But none of it had been real: not the love, the loss, or . . .

. . . the werewolves.

"You okay?"

I nodded my head. Hard. It was an attempt to convince Amy as much as it was an attempt to convince myself.

Of course, if he was just a character—an invention of my overactive imagination—I could revisit him anytime I opened my notebook and flipped through the pages. I could write us a future that would make other romance novels pale in comparison.

But it would never be the same.

Imagining. Or having.

"I can get a blanket from Annabelle Lee, if that helps. . . . I just didn't want to wake the adults."

Adults. Plural. That was it then. Mom still existed.

But Pietr didn't.

"No. No," I said, standing up. "It's no trouble." The sheet and blankets dropped away from me as night wrapped her icy fingers around me.

Maybe Mom and I hadn't even had that final argument. . . . If I had to lose Pietr but I still had my mom . . . I sucked in a deep breath and padded over to the closet. I dug around a moment before tugging free a blanket that somehow still smelled like mothballs. I spun, holding it high so it draped down and briefly obscured my vision of the rest of the room.

"Here," I said.

Amy took it and I gasped as it folded into her arms and I saw him standing there in my doorway.

His silhouette was stark. All angles and strength, with an easy grace that made him seem fluid even when standing still.

Pietr.

In his jammies.

I blinked.

Amy waved a hand in front of my face.

"What?" Pietr asked, his voice as deep as the room was dark. "I had to pee."

I laughed. Loudly.

"It's a natural bodily function," he said, perplexed. "Not particularly a funny one, that I know of. . . ." He looked at Amy for support, but she just shrugged.

"You're for real," I whispered, still stunned.

"*Daaa*. I *for real* had to sneak out of your room to use the bathroom."

That wasn't what I meant, but I didn't correct him, I just stood there gawking at him. Watching him talk. He was gorgeous when he did that, too.

"I didn't want to wake you. Or anyone else," he muttered, casting a glance at the still-open door.

"How'd you get in here?"

"Door . . ." He pointed back the way he'd come.

"No, I mean . . ." I widened my eyes and peered at Pietr in pajamas.

"You don't remember? Through the window." He scrunched his face up at Amy. "It's not like your father would let me stay with you—in *your bedroom*," he emphasized.

True.

"Are you okay?" he asked, stepping closer.

I grinned. "I'll be fine."

He looked at Amy again, but she was no help.

She simply shook her head and headed out of the room with the blanket over her arm.

"Good luck," she wished Pietr softly. "I've known her for years and I still haven't figured her out."

He was real. My Pietr was flesh and blood and . . . He wrapped an arm around me as soon as the door clicked shut, his skin hot as if glowing embers lined his bones.

And very much werewolf.

My heart skipped a beat as my brain puzzled the pieces back together and I leaned my head on his broad chest.

Pietr was alive, which meant Mom was dead.

But people died—even people like my mom, someone I'd loved and thought I couldn't live without. And somehow I'd gone on in her absence; I'd have to go on, living, learning and growing, making mistakes so I could make better choices later.

My life in small-town America was exactly like what most people thought real life *should* be.

Plus werewolves.

ACKNOWLEDGMENTS

Strangely, these are even harder to write in the last book of my debut series than they were in the first. So many people have helped me along the way, and inevitably, I will forget to thank a half dozen of you. Or more. For that I apologize.

Of the people who started this journey with me, only a few have stayed by my side, and they are truly of the most remarkable sort. I should mention Karl and Jaiden, who ask me how the writing or the revising or the proofreading or the copyedits are going and keep coffee in the house and remind me from time to time that things beyond the publishing world exist. The Morgans (both of them) just for being who they are and listening or talking at the right times. Robin, who is one of the first people I call about any of the madness that comes from this business. She is my shoulder to cry on, my listening ear, and simply put, a tremendous friend. My editor, Michael Homler, who is simply the best editor anyone could work with (if I explained all the reasons why, I firmly believe this section would have to be trimmed because there are so many reasons). My cover designer for the entire series, Ervin Serrano (yes, you've loved his eye-catching work throughout and there are plenty of reasons to adore it).

Then there are the people who are relatively new to me but very much appreciated: the publicity and marketing staff at St. Martin's Press—all of whom have been easy to talk to, quick to respond, courteous, and tremendously helpful; the proofreading and copyediting staff at St. Martin's Press—people with sharp eyes and a great attention to detail; the bloggers and booksellers who have become my friends during the course of this crazy journey; the aspiring authors I've had the pleasure of meeting and teaching—especially through RWA and my Fall into Writing Class of 2011; they met with me weekly at the Harris Memorial Library and inspired me as much as I hope I inspired them! Special thanks to my agent, the amazing Richard Curtis. And last, but far from least—YOU: my readers, my cheering section, my fans. I hope you adore this series as much as I adore YOU! And I sincerely hope we meet again and again over action-packed scenes involving hot heroes and bright and daring heroines and the quirky characters in their circles of friends. Much love to you all!

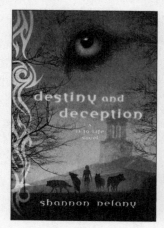